STARBOUND

The Persephone Adventures Book 2

JOHN NOBLE

Cover Produced by Damonza

Editing by Carol Noble

For Sarah, my Melissa, who is always stressed and yet always
reminds me what it means to have fun

Contents

Prologue

Three million dollars. That was a lot of money, the technician mused. Might not buy as much as before the war, but it was still a lot. Enough to pay off his truck, keep the bankers from getting their hand son his parent shouse, and definitely enough to go on that vacation to London his girlfriend kept talking about. Better than the pittance the military paid him, that was for sure.

Beneath him the shuttle rumbled in preparation for takeoff. Strapping into his seat, the technician couldn't help but wonder what exactly was in the suitcase he had boxed away with the other spare parts.

Probably drugs.

His curiosity had gotten the better of him that morning. Upon popping open the case, he'd found tightly packed rectangular blocks packaged in brown paper with green saran wrap beneath. He didn't know enough to tell which drug in particular. He was fairly certain Ecstasy came in the form of pills, so maybe, cocaine or Serenity.

Probably Serenity. It was popular with the college crowd, and there were certainly enough young people that passed though Medea Station, no doubt some of them were looking to get high.

An unconscious scowl crossed his face. Ungrateful brats. Back when he'd graduated high school, there hadn't been a choice, if you weren't top ten-percent it was the draft, then boot camp, then straight to Taiwan to fight the Chinese because...

freedom, or something. And apparently this was that *freedom* his friends had all died for—so a bunch of idiot kids could trip their way straight into the stratosphere.

Oh well, he sighed, if stupid people were going to blow their money on synthetic poison, better that he at least got his cut.

Beneath him the Technician felt the shuttle lurch as it was loaded onto the electromagnetic launch rails. A moment later the captain's voice came over the intercom with the usual admonitions to buckle in and prepare for launch. The first time he'd been up to Medea Station, he'd listened to all the announcements with rapt attention. But anymore, the man just popped in his ear buds, cranked up some synth-rock, and leaned back into the stiff seat that the military hadn't even bothered to pad. A moment later there was a barely audible countdown, then a sustained jerk that slammed his body back so hard the metal frame dug hard into his shoulders. Normally, the pain would have provoked a cynical scowl at the DoD's penny pinching. But this time, he just thought of all the money he was about to have and smiled.

Chapter 1
Launch

March 5th, 2067
Spaceport America
New Mexico

The maglev train had been slowing for a couple of minutes now. Staring out the thick window, Devon could start to pick out the little details along the side of the track that all blurred together at the 180-mph cruising speed. There wasn't much to look at in the desert – just rocks, dirt, and clumps of brownish grass. Still, he wouldn't get to see anything but cold steel walls for the next six months, so the sixteen-year-old pressed his face a little closer to the glass to take in the view.

In the seat next to him, his younger sister Evie wasn't concerned with the dirt at all. Instead, her eyes were focused on the sprawling spaceport that sprouted out of the desert as they hummed closer, a hill of chrome steel and dark glass. Toward the horizon, he saw a flare zip skyward, cutting a burning arc in the crystal-clear air, like a meteor in reverse. He stared for an instant, his stomach knotting as he realized they would shortly be riding that fireball into the beyond also. Then he jolted in surprise as the windows shuddered from the far off sonic boom.

"What was that?" Evie's voice intruded on his thoughts.

In a better mood, Devon might have said something to reassure his nine-year-old sister. Instead he remarked, deadpan, "That's how we're going to die."

The color drained from Evie's face, but Devon didn't really care. His gaze shifted back towards the front of the maglev car where a digital display was ticking down. It currently read fifty-two miles per hour, dropping fast, and when it hit zero, that meant they had arrived and his life was officially over.

"Mom," Evie asked nervously, "are we going to die?"

"What? Of course not, Evie. Why would you think that?"

"Well, Devon said that…"

He glanced across the aisle right as his father shot him a disappointed frown that pretty much guaranteed he would be in trouble later.

Whatever. What could his parents do? Lock him up in a steel box with nothing to do, no friends, and no working internet for three months? Nope, they were already doing that. Short of food and water, there wasn't much more they could take away.

Focusing back toward the front of the train car, he saw the speed ticking down to twenty miles an hour, then ten…five. Finally, a concrete rail platform inched into view, and the maglev coasted to a stop. Devon watched for a second as the people in the front stood to leave, before his eyes wandered back to the four-inch screen in his lap. He wasted a few moments flicking through old messages, wishing that something new would pop up to distract him. Normally he had dozens of updates vying for his attention, except he had spent most of the ride out anxiously checking through everything. For once his phone was oddly quiet, like even it had deserted him.

Eventually it was their turn to go. Devon was only barely aware of his dad standing in the aisle and digging their luggage out of the overhead bin. He started though when Dad roughly dropped a backpack into his lap with a curt, "Come on, let's go."

Devon waited there a single defiant moment, just long enough to make a point, but not long enough to actually land himself in more trouble. Then, with a resentful sigh, he rose to follow his dad.

Despite the constant signs billing it as *America's #1 Launch Choice*, he couldn't help but feel that Spaceport America was surprisingly spartan. From the outside it looked like a shining hub of human progress set amidst the barren desert, but inside it was all just tinted glass with gray steel framing. The roof soared to an entirely unnecessary height, probably to give the feeling of an aircraft hangar, and with all the beaming still exposed, it seemed almost half-finished.

And it was small. Even despite the airy feel offered by the vaulted ceiling, the entire spaceport wasn't a quarter the size of the O'Hare terminal they had flown out of a few days before. Back in Chicago, they'd had a twenty-minute hike just to get from the Blue-Line train stop to their gate. But here, they were departing from 'Gate 3' out of 4 in total, literally a minute and a half walk away.

They had arrived early too, which meant for the next hour, Devon had literally *nothing* to do. They had the news broadcasting on several suspended screens and he tried to watch for a while as a distraction.

Unfortunately, it wasn't much of a distraction at all. There'd been more bluster from the Chinese government about Mars Expedition 11 last night, and all the talking heads were busy trying to sort out what that *meant*. Devon felt it was pretty self-evident. They were pissed, so… same as usual. He watched a few minutes before retreating to his phone. He idly scrolled through a few forums but failed to find anything stimulating there either. Eventually he found himself staring out across the tarmac, trying to appreciate his last view of Earth, while the same relentless thought drummed in his head. *Why is this happening to me?*

Eventually, he saw their little shuttle being towed up to the gate and the knot in his stomach tightened when he realized just how small it was. The shuttle was absolutely dwarfed by the jet-liner they'd flown out in, nothing more than a flattened cylinder with swept wings toward the back. It was essentially a sleeker, smaller version of the old space shuttle they'd seen on their trip to Florida a few years before. It didn't look particularly safe either. The top half appeared decent enough, but the bottom was streaked with char-black scorch marks from numerous atmospheric reentries.

Evie saw the burn marks too, and Devon felt her latch onto his arm. "Are we going to be okay in *that*?"

He was sorely tempted to say no and send her scurrying back to Mom and Dad in tears. Make them regret this ridiculous trip. That would land him in even more trouble though, and... he rubbed his forehead, frustrated. There was no point being nasty to Evie. None of this was her fault.

"I'm sure we'll be fine." He gave her shoulder a squeeze. "Lots of people fly on these shuttles, and they wouldn't let them go up if they weren't safe."

Honestly, he wasn't sure if he believed that or not, but it was an encouraging thought as they filed down the jet-bridge and found their seats inside. He and Evie had a pair of seats to themselves, with Mom and Dad one row up.

The other encouraging thing was the cute girl about his own age with short, slightly curly hair. She came in a moment later, fighting to squeeze a worn, camouflage pattern backpack into the cramped overhead bin, before finding a seat right across the aisle from him. That was a surprise. He wouldn't have guessed there were many other kids going up to Medea Station, maybe–

"Devon," Evie shattered his thoughts, her hands latching onto his arm, "where are the windows?"

"Umm..." He glanced around at the bare, windowless interior of the launch craft and gave the obvious answer. "There aren't any."

"But you said I could have the window seat on this flight." Evie had a cheated expression. "You got it on the Chicago flight."

Devon sighed. He should have realized that bargain would come back to haunt him. "Look, Evie, I didn't realize there wouldn't be windows on the shuttle flight. Okay?"

"Well...why don't they have windows?" the nine-year-old insisted.

He didn't really want to get into a drawn-out explanation of re-entry heating so, "It's a way to save money, okay?"

"But they have windows on planes."

"Yeah, and this is a *space ship*."

"So, why not."

"Well," a helpful feminine voice intruded from nearby. "I think it's because we'd all die if there were windows."

"Huh?" Devon turned and found the girl from earlier looking at him.

"The windows," she said with an oddly cheerful smile given the topic. "When the ship re-enters the atmosphere, from what I read it's like being in the center of a giant fireball. I don't think windows are good for that."

Evie's eyes fixated on the strange girl for a second. "So, the ship's going to blow up?" she finally asked with a terrified face.

"Oh, ummm... I mean, probably not." The girl's tone was sympathetic, but Devon got the feeling she was trying not to giggle at the same time. "The air just gets really hot when the ship re-enters the atmosphere and windows might melt or crack."

Devon saw from the way Evie scrunched her brow that she was still confused and probably on the verge of asking why it got hot. "Look, Evie, there aren't a lot of windows on space-ships, okay. Except in the cockpit, and those are a special, really expensive glass." He settled the argument before she could get off any more irritating questions.

Evie didn't seem very happy, but she finally accepted his answer, crossed her arms, and glared at the white painted interior wall where the window should have been. Devon turned back to the girl across from him to find her idly fidgeting with a strand of her shoulder length, brown hair. "Sorry about my sister," he explained. "She's a little excitable."

"She's cute." The girl smiled. "I didn't scare her, did I?"

"She'll be fine, she just needs a few minutes to sulk." As he spoke, Evie jabbed her elbow into his side as hard as she could. "Owww..." Devon glared at her. "What was that for?"

"Humph."

"Fine, be that way." He shook his head and turned back toward the girl. "I don't think I got your name, I'm Devon."

"Melissa." Her gaze drifted back and forth between him and Evie. "So, is this your first trip up to Medea Station?"

Devon nodded, "You?"

"Same. What are you going up there for?"

He scowled, "My family's going into permanent exile on the other side of the solar system."

She blinked, "What?"

"The colony ship thing for Mars," he explained, "the Persephone."

"Oh," Melissa answered, her own expression tinging with bitterness. "That's where we're going too. I didn't think there would be other people our age there."

"Me neither, but I guess with two thousand people on the ship…"

"Yeah."

Devon was still trying to summon up something intelligent to say when the shuttle abruptly shifted beneath them, and the captain's voice came over the intercom for the preflight announcements. He watched for a few minutes as a young woman in the center aisle did the little flight attendant dance, just in case you'd somehow forgotten how to buckle your seatbelt. Over it all, a prerecorded, woman's voice droned on about the 'safety features' of their launch ship. Everything from what to do in a water landing, to *unexpected decompression.* Hopefully that last one didn't happen though, because listening between the lines of that peppy safety optimism, Devon got the ominous sense that it all really translated to, *if something goes wrong, at least you will die quickly.*

The pre-flight ended with a cheerful, *Sit back, and enjoy your flight on American Starlines.* Beneath them, the launch ship continued to move, pause, and jerk as it was tugged out across the asphalt tarmac. There it would be quick-coupled together with a liquid fuel booster rocket, and the whole assembly would be used to form the fuselage on a huge airframe that was little more than two massive wings loaded down with about a dozen scramjet engines. The last step would be to mount the entire assembly on a detachable firing sled for the railgun launch stage.

Without windows, Devon couldn't see any of that, but he'd played around with spaceflight simulators before. After crashing entirely too many ships just like this one in KSP-VR, he knew exactly what the final assembly would look like – a massive, delta winged airship mounted on two leaded steel crossbars. All that just to get thirty people up into orbit.

The prelaunch assembly was shockingly fast, maybe five…ten minutes to put all the pieces together. Given that the preflight barely finished before they were back to taxiing again, Devon wasn't sure if he should be impressed or terrified.

Soon enough, the pilot's voice came back on the intercom, warning them to keep their hands and arms close at all times. The flight attendant made one last trip down the aisle checking seatbelts, and Mom poked her head over the seatback, making triple sure that Evie had her arms positioned right, before finally settling back into her own seat. Devon glanced over at his sister, who was still fuming about the window thing, her arms immediately crossing again now that Mom was gone. "Evie, hands in the arm rests. For real."

This was the one *actually* dangerous part of the flight. If Evie didn't have her hands in the gel padded slots, she could easily end up with a broken arm when all five g's of acceleration kicked in. She sullenly glared at him, but Devon just glared right back. He could win that game, especially over something like this. Finally, Evie blinked. His little sister frowned but reluctantly situated her arms in the rests. She leaned back in her seat as the final twenty second countdown commenced.

"Whatever you do," Devon warned her, "Don't move." His sister nodded, suddenly looking nervous, and the final words rang out, "Four…three…two…one…launch!"

The whole world turned sideways as the two-and-a-half-kilometer railgun beneath them sparked to life. Devon was smashed back into his seat's padding as the shuttle catapulted forward with so much force that he struggled to even breathe. For the next ten seconds, he felt like he was being continuously body slammed, as the railgun pulsed their speed up to eleven hundred miles per hour.

But even if the acceleration made it a struggle to so much lift a finger, Devon couldn't keep his mind from racing through all the times he had wrecked ships just like this on the computer. It was usually stupid things, like getting his center of mass a bit off, or having the wings too far back and boom – dead.

It had happened in real life too. He'd seen the videos – a giant fireball when the booster rocket detonated, and whatever charred wreckage that survived littered across the desert like someone had dumped out a bucket of Legos. The rational part of his brain knew that had only happened twice, out of hundreds of launches, but the knowledge didn't stop tendrils of cold panic from lacing around his chest as the ship violently jostled side to side.

There came a final heart-wrenching lurch as the launch bar detached. Suddenly he could breathe again as the five g's of acceleration were replaced by less than one. Beneath him the airframe shivered as a battery of supersonic ramjet engines blazed to life, boosting the launch ship up to about Mach 12 and ever higher into the thinning atmosphere.

For a moment, Devon felt a surge of relief at the simple fact they were still alive, but that was quickly drowned out by the thunderous roar of the air outside. Combined with the buzzing vibrations from the engines, it sounded like they were flying through a hurricane. As they ascended higher, the volume rose to a crescendo so loud he could barely hear his own thoughts.

Then, slowly but steadily, the noise began to die away. He knew what that meant. The air outside was getting thin, and at some point, even the scramjet engines would begin to starve if they went much higher.

As if on cue, there was a bump and an instant of terrifying weightlessness. Next to him Evie glanced over, scared, and Devon just nodded, trying to keep his own heart calm. That would be the winged airframe detaching to glide on down to a recovery field below.

For a second there was an almost surreal stillness, like the ship catching its breath. Then the shuttle jerked as the second stage of the orbital ascension vehicle flared to life. Loud vibrations pulsed through the craft as the powerful rocket engine boosted them out of the mesosphere, right past the Karman line, and into space.

Devon didn't immediately start floating though. The relentless acceleration from the rocket burn kept a mounting pressure on him, almost like Evie standing on his chest. At first it wasn't that different from laying on the ground, but as they burned more fuel and grew lighter, the acceleration came faster and faster. The acceleration gravity piled on his chest until he had to focus just on breathing in and out.

Until…it all stopped

The titanic shivers from the engine cut out and the pressure on his chest instantly vanished. The ship gave one last jarring shudder as the booster detached to de-orbit itself.

Then, a motionless quiet.

As the gel padding on their seats rebounded, he gradually drifted forwards until the body harness seat belt gently tugged him to a stop. A few feet away, he heard Evie's awed whisper as she had her first taste of weightlessness. "Devon, are we there?"

"Yeah, Evie," he said, "we're in space."

He glanced across the aisle as Melissa shifted, experimentally holding out one arm in the null gravity. Her hair splayed out in a wild, messy halo around her face, like she was drifting underwater. Earlier, he had caught the same sort of melancholy in her voice that he was feeling about the whole trip, but now, despite all that, there was an excited gleam in her eyes. "This is cool," she murmured like she had just stepped off a giant roller coaster.

Devon didn't want to admit it aloud, especially not where his parents might overhear him, but – it was.

Chapter 2
Medea Station

The pilot's voice came back over the intercom. "Well, everyone, I hope you enjoyed the ride up. We were a tad late getting off the ground, so we'll be holding a low orbit here for a few moments while we catch up with Medea Station. Then we'll be conducting a brief transfer burn. I would ask that you all stay strapped in while we wait. Hopefully we should be station-side in less than ten minutes."

With nothing better to do, Devon turned to Melissa. "So, where are you from?"

Apparently there was something wrong with that question, because a frown creased her face as she answered, "Ummm… Texas… I guess. What about you?"

"Chicago… well, technically we live on the Indiana side of the border, but it's basically just the nice part of Chicago. Have you ever been up that way?"

She shook her head. "Not really. I think we flew through the airport once."

"Oh, well if you ever–" He never got to finish, because once again his sister cheerfully chimed in.

"Look, Devon."

"Wha…" He turned to see his little sister cheerfully hovering a foot off the seat cushion.

"Evie, get down." He hissed, grabbing her wrist and tugging her back into the seat before their parents could turn around and notice. "You're going to get yourself hurt."

Evie pouted. "Well, what's the point of being in space if you can't float?"

"Look," Devon explained in a hushed voice, "in a minute or two they're going to turn the engine back on, and the ship is going to start moving because *it's* attached to the engine. But if you aren't strapped in, then *you* aren't attached to the ship and when thrust gravity kicks back in, it'll be like jumping off a second story roof. So strap in, okay. You'll have plenty of time to float around later."

Evie bit her lip and crossed her arms before apparently deciding he might have a point. "Fine," she muttered, clicking the seat harness back into place. "Can I at least play a game while we wait?"

"*Noooo*," he wanted to throw up his hands. It was like she hadn't bothered to listen to the safety announcements at all. Obviously, trying to hold onto a tablet in an environment where a sudden change of gravity could send it flying out of your hands and into the person behind you wasn't a good idea. "Just wait."

As if to emphasize the point, vibrations suddenly raced through the shuttle as the main engine pulsed to life. Devon went from floating a quarter inch off his seat to being pressed back against it at a leisurely half g.

He shot Evie a smug side glance, "See."

***

While Devon kept his sister from bouncing off the walls, Melissa leaned back in her seat, savoring the bizarrely weak thrust gravity. The sensation occupied an odd realm, kind of like floating in a pool, except every movement was strangely easy without the water resistance.

With the thrust at her back, she might as well have been laying in bed and…

The thrust abruptly cut off and her whole figure rebounded into weightlessness, leaving a vague disappointment in her voice, "That was fast."

"Don't worry, there'll be another one in a few minutes." Devon said from across the aisle.

Melissa blinked, "There will be?"

"Yeah, that first one was a transfer burn." Devon explained "But we'll still have to circularize."

"Okaaaay," she nodded with a sly, "do we have to square something after that?"

Devon laughed and shook his head, "I'm pretty sure that's not a thing. I mean, outside of Algebra. Just wait, you'll feel the turn, or…"

He paused, wetting his lips, then pulled his phone out of his pocket, a sleek, chrome-silver Lexa HI. He positioned the phone so it hovered motionless, right in front of him.

Evie frowned, "Wait, so I can't use *my* tablet, but *you* get to pull out your phone and–"

"It's just an experiment," Devon warded her off with one hand while his other hovered close to grab it. "Besides, it won't get away. In a second, it'll start moving and we'll be able to see–

"Devon," A severe woman's voice from the row ahead sliced into their conversation, "stop showing off, and put up your phone."

Devon froze, his face turning an embarrassed scarlet and Melissa fought back a snort of laughter as he hurriedly shoved his phone into his pocket with a chagrined. "Yeah, mom."

Ouch.

Beneath them, the shuttle abruptly shifted, nudging Melissa to the side and back. A moment later came another quick pulse from the engines, followed by a few erratic jerks.

"That's the maneuvering thrusters making the final docking adjustments." Devon added, more quietly.

She nodded, one knee bouncing in anticipation as…

Thunk

The shuttle lurched beneath them.

Then everything went perfectly still. The familiar, but strangely weak tug of gravity returned, gently dragging Melissa back into her seat. Something about it felt very… wrong though, like her head was being constantly pushed to the side.

The captain's voice returned with an upbeat, "Alright folks, we're officially docked. Welcome to Medea Station. Please be careful as…"

He kept speaking but Melissa only half heard.

Seemingly at once, everyone stood. A few bounced slightly in the weak gravity, and a man five rows up managed to bump his head on the ceiling. But most just went about the familiar post-flight ritual of digging into the overhead bins and crowding into the aisle. Personally, she'd never understood the logic, you didn't get off any faster by standing. Mainly you just crowded awkwardly close to everyone else and waited for the flight crew to get the cabin door opened. But whatever.

Across from her Devon was up in a flash also. He wobbled an instant with an, "Oh that's… weird." But collecting his balance, he grabbed his own bag out of the storage compartment, then a second, pastel green one that he tossed to Evie, "Catch."

Evie did, hugging it to her chest as they waited.

"I like the backpack." Melissa offered, "The green's a good color."

"Really?" Evie's face brightened. "I just got it. My old one was pink, but I wanted something different for Mars. This one's way nicer."

Up from front came a sharp hiss of pressure, and looking over the seat back, Melissa saw people starting to move. Next to her Devon lowered his voice a touch. "So ummm… if we're going to be stuck on a ship for the next several months, do you want to hang out sometime?"

"Uhhh…" Melissa glanced up at her parents, who were sitting three rows up, and didn't look like they were watching her. "Yeah, sure." She nodded and held out her wrist, trying not to feel too self-conscious as she double tapped her dumpy little GlowNote wristlet against his smart-watch to swap contact cards.

By now it was nearly their turn to go, "I'll see you around then." Devon nodded.

Yeah, she smiled. Sounded like fun.

Behind him, his little sister unstrapped and forgot to stand up slowly. She slow motion bounced all the way up to tap her head against the ceiling in the low gravity. "Oww."

He sighed, exasperated, "Careful, Evie."

Melissa grinned. His sister really was cute. Standing more slowly than usual, she wobbled at a sudden dizziness, like her brain doing a somersault in her head. For a second she froze, swaying slightly and trying to keep up with the weird spin gravity of Medea Station. Finally though, she took a cautious step, and when the feeling didn't return, she grabbed her own backpack from the overhead bin and hurried to catch up with her parents.

Melissa didn't regard herself as a space nerd in *any* sense of the word, mainly she knew stuff from movies and whatever weird documentaries Dad forced her to suffer through. However, everyone even *remotely* associated with the Space Force knew the basics of Medea Station. At a half kilometer wide, the station was set up like a giant wheel, constantly spinning to maintain the feel of gravity along the outer rim. Meanwhile, the hub of the wheel served as a relatively stationary docking bay where the numerous shuttles zipping in and out of the station on a daily basis could land, refuel, and take on passengers.

Given the amount of traffic, the main hangar bay apparently wasn't pressurized. Instead, a collapsible tube of transparent plastic had been run from an airlock about ten feet away, forming a pressure seal around the shuttle exit door. Stepping out into the ribbed frame, Melissa peeked into an alien world of steel and stars. Overhead the huge hangar bay curved upwards in a vast arc. She might as well have been standing on the inside of a massive hamster wheel with numerous other shuttlecraft latched on at various points overhead.

A subconscious part of Melissa's brain kept screaming that the ceiling was about to fall on her, even as she bounced with each step in the low gravity. Up above, another ship detached from the cylinder, spitting out white puffs of gas from stabilizing jets. It drifted to the center of the hangar bay, then fired a long white burst to accelerate out of the hangar bay entrance, beyond which she could just barely glimpse the bluish edge of Earth's atmosphere far below. For about ten seconds it was an absolutely captivating sight, until eventually she found herself shuffled along out of the plastic entryway, and past the airlock. There they found a set of stairs leading downwards, with at least *four* different signs warning them to use the handrail. At first she didn't pay much attention, just more overzealous busybodies posting warnings everywhere.

Then she took her first few steps.

Or not.

A wave of nausea swamped her with the disconcerting sensation like she was about to fall over and throw up all at the same time.

What the...

Her hands latched onto the railing as tight as they could for the next wary step. She cautiously probed downwards with her foot. All good. Then she shifted her weight down, her body dropped and...

There it was again, that disconcerting sensation like someone was pushing her. But after a few more tentative steps, she found that if she moved slowly enough, she could keep the wackiness to a tolerable level.

As dumb as it felt, she breathed a sigh of relief when she reached the bottom of what should have been a simple staircase. She had read a little about this beforehand – the unsteadiness that came with changing height in a rotating station. The Coriolis Force... or something like that.

She glanced back to see Devon, also struggling his way down, and felt a flicker of reassurance. Oh well, at least she wasn't the only klutz up here who suddenly couldn't manage stairs.

A few more flights of stairs like that might have made her give up on the whole space thing entirely. Thankfully though, she saw her parents up ahead waiting at what looked like an elevator. Presumably that would ferry them from the station's inner docking hub to the outer rim. Hopefully down there the spin-gravity was a bit less disorienting.

Catching up with her Mom and Dad, Melissa waited as a man in military fatigues counted them off in groups of ten to enter the elevator. Inside she found a long, narrow elevator car with seating benches along opposite walls. A gigantic white arrow that pointed towards the floor was painted on one wall, with another arrow directly across from it except pointing at the ceiling. A constantly looping feminine voice kept repeating, "This elevator is going *down*, please take a seat, and secure any belongings. Be warned, gravity may shift unexpectedly."

Uh… what? Melissa had exactly zero clue how that was supposed to happen, but whatever. She crowded in beside her Mom at the end of the *down* arrow bench, her backpack in her lap.

She was still trying to riddle out why they'd left the other half of the elevator empty, when the car began to move. Her stomach jumped into her chest as the feeling of weight disappeared almost entirely. A second later though, gravity was back. As they picked up speed the room twisted sideways like a theme park ride, one force pulling her down towards the floor, while another shoved her back into her seat. Suddenly she understood exactly why the other half of the elevator was empty, anyone in the up arrow seats would have fallen right onto them.

For about a minute they kept moving, with the down gravity slowly increasing. When the elevator eventually slid to a stop, things finally leveled out again. Melissa was still careful when she stood, but now gravity was back to a familiar Earth level, and the weird vertigo when she rose was much reduced.

Stepping out of the elevator, she emerged into a broad concourse, with colorful storefronts lining both sides. Instantly she was surrounded by the chaotic jumble of a hundred voices all talking over each other as waves of people milled on by. It almost reminded her of the mall back home… Well, so long as she ignored the way the floor curved upwards in the distance. Even so it was just so… big.

In front of them people streamed by at a steady clip, a few carrying shopping bags. A quick glance to either side revealed at least four different places to eat, while a theater a little to their left oozed the rich scent of buttered popcorn.

Behind them the elevator doors dinged shut, and Melissa glanced over at her mom. "So, can we get food?" she asked hesitantly.

"Sweetheart," her mom said, "didn't you eat something at the hotel?"

"No," Melissa mumbled, defensive. They'd had to check out at seven in the morning to catch the maglev. She considered it a minor miracle that she'd managed to stumble out of bed, shower and comb her hair, let alone eat.

From her mom's strained expression though, she was apparently the only one with that perspective. Her mom let out a long breath. "Your father needs to report in before we do anything else."

"Oh… okay." Melissa tried to make the best of it and keep the disappointment from her face but couldn't hide it in her voice. She'd learned a long time ago, when it came to Dad's job, she wasn't allowed to argue. "Which way is that?"

Her father had been scanning the various signs and arrows pointing the directions to everything on the station. "This way," he declared, setting off at a quick pace that had her nearly jogging to keep up.

She should have guessed that there would be something to do… there was *always* something to do. Her dad was a Lieutenant Colonel in the Space Force, so whenever they went to a new post, he always had to check in. Apparently, despite feeling like the slowest organization in the solar system, the United States Space Force couldn't be bothered to wait half an hour for anything.

At least it wasn't far to the station post. A short walk took them past most of the friendly storefronts and into a more spartan part of the concourse complete with the requisite *Authorized Personnel Only s*igns. Five minutes later, Melissa and her mother were sitting on a couch outside the office of a 'Colonel Mark Perry' while her dad introduced himself to Medea Station's senior officer.

Her phone didn't have service and sitting there with nothing to do, Melissa let her gaze wander across the waiting room. It was surprisingly spacious. She'd been imagining space as a bunch of tight, cold, metal rooms that she'd be trapped in for the next six months.

Perry's office was nice though, almost lavish. The couch was the typical Space Force spartan, but the entire far wall had been covered over with a giant flex-screen that might as well have been a window into another world. Currently it radiated out the warm vibrance of the Serengeti. Melissa found herself staring as a pride of lions padded by, so close she could have reached through to touch one.

The nature ascetic was only slightly spoiled by the TV wedged into an upper corner and quietly broadcasting the news. The news snippet was basically the same as she'd caught back in Space Port America, more threats and–

The channel abruptly changed and Melissa glanced over to see Mom had the remote, a trace of a scowl on her face at the news. She flipped past Disney, Anime Network and finally paused on the financial channel.

"...flagship product is a hybridized variety of corn that can grow in pressures down to a third of Earth's atmosphere. Which, for your viewers, is comparable to the pressure at the peak of Everest. It can survive transient pressures down to a tenth of an atmosphere which gives considerable flexibility to deal with habitat breaches. We believe StarCorn 3 will be a game changer in terms of being able to construct lighter growing habitats and transition to a more self-sufficient colony."

"That does sound extremely promising. Now, I'd be remiss not to mention that BioStellar stock is down seven percent this morning following the overnight remarks by China's top diplomat. What's your message to shareholders who woke up to a pretty ugly loss this morning?"

"Well, regardless of all the saber rattling going on, we think our fundamental case is extremely strong. Our R&D pipeline is–

The TV abruptly flicked off and Melissa looked over to see Mom toss the remote aside with a frown. But then Mom turned to her, forcing a smile "So, Melissa," Mom asked, "who was that boy you were talking with on the shuttle?"

Her face heated in embarrassment. Really?

"He was just… someone."

Apparently the universe hated her, because her bracelet picked that moment to glow a soft blue, which meant, incoming text. "Ohhh, is that him now?" Her mom leaned over to look.

Melissa looked away, blushing furiously, and tried to pull her sleeve down over the GlowNote. Suddenly she really hated the thing and wondered why the fourteen-year-old version of herself had settled for it as a birthday gift. She at least should have picked something that did more than just log her biometrics. "I umm... I need to get a drink." She excused herself before Mom could do any more prying.

It took her a few minutes to find the nearest water fountain, which happened to be right outside the officers' club. After a few sips she found herself watching through the window. Inside a bunch of first lieutenants and captains were apparently having a great time and crowded around a lady whose dress was cut a bit shorter than Melissa felt was really appropriate.

For a moment she skimmed through her phone. It *had* been Devon texting her. 'Going exploring later, want to come?'

She mulled over the idea for a minute. That might be fun. It wasn't like she had anything else to do. What was the alternative? Spend the rest of the night with Mom and Dad looking over her shoulder? She spent a few moments typing a response and struggling to think through all the nuanced intricacies of *Sure.* For a single word it felt pretty complicated and she was still working on it when her parents showed up in the hall behind her. "Melissa, there you are." Her dad was holding her backpack. "Ready to go?"

As long as it meant they could get food, heck yeah she was. A few minutes later they were back out in the main concourse that ringed around the entire station. Stepping past the soldiers guarding the post entrance, she noticed the hallway seemed more crowded now. Assuming her phone had updated to the correct time zone, it was currently a little before 5:00 PM station time, and the concourse was crammed with a swelling mixture of servicemen rotating off duty, and a crowd of people in civilian clothes. Probably more crowded than normal, she figured. Along with all the people who typically worked on Medea station, there were an extra two thousand others like herself, busy being shuttled out to the Persephone for their trip to Mars. Her family wasn't scheduled to leave Medea for another two days, and she guessed there were plenty of others in a similar situation.

"So, can we get food now?" Melissa's stomach growled. They'd gained five or six hours going from New Mexico time to… whatever wacko time zone outer space was. Regardless, she was running on zero breakfast and it was almost dinner time. She was starving, and there was a flashing sign for:

Trio Pasta
Three Hundred Feet Spinward

Whatever that meant.

Chapter 3
The Missing Necklace

By the time Devon got back from early dinner with his family, the novelty of being in space was quickly wearing off. The hamburgers on Medea tasted like a mix of tofu and over-spiced chicken, while just a soft drink cost more than a whole meal back home. The Wi-Fi worked slower than old fashioned carrier pigeons, and to top it off, their cabin was little more than a cramped hotel with pull-down beds for him and Evie. He was lying on his sorry excuse for a mattress watching a video buffer at an agonizing half megabyte per second when Melissa finally texted him back, 'Sure, gtg whenever'

"Hey, dad," Devon looked across the room, "I'm going to look around."

"As long as you don't get in trouble," his father answered, distractedly skimming through something on his tablet.

"Ooooh, can I go too?" Evie chimed in with an uncharacteristic eagerness.

"No."

"But I want to go!"

His mom cut off any argument. "Devon, take your sister with you."

"But…?"

"No buts, you can either take Evie or stay here. Your father and I are going to the earth viewing theater in twenty minutes, so you'll have to watch her."

Devon didn't see why that should be *his* problem, but from his mom's expression he didn't have much choice.

"Fine," he grumbled, roughly pocketing his phone, heading for the door and gesturing his oddly anxious little sister to follow. "Come on, Evie."

Outside, the hallway wasn't much better than their room. Stark grey-white walls lined a corridor where the floor curved upwards the further he looked, so it always felt like he was standing in the middle of a giant bowl. The ceiling was studded with harsh white LED lights, and crisscrossed with exposed pipes and wiring that lent the whole station an unfinished feel.

Evie kept fretting as they walked, saying something about packing and trouble with a sink, but Devon was too preoccupied to listen. Melissa was waiting at '-TT 250.140.0+' which would be... he honestly had no idea. He wasted a good five minutes being lost until he eventually found elevator 'E125'. He took it down to the main concourse, where, after the cramped rooms and claustrophobic halls, he finally felt like he could breathe again. With a main floor below and a wide walkway above, this part of the station wasn't entirely different from downtown Chicago where all the towering high rises crowded out the sun. Lining both sides were rows of stores and restaurants, each adding a cheerful splash of color.

His dad had tried to explain the numbering system on the station during dinner, something about polar coordinates and a rotating reference frame. In the end Devon just headed left and hoped that was the right direction. Everywhere, the concourse was packed with milling crowds of people, and despite the occasional scent of air freshener from some shops, the place smelled uncomfortably like a gym.

Fortunately, he didn't have to go far to find Melissa. In a few moments he caught sight of her peering through a dress store window.

"So, anyway," Evie was still busy explaining... something... most of it had been washed out amid the drone of background noise, "We need to find it before we leave the station, or else it'll be gone forever."

"Sure… whatever, Evie." Devon muttered. He quickly put his sister out of his mind as he walked up and tapped Melissa on the shoulder. "Hey."

"Oh, hi," she whirled around with a smile. "You found me."

"Barely, the directions around here are a little strange."

"Yeah," she nodded, "I still haven't sorted out the whole spinward, anti-spinward thing. Someone told me that you could feel the gravity change when you walk, but I sure can't. Anyway, did you want to do something?"

"Well, I heard…" Devon felt an urgent tug at his arm. "What, Evie?" He wheeled on his sister who suddenly seemed like she was about to cry.

"Well, are we going to do anything?' she asked nervously.

"About what?"

"Mom's necklace."

"Huh?"

Evie's face twisted in worry, "Were you even listening?"

"Ummm…" There was no good answer to that question. Off to his left he was vaguely aware of Melissa giving Evie a sympathetic look. Apparently ignoring your little sister didn't go over well with girls.

Evie bit her lip in frustration. "You know the necklace mom gave me for my birthday last month, the one that grandma gave her when she was my age?"

Devon honestly didn't. Evie might as well have been talking about their secret moonbase. He tried to nod along, but apparently Evie saw the blank look in his eyes and frowned. "The one with the little butterfly charms?"

"Oh, the really ugly… I mean," he paused and kept his voice flat. "Yes, I do recall it now. Why does it matter?"

Evie shuffled her feet like she wanted the floor to just swallow her up. "When I was in the bathroom earlier, I dropped it down the sink."

"Well, that was dumb."

There was a gasp next to him, and he turned to see Melissa with a horrified expression.

Devon's breath hissed between his teeth at the melodrama. "Oh, not you too."

Melissa glowered and hurried over to where tears were pooling in Evie's eyes, wrapping her arm around the distraught girl. "She is your *sister*," Melissa hissed. "You're supposed to help her."

Devon's exasperation came out as a sigh that sounded more like a growl of frustration. "Evie, why didn't you just tell mom and dad?"

"Because mom told me not to wear it," she murmured in an abashed voice. "But it was so pretty and… well, if I tell them, I'm going to be in trouble."

Normally, Devon might have just dragged his sister back to their room to face the proverbial music. But from the look on Melissa's face, he suspected that doing so would also torpedo any chance of them hanging out later. Apparently, it was Evie's lucky day.

"Look," he noticed he was wringing his hands in frustration and made a conscious effort to stop. "Mom and dad are off Earth-watching, so if we head back, we can probably just fish the necklace out of the sink before anyone notices."

Melissa's glare softened a little when he agreed to help, and now he met her gaze, guessing the answer before he even asked, "You want to come along, too?"

The older girl pulled Evie close with a protective gleam in her eyes, "Definitely."

Ten minutes later, all three were crowded into the tiny excuse for a bathroom, peering down a dark, grimy sink drain and trying to ignore the overpowering scent of bleach from the toilet.

"Soooo, any ideas?" Devon asked after a moment. He knew well enough where the necklace was. The sink had a small U-bend designed to trap falling objects, which also acted as a water seal to keep noxious sewer gas from bubbling back up into the room. His dad had even shown him how to take one apart. Unfortunately, that required a pipe wrench, which they didn't have.

"Would a magnet work?" Melissa suggested.

"I don't think silver is magnetic." Devon paced out into the room for a moment to think things through. He needed something long, thin and with a small hook, something like... his gaze came to rest on the diminutive closet in the corner. That could work.

The room had a few spare wire clothes hangers he'd seen when helping Dad hang up some of his nicer clothes earlier. In a few seconds Devon grabbed one out of the closet, then beelined over to Dad's travel bag. His dad usually kept a multi-tool in his bag, basically a Swiss Army knife with a pair of pliers on the end. Devon wasn't sure he had ever *actually* seen his dad use it for much beyond showing off that he had it, but now it was finally coming in handy. He held one end with the pliers and a few quick twists later, he had himself a basic wire hook.

"You think that'll work?" Melissa intruded from behind him.

He jumped a little and glanced back to see the girl peering over his shoulder with a dubious expression.

"Only one way to find out." Devon confidently strolled back into the bathroom and slid the wire hook down the drain. There was a soft chink as it threaded down the PVC pipe, and the two girls crowded around, Evie watching with wide, anxious eyes and Melissa holding out her phone to use the flashbulb for light.

"Okay," Devon felt the hook go down until it met some resistance and they heard a faint rattle from the pipe. "There it is, so..." He twisted the wire trying to hook onto the necklace. "It just needs..." he slid it in and out several times, never quite getting the hook to latch on.

"You want me to try?" Melissa offered.

Devon wasn't really in the mood to be upstaged by a girl, but after another moment of her questioning glances, he decided to let her have a go and see how hard it was. "Sure, give it a shot."

Melissa went at it for about two minutes with no luck. She came close a few times, but the hook kept barely missing. Finally, she gave it a frustrated shove, maybe hoping to stir up the necklace. Without noticing though, they had been gradually feeding the hook further and further down the drain and with that last push there was suddenly a hollow ting and a rattling from behind the wall.

Melissa's face went pale. "Oh no." The rattling moved along the wall for a moment before fading away. It wasn't hard to guess what had happened. They had pushed the necklace all the way back into the main pipe where it was caught up with the water flow from a hundred other rooms linked together around the station.

Tears welled up in Evie's eyes. "My necklace," she moaned.

Normally Devon might have just left Evie to her fate, but at the moment there was a girl to impress and his mind was working in overdrive. "Oh, give it a rest," he muttered, not a trace of concern in his voice. "We'll get your necklace back."

Melissa narrowed her eyes, doubtful and gestured him outside to talk. "You shouldn't promise her things like that," she whispered.

"Don't worry," Devon waved aside her objection, "Evie loses her stuff all the time, and except for when she dropped her purse in Lake Michigan, we always get it back."

"It's in the pipes," Melissa lips bent in a sharp frown. "How are we supposed to *get it back*?'"

"Easy," he cut her off, "this is a space station, which means that all the water should get recycled. Right? We just need to find where water reclamation is. The necklace should be filtered out there and we can just pick it up."

Melissa thought about it for a moment, eyeing him suspiciously. "I suppose that could work," she finally agreed.

"Of course it will, we just need a map." Devon already had his phone out. "Search for Medea Station Schematic," he said aloud.

His phone was a special one with the brand-new Holographic Interface option. And a quick flick of his hand flashed the display out into a 3D picture that hovered above the phone like a semi-transparent mist. The two stared at the loading screen for an agonizing moment, as though that would make it load faster. The painfully slow station internet had different ideas.

"This is taking forever," Melissa muttered, pacing back and forth as though it would speed things up somehow.

"Well, I don't see you coming up with ideas."

"Actually," his sarcasm looked to shake an idea loose in her mind, "Water reclamation would be in engineering, right? Near the reactor and all that stuff?"

"I don't know… probably."

"I think I know where that is."

"You do?"

"Just come on." She headed for the door.

Devon sighed, "Evie, come on. We're going."

"What?" the girl looked up, teary eyed. "Where?"

"We're getting your stupid necklace back, so stop moping and move it."

Fifteen minutes and several doors later found the three wandering down a starkly lit, narrow hallway. The walls were lined with caution signs and studded with valves and gauges crammed wherever they would fit. Overhead, a maze of pipes radiated off a constant damp heat that turned the hallway into a sauna. If that wasn't oppressive enough, Devon couldn't escape the strange sensation that he had gained a few pounds. That was a very real possibility. In a station with variable gravity, the further 'down' they went, the closer they were to the outer ring and the more the spin gravity increased.

"How did you know this was here?" Devon asked.

"Just a guess," Melissa shrugged, like she didn't find it very remarkable. "This whole station was built as a military base, and given how big and immobile it is, they probably expect to defend it in close quarters fighting. Logically, you put all the important stuff close together to keep it easily defensible, and this is right next to the command post. You'd probably do it differently on an actual warship. But if the Chinese want Medea Station, they either have to destroy it, which can't really be stopped, or they have to fight for it level by level. In that case, this layout makes sense."

Melissa might not have thought that was very impressive, but Devon sure did. He didn't say much as they crept through the hall, following the occasional signs, and carefully listening for the sounds of anyone coming their way. Soon enough they found themselves in front of a heavy steel sliding door set in a wide curved frame with 'Sewage Treatment' painted in big blue letters overhead and a small keypad on the wall nearby.

"My necklace is in there?" Evie's face fell when she saw the word sewage.

"Cheer up," Devon patted her on the head, "Silver is anti-microbial, so it'll be fine." He focused on the keypad for a half second then turned to Melissa. "Do you have a makeup kit?"

"Ummm, sort of." She looked confused, but after a moment rummaging through her bag she pulled out a little compact mirror with some blush and a small makeup brush in the lower half. "Does this work?" He nodded, swabbing the brush in the powder, and started dabbing it on the number keys.

She watched for a second in absolute bewilderment. "What are you doing?"

"Cracking the lock." He gently blew on the keypad, producing a fine cloud of pinkish powder. "The powder sticks to any recent fingerprints, so we should be able to figure out which numbers to use and narrow down the possible combinations." He pulled out his phone to give extra light and leaned in close, squinting at the keypad. It took a few seconds but eventually he tapped out four digits on his phone and began rapidly entering sequential combinations.

Behind him, Melissa anxiously bit at her lip. "You know, maybe we should go back and ask somebody to help."

Devon shot her a sharp glance, between attempts. "You're not going to wimp out now?"

"Well, all the doors before were unlocked, so we haven't technically done anything wrong… yet."

"Riiiiight," Devon let the word hang for a moment as he kept punching in numbers, "because all those signs saying 'Authorized Personnel Only' were clearly just for show. Besides, what's the worst that can happen if we get caught?"

"Well, at minimum we get hauled in front of Colonel Perry, and then dad spends an hour shouting at me for being an idiot."

"Who's Colonel Perry?"

"The Medea Station CO."

"Huh?"

"Commanding officer."

"Ohhhh," Devon punched in yet another series of numbers and suddenly the indicator light flashed green. The double doors slid open. "Well, I'm sure he'll understand."

Behind him Melissa skeptically shook her head as they walked inside. "No," she whispered, "he won't."

The wastewater treatment plant wasn't quite what Devon had expected. He had imagined a toxic sludge pool. The biohazard sign on the door did nothing to dispell that impression. What they found though was a sprawling room crammed full of industrial machinery. Pipes painted various colors crisscrossed everywhere, with a few massive holding tanks thrown in for variety. The room hummed from all the pumps persistently whirring away, and Devon could swear he caught a faint scent of roses, like someone had left an air freshener lying around.

"So, should we be worried that it was so easy to break in here?" Devon asked after a moment of staring at the pipes in confusion. "I mean, judging from all the radioactivity warning signs we passed, there's a fusion reactor somewhere around here."

"I'm sure they have guards at the reactor," Melissa shrugged. "Sewage treatment probably isn't a major priority. Anyway, let's get Evie's necklace and get out of here before someone finds us."

They both stared at the 'Process Diagram Flowchart' pasted on the wall a few feet away, trying to sort out what it meant. As far as Devon could tell, sewage treatment was just a bunch of lines leading to boxes, leading to more lines. The diagram lines weaved around like downtown traffic and occasionally doubled back on themselves.

"Ummm, is this it?" Melissa finally pointed to something with the word 'Inflow' marked next to it.

"Maybe," Devon wheeled around to try and line up the diagram with the rest of the room. Fortunately, all the pipes had arrows showing the flow direction on them, so he just had to work backwards until, "There." He pointed to a gray tank with several green painted sewage lines running from it, but only one large line running in, which emerged from the wall. "That should be the…'Greywater Coarse Screens' tank, the necklace ought to have been filtered out there."

The three hurried over. There was a small viewing port on one side, but all that was visible was a swirl of brownish sludge. Fortunately, the tank tapered off towards the base, with a small transparent chamber sitting right at the bottom labeled 'Secondary Flush,' with a screen and an oversized drain pipe beneath.

For a minute they tried to puzzle out what all the various levers and valves did. That was, until Devon realized they weren't getting anywhere and decided to just pull levers and see what happened. He had a vague idea what he was doing, and the first open valve sent a deluge of brackish water mixed with several bits of trash down into the chamber. He closed it up quickly, while Melissa watched with the terrified face of someone who expected an alarm klaxon to start blaring any second. Pulling another lever below he opened a…butterfly valve? His dad had shown him different types of valves on a few occasions, and that seemed like the correct name. Regardless, it inched open, and in a moment all the water had drained away leaving a lump of trash on the wire screen.

Evie had been watching the whole thing, her face pressed close to the transparent glass. Suddenly she burst out, "I see it!"

"Told you we'd find it." Devon couldn't suppress a conceited grin as he closed the valve and began opening up a small access port to get at the gleaming bit of silver that poked out of the soggy trash.

When Devon finally tugged loose the access panel, and rolled up his sleeves to fish around inside, the smell that flooded out was enough to make Melissa wrinkle her nose in disgust. She recoiled, taking a few steps back while he tried to pick Evie's necklace out of that pile of revolting garbage. For a moment she let her gaze wander across the room.

In a way, having all this on a space station was remarkable, except–

Something caught her eye, a little white-grey block stuck on the wall that almost blended in with the beige of everything else.

Melissa took a few steps closer. She knew she had seen something like that somewhere but couldn't quite recall…

"Got it!" Devon proudly proclaimed behind her.

She wasn't paying attention. Stepping closer to the lump tacked on the wall, Melissa bit at her lip. It looked like putty, except putty would have been more colorful than the off-white blob. It did remind her of the time her dad had accidentally brought home an old brick of plastic explosive, and she had tried to use it as modeling clay. Her mom had freaked out when she realized and – her mind screeched to a halt as all the pieces locked into place.

"It's a bomb."

"What?" Devon looked up from handing the necklace to Evie.

"It's a bomb!" Her voice was louder this time, and more terrified.

"A bomb?"

"Yes, you idiot!" she panicked. "Over there on the wall, we need to get out of here!"

Abruptly, a woman's voice calmly intruded from back by the door. "Oh good, you found it."

Melissa wheeled around to find herself facing the same woman she had seen back in the officers' club on base, the one with the shimmering chestnut hair, who'd been cozying up with one of the captains. She had switched out of that ridiculous short skirt since then. Now she was wearing a red lacy top with a pair of tight-fitting jeans and a leather crossbody satchel slung over one shoulder.

Melissa stared a moment, trying to put the pieces together and coming up with a blank.. "Who are you?" she finally stammered.

"The name's Andrews, Kristina Andrews." She brushed back her chestnut hair and strode over with a no-nonsense, "Now, where is this bomb of yours?"

"Over there," Melissa said, shakily pointing at the wall. "But it isn't ours, I swear, we were just here trying to–"

"Yes, yes," she waved dismissively, "I sincerely doubt you three are saboteurs."

Radiating calm, the woman strode over to the large lump of plastic explosive stuck on the wall. Melissa inched towards Devon and Evie, watching with rapt attention as Kristina examined the bomb for a couple seconds. Then she pulled a black stick out of the malleable plastic and deftly snipped two wires sprouting from its end. The woman dropped the small control box along with what must have been the detonator rod in her bag. Then she peeled the lump of plastic explosive off the wall, tossing it in her hands like it was a toy.

Finally, she slid the bomb into her bag and turned back towards them. "So then," Kristina strode over with a bemused, almost condescending glare, "assuming you three aren't working for the Chinese, how did you end up down here? Or is sewage treatment just where all the teenagers go to make out these days?"

It was funny how fast one worry could replace another. The bomb was gone, but now Melissa gulped back another lump dread slowly gathering in her chest. They were about to be in *soooo* much trouble. Mom and Dad were going to kill her when they heard about this.

"We're so sorry," the words spilled out desperately, "I'm Melissa and this is Devon and his sister Evie, we were just here to get Evie's necklace. You see, it got lost in the sink and…ummm well, we came down here to get it back and…" she ran out of words.

"Hmmm," Kristina fixed them with a long, penetrating glare, like her eyes were giving them a polygraph test right on the spot. "Did you notice anyone suspicious on your way in?"

Melissa shook her head. "No, we tried to avoid everyone coming in."

"Fair enough," Kristina finally broke her iron gaze. "I take it you three can keep a secret?"

Hold on, they *weren't* in trouble? Before she could think it through though, Devon and Evie were both nodding and Melissa found herself joining the chorus.

"Good," Kristina said, with a calculating glint in her eyes. "In that case, we never saw each other. I suggest you all…"

Kristina's voice was abruptly drowned out amid an ear shattering blast. For Melissa everything seemed to happen at once, a blinding flash, coupled with a thunderclap roar. A shockwave slammed her into the ground, and her head hammered against the hard steel floor. The whole world went black.

Chapter 4
A Jump in the Deep End

Melissa's eyes flickered open. She had no idea how long she had been out. It felt like hours but judging from the rapidly dispersing cloud of smoke and the ringing in her ears, it couldn't have been more than a few seconds. Off to her left, Devon was huddled over his sister. The blast had punched them both several feet from where they'd been standing. Melissa felt a surge of icy terror when she saw that neither was moving, and Devon had a wide gash on his arm.

For a half second she had a terrible flashback. This was Frankfurt all over again. Except then Devon rolled over with a muffled groan and Evie scrambled out from beneath him, apparently unhurt, except for the dazed panic in her eyes.

Kristina, meanwhile, seemed to have fared much better. She was further from the blast, had avoided the worst of the shock wave, and looked almost unfazed. Back at the post, Melissa had pegged the lady as a civilian. Now the thought dimly crossed her mind that maybe Kristina was military after all.

Kristina was back on her feet in a flash and heading straight for the exit. Melissa tried to struggle upright to go after her, but when she moved, pain lanced through every joint in her body, and she collapsed back on the floor in agony.

"Wait," she called, barely able to hear herself past the ringing in her ears.

Somehow Kristina heard though. She glanced back at the three with a scowl, her eyes fixing on something behind them. Melissa was sure she was going to leave them, but three seconds later Kristina was right there pulling her to her feet, before turning her attention to Devon and Evie. "Get up!"

As the ringing in her ears began to fade, Melissa felt a stiff breeze rippling across her skin. She turned toward the site of the detonation. Most of the smoke was gone. What had once been a maze of piping had been reduced to jagged, twisted wreckage spilling brown sludge across the floor. Her first thought was that the room was going to flood, until she saw something else behind the ruined pipes – a pitch black void two feet wide. As she watched, the last of the smoke swirled above it like a tornado before being sucked down out of view.

It all took a second to register, then her breath caught in her throat as icy panic flooded back. That was a hole into outer space… they were going to die!

"Run!" Kristina's shout sounded faint and far away, despite standing not five feet from her. A hand on Melissa's back shoved her forward while Devon and Evie staggered for the exit. It couldn't have been more than ten or twenty seconds since the blast, but already the air seemed thin to the point where she struggled to catch her breath.

Near the door, what had been a simple breeze funneled into a stiff gust as the atmosphere thickened. They rushed through, and Melissa gulped down the fresh air.

Outside, the hallway screamed at the rush of air being sucked past them. Behind the roar of the gale Melissa could barely make out that same feminine voice from back at the landing bay, "Warning, Decompression: Doors Automatically Sealing in 5, 4, 3, 2, 1."

Next to them, two heavy steel doors with thick rubber seals slid forward and clamped shut. Instantly the wind stopped.

Everything fell eerily quiet. There was still a sharp ringing in Melissa's ears, and in the thin air, voices sounded muffled and far away. The ringing in her ears was dying away though, and her skin tingled… hopefully that was the air pressure being restored.

Melissa's hands were still shaking in terror, Devon's face was deathly pale, and huddled at his side, Evie looked like she wasn't sure if she should cry or scream. Somehow, Kristina seemed perfectly composed though. She paced in front of them, muttering to herself. "Thirty seconds to airlocks automatically closing, and probably a minute until they realize what happened." She focused back on the three kids with a frown creasing her face. "We need to go. Now."

"No," Devon didn't budge. "What's going on?" He glared right back at her.

Kristina muttered some word Melissa couldn't make out, but the way she said it seemed like a curse.

"Look," the woman's dark blue eyes narrowed, "you can either come with me, or be thrown in a military prison for terrorism. Your choice."

Well, that wasn't much of a choice, at least as far as Melissa was concerned. Kristina had a point. If anyone found them, it wouldn't matter what had happened. They were in the wrong place at the wrong time, and Melissa had no intention of being blamed for blasting a giant hole in the space station. "She's right," she grabbed Devon's arm before he could protest. "We don't want to be here when more people show up."

He resisted, but for only a second, "Fine."

"Excellent." Now that she had gotten her way, Kristina seemed almost cheerful, despite having nearly just died. She reached into her satchel and pulled out a small handgun. "Follow me."

Melissa had no idea how Kristina could be so chipper. When she tried to move again, she gasped at the horrible cramp in her stomach. Somewhere in the back of her mind, she knew what was happening – decompression sickness, or 'the bends' as navy people called it. It had something to do with nitrogen bubbling in her blood when the pressure dropped. Regardless, it made her want to cry, cringe, and puke all at once.

Kristina seemed fine though, nothing more than a grimace on her face. That might have signified pain, but probably just impatience. She even held her pistol at the military specified ready position, both hands on the grip, with arms locked and angled down. She strode on ahead while Devon and Melissa stumbled behind, trying to help Evie as best they could.

Up ahead a technician dashed into the corridor. In a flash Kristina's pistol snapped up to eye level, and there was a soft pop of compressed air as she fired off a dart. Not like any dart Melissa had ever seen, two wire strands popped out from the side, and it hit with an electric taser clicking sound. The man convulsed at the shock and dropped to his knees.

Before he could rise, Kristina dashed forwards and caught him in a sleeper hold. She held him tight around the neck until he went limp, then coolly let his body thump to the ground. Reaching down she tugged her taser-dart loose, revealing something similar to a large caliber bullet with a hypodermic needle where the tip should have been. Two wire strands spooled out of little side chambers in the bullet with pointed electrodes stuck on the tips.

Kristina barely paused as she dropped the depleted dart in her bag, then pulled out another, calmly chambering it into her single shot pistol as she gestured them forward. "Come on, move."

Hurrying past, Melissa couldn't avoid a pang of guilt when she glanced down at the man in dark blue Space Force fatigues. What was going on? And more terrifying, who was this lady who didn't think twice about coldly pumping a tranquilizer round into a serviceman? That was–

Stalking ahead, Kristina made a sharp turn at the next intersection and weaved down a hall packed so tightly with multicolored pipes and wheel valves that they had to wiggle past in places. In a moment they were through, emerging into a short dim hallway that Melissa didn't recognize. Judging from the rust pitting the pipes and the flaking paint, this was an older section, probably a module from one of the first stations that had been incorporated into Medea.

There were faint voices that seemed to reverberate from everywhere now, the tight halls creating eerie echoes. But the jumble of sounds was far away, half masked by the constant drone of pumps and motors.

"Where are we going?" Devon's question echoed more loudly than he had probably intended.

"Quiet," Kristina hissed at him. "Are you *trying* to get us caught?"

"Sorry," he whispered with an abashed face. "But seriously, where are we going?"

"*Dieti...*" Kristina muttered to herself.

"Hey! You there! Stop!" An outraged shout echoed in the hall.

Melissa saw Kristina roll her eyes as though the command had come from a five-year-old who didn't appreciate the gravity of the situation. She let her gun drop to one side and half turned so it wouldn't be visible.

"What are you all doing here!" An angry woman in uniform stomped up with a harsh expression. "This is a restricted area and–"

She didn't get further than that. Kristina whipped her other hand up and got off a shot almost before the woman could blink. The miniature taser round dropped her in bare seconds. Before she could call out, Kristina was right there pinning her down, with one hand over the woman's mouth. "Shhhh...." Kristina murmured, almost like she was talking to a child. "No need to scream, dear. Just a couple minutes, then you won't have to remember any of this."

The other woman struggled for about ten seconds, but her frantic jerks slowed and finally ceased as the lack of air sent her spiraling off into unconsciousness. When she stopped moving, Kristina lifted her hand and tugged the dart free from the lady's chest. "That should keep her down for a while."

She glanced back and must have noticed the way all three of them were staring at the dart in her hand. "A Dusha round," Kristina explained, dropping the spent syringe bullet into her satchel. "The electrodes work like a short burst taser, and the needle doses them with a drug that causes short term memory loss. When she wakes up, she won't remember breakfast, let alone any of this."

She stood and rubbed at her forehead. "We need to get out of here though. Quickly. They've probably already found that first man and it won't take long to realize he was drugged."

"Well, we just walked in," Devon suggested after a moment. "Couldn't we just – walk out?"

The way Kristina glared at him, he might as well have suggested they teleport up to the launch bay and hop the next shuttle for Pluto. "*Really*? I never thought of that."

Her gaze drifted back at the limp woman lying on the floor, and Melissa saw an idea spark to life in her eyes. "Although… think you all could manage to look scared and ashamed for a few minutes?" She glanced toward Devon and Melissa, and added a sarcastic, "Given the mess you're already in, it shouldn't be too difficult."

Melissa bit back the protest that welled in her throat. No point arguing with the one person who could save them, especially not with an unconscious staff sergeant lying ten feet away. How did this mess just keep getting infinitely worse? She squeezed her eyes shut in frustration… and nodded.

"Excellent," Kristina was all smiles when she saw Melissa's reluctant assent. "Now, this'll just take a second. Don't look or I'll shoot you." She gestured for them to turn around with a quick flick of her finger.

It took a half second for Kristina's deadpan threat to register, but when it did all three had their backs to her in a flash. Meanwhile, Kristina… well, from the sound of things she was getting dressed?

"So, what's the plan?" Devon finally asked, still staring off the other direction.

"The plan is whatever I say it is," Kristina remarked wryly. "Right now, it involves you all *not* asking questions."

A moment later she strode back into view wearing a loose-fitting blue camouflage uniform, with her hair done up in a tight bun. Her lacy red top and jeans were buried beneath the military fatigues, and her face seemed starkly different, more severe without her waterfall of silky chestnut hair to frame it. She'd done something with her makeup too. Her cheeks seemed darker and it lent her eyes a sunken, haggard look, like she'd instantly aged five years.

"Did you just…" Devon glanced back towards the other woman, who had, fortunately, been wearing *some* clothes under her uniform.

"Hey!" Kristina snapped her fingers right in his face and drew his eyes straight back to hers. "Did I say you could turn around? Show some respect for your own soldier."

"Respect…" Devon's mouth fell open, "you just shot her and stole her clothes."

"And I'd do the same to you, except you wouldn't remember the lesson when you woke up." Kristina rolled her eyes with a growl and turned towards Melissa. "And you," she tried to recall the name, but her glare settled on Melissa's short, brown hair. "Curls, or whatever your name is… take this." She pulled out a card, slipped it into her pocket, then shoved her satchel purse into Melissa's arms. "Don't lose it, and don't touch anything. You understand?"

"Yes, Ma'am." Melissa was quick to nod. Honestly, after seeing the lady drop a bomb, a detonator rod, and several loose tranquilizer darts into the thing, she wouldn't have reached a hand inside if she was getting paid. As it was, she held the satchel at a nervous arm's length, like it might have held a miniature nuke… which wasn't totally unreasonable.

"Okay then," Kristina went right on spouting off orders, "Curls, give your purse to…Evie? Right?" She glanced at the young girl who gave a quick nod. "Give your purse to Evie so you aren't walking around with two of them like a fool. Then all of you stare at the floor and look sad like you just got grounded… forever."

Melissa reluctantly handed her bag to Evie, and looped Kristina's much heavier 'purse of death' across her shoulder, still glaring sullenly at the floor over being called 'Curls'. Her hair wasn't even that curly.

"Now remember," Kristina latched a surprisingly tight grip around her and Devon's arms, "look *very* scared, because if you don't pull this off, then you're going to end up in front of Colonel Perry and in that case, you won't have to pretend."

Just the thought of being hauled in front of the station CO was enough to send a shudder through Melissa, and it wasn't hard to translate that into a downcast face. "What about cameras?" Melissa asked quietly.

"Well, I assume you avoided them on the way in?" Kristina shoved them down the hall, with Devon's free hand tightly gripping Evie's. "It won't be that difficult to avoid them on the way out. Besides, odds are, the cameras aren't even working. Whoever came through to plant those bombs didn't want to be seen either, and if my suspicions are correct, well…let's just say the PLA has some excellent hackers."

That wasn't very reassuring. Although, with that said, Melissa wasn't entirely convinced that the Chinese could hack Medea Station as easily as Kristina implied. If they could have, they would have overloaded the fusion reactor and vaporized the place ages ago.

That said, they might have been able to knock out the cameras for a short time. Just long enough to get someone in and out. She'd heard of stuff like that before, and the possibility that they were basically under attack was enough to make her stomach churn.

Regardless, all those questions were quickly dispelled when Kristina turned them down another hall with a sharp jerk, and they found themselves facing a flight of stairs. Melissa's stomach still churned, but now for a different reason. She might only have been on Medea for a few hours, but already, she'd come to loathe stairs. Just the act of standing up was bad enough, like someone was lightly trying to shove her over, but stairs were worse. No matter how smoothly she tried to walk, her head felt like a rubber band being constantly snapped back and forth with every step. She didn't know what she was doing wrong, but by the time they reached the top she was so dizzy she might have fallen over if not for Kristina's grip on her arm. Stupid Coriolis Force.

Those weren't the last stairs either, and Kristina apparently wanted to dash up every flight three times faster than Melissa would have liked. Two stairways and several halls later, they stood aside as four soldiers dashed by in a blur of camouflage service uniforms that all matched the one Kristina was wearing. This time Melissa didn't need to pretend to be scared or ashamed. The way her heart leapt into her throat when she saw them turn the corner, combined with the urge to puke after running up all those stairs, left her cheeks pale and forlorn.

Apparently, that was exactly the right look too, because the soldiers trotted on by, shooting confused glances at the teenagers, but not lingering too long given the deep scowl on Kristina's features. They probably had better things to do, like fixing the hole in the space station. So as long as a lady in uniform appeared to have the situation well in hand, they kept on moving.

Kristina pushed them forward again, picking up the pace even more, and Melissa could swear she felt the woman's hand shiver. In a way it was kind of reassuring. Up until now the lady had seemed like an invincible hybrid of Batman and Wonder Woman. The thought that Kristina might just be human too helped Melissa relax, and when they came to the sentry guarding their way out of the engineering spaces, she managed to put on a perfectly contrite expression.

"Excuse me ma'am." The sentry stepped out in front of them, fingering a holstered pistol that made Melissa gulp nervously.

"I found these three downstairs," Kristina answered sharply as she shoved Devon and Melissa a step forward. "Not sure what they're up to, but I'm hauling them straight to Colonel Perry to let him sort things out."

The sentry regarded them for a second, before giving a stiff nod and gesturing them on through. "Don't keep the colonel waiting."

As they walked away Melissa kept expecting to hear the guard suddenly shout at them to stop… but there was nothing. A moment later they turned the corner out of sight, and she finally felt the tension begin to drain away. Kristina's grip on her arm didn't loosen though.

Devon tried to pull free, testing her grip, but Kristina just scowled and dug her fingers into both their arms so much it hurt. "Where are we going?" Melissa tried not to wince.

"To talk," Kristina answered bluntly. "Now hurry up, before that guard back there wizens up and raises the alarm."

Chapter 5
The Maze of Questions

Melissa had never imagined that beneath the single sprawling corridor that ringed Medea station there would be such a maze of hallways. They must have spent five minutes weaving through the labyrinth, and in half that time she was completely lost. Abruptly, Kristina shoved them into a side room that was little more than a steel box with white plastic crates stacked against the far wall and a single, glaringly bright light studded into the ceiling. Finally releasing her painfully tight grip, Kristina quickly closed the door behind them before turning to glower at the three.

"What just happened?" Melissa gulped, her face a swirl of terror and confusion. "Why is someone trying to blow up the station?"

Something about her question caused Kristina's hard glare to soften. "I'm sorry you three had to be involved in all that. It was supposed to be a lot simpler."

"What do you mean?" Devon asked, as if he wasn't sure he really wanted the answer.

Kristina sighed, then dug around in her satchel until her hand re-emerged holding the block of white plastic explosives she had peeled off the wall earlier. "Do you all know what this is?"

"A bomb?" Devon stated the obvious.

Next to him Melissa spoke up, "C-4B," she said in a flat voice, "a second-generation plastic explosive, American made, developed sometime around 2035 I think. It's got… HMX?" She didn't know exactly what that was, but she'd heard it thrown around.

Kristina gave a smile at the girl's knowledge. "Very good, dearie. But there's one other thing." She pulled out a small black box and waved it near the lump of explosives…nothing happened. "This C-4B is special. It's missing something, a taggant."

"A what?"

"A taggant, it's a trace chemical that evaporates very slowly. It allows you to detect the explosive," Kristina explained. "That's likely how they were able to smuggle it onboard and means that someone went to a lot of effort to get this specific C-4B up here to Medea. As I said, I'm sorry you three got caught up in that. I was planning on disarming the bomb and leaving, simple enough. I didn't realize there was a second one, or that it was quite so powerful."

"Are you like…with the CIA or something?" Devon suddenly asked.

For an instant Kristina's lips tightened with a hint of a frown, and the terrifying possibility echoed through Melissa's head that she was about to kill them for asking that question. But instead the woman turned and paced to the other side of the room. "Something like that." Kristina wheeled back with a serious face. "I assume you both understand that you can't talk about this…to anyone."

"Umm," Melissa glanced at Devon who clutched Evie a bit closer, "sure."

"That means no talking to mommy and daddy either." Kristina arched her eyebrows and gave young Evie a pointed look.

Devon took a small step forward as if to guard his little sister. "We understand," he nodded.

"Good," Kristina's eyes fixed on his upper arm, still bleeding from the shrapnel gash. "Now, assuming you don't want to field too many questions, we'll need to do something about that cut."

"Huh..?" His gaze drifted to his arm and Devon's mouth gaped open, like he had only just noticed.

"Are you okay?" Melissa stepped closer, trying to think of what to do.

Kristina didn't seem very concerned though. She rummaged through her bag, pulling out a pouch of baby wipes, a miniature tube of something that looked like toothpaste, a bandage roll, and an aerosol spray can. "All right, sit down." She pointed him to take a seat over on one of the nearby crates, where she deftly began cleaning and bandaging the wound.

"Shouldn't we find a doctor or something?" Melissa reached down and gripped Evie's hand with an anxious voice.

"Doctors ask questions," Kristina declared bluntly. "Especially on this station." She waved Melissa closer and shoved the bandage wrap into her hands, "Hold this."

For a moment Melissa watched as Devon gritted his teeth whenever Kristina dabbed at the wound. Now that she had time to think, a swirl of questions began popping into her head. "Why would they try to blow up the sewage plant?" she asked, nervously biting at her lip. As far as she was concerned, asking Kristina a question wasn't that different from poking a mountain lion with a stick.

Kristina smirked, "Well, I can think of a few humorous reasons. But I suspect the real answer has little to do with the sewage plant and more to do with what was on the other side of that wall."

"Which was?"

"Reactor coolant, more commonly known as water."

"They were trying to blow up the reactor?" Melissa's breath caught in her throat.

Kristina rolled her eyes. "Sweetie, a fusion reactor and the coolant for it are two *very* different things," she explained in a patronizing voice.

"So ummm…." Devon grimaced as Kristina finished cleaning the blood off his arm and began rubbing gel in the gash. "What would have happened if the bomb had gone off?"

"Probably something bad." She gestured for Melissa to hand her the bandage and began wrapping it around Devon's arm. "At the very least, a reactor shutdown. Who knows, if they lost enough coolant, they might not even be able to restart it."

"You said it was just water," Melissa muttered, still fuming over Kristina treating her like a child. "Don't they have lots of that up here."

"Look, Curls," Kristina said pointedly, "I'm not a scientist, but even I know that you do not simply get a garden hose and *top off* a tokamak fusion reactor like your backyard pool. And even if you could, you're used to Earth where water magically falls from the sky for you to frolic in, but up here it's a little harder to come by and a lot more expensive, because you have to ship it up from Earth. Just the sewage water venting out into space will probably cost millions to replace. It's not *just water*."

Kristina expertly tied off Devon's bandages, then reached for the spray can labeled 'Spray on Skin.'

"Hold out your arm."

Devon did and she began spraying the light beige mist over his bandages. "This is going to look a little off," she said. "It's meant to match my skin tone, but yours is close enough that no one should notice. It'll last about three days. By then the antiseptic gel ought to have your cut mostly healed. Just try not to rub it too hard when you wash."

Kristina finished up and stepped back to assess her handiwork. "Well," her gaze lingered at the spot where Devon's skin was now a shade lighter, "that should help, although you might want to wear long sleeves for a couple of days."

It was hard to be certain, given the way the harsh lighting washed out all the color, but Melissa thought it looked pretty convincing. "Why do you have all this stuff?"

"Like I said, doctors ask questions." Kristina paced over to the door and swung it open. "Okay you three, get out of here," she gestured them outside. "Remember, this never happened, you never saw me, and you probably ought to work out a cover story before getting back to your rooms."

"Wait," Devon insisted as she shooed them out of the room, "What about the station? Is it safe?"

"Let's hope so," Kristina said with an inscrutable expression. "Either way, you should hope you don't see me again."

Devon dug in his heels even as Kristina herded them outside. "Why? Does that mean everything's ok, or are we in trouble or... Oww!" Melissa jabbed him with her elbow.

Kristina glared at the boy. "And if you *were* in trouble?" Her eyes narrowed like an irritated panther watching her next meal.

"Umm..."

"Just go already," Kristina pushed the door shut, turned and walked off the other direction. "And try to be more like Curls," she added. "At least she knows when to stop asking questions."

In a moment, Kristina vanished down a branching side hall, and it was just Devon, Evie, and Melissa. Melissa was the first to say anything. "I don't like her."

"I don't know, I thought she was... interesting," Devon said with an admiring gleam in his eyes.

Melissa wrinkled her nose. It felt like Kristina had left a bad aftertaste. "So, what's our cover story?"

"We went to see a movie," Devon said without any hesitation. "How about...*The Pool?*"

"Isn't Evie kind of young for that?"

"Nah, she's fine." Devon glanced down at his terrified little sister with an attempted grin. "Aren't you, Evie?"

The scared girl didn't even feign a smile. "Devon, are we going to die?"

"What?" He tried to sound optimistic. "No, we're going to be just fine."

Melissa glowered and crossed her arms, "Don't lie to her."

Devon pressed his hands over Evie's ears before giving a terse answer, "We aren't going to die. Okay? We just need to think this through."

Before he could say more, Evie got frustrated and jerked her brother's hands off her ears. She slid over to Melissa who put an arm around her, pulling her close.

Melissa arched her eyebrows, "Great job."

Devon's breath came out as a low growl, and he shot her a glare as he knelt down beside his sister. "Evie just... please, it'll be alright."

Melissa rolled her eyes. *Riiiiight,* they'd almost gotten sucked into space, but everything would be *fine.*

Down at her side Evie shook her head, with a mumbled, "I just want Mom."

Devon let out a frustrated hiss, "Well, if you'll just come on…"

He grabbed her hand but Evie jerked away, nearly in tears, "I want Mom!"

"Evie" Devon pleaded, frustrated, "we're going, just–"

"Devon, leave her be." Melissa snapped, giving the girl a tight hug, "Just give her a minute to–"

Devon stood, "I'm just trying to help. Okay?" He spun away, pacing in frustration.

Yeah sure, Melissa glared after him.

It was a couple minutes to get Evie calmed down enough to move. By the time the three found their way through the maze of halls and back to the main concourse, both their tempers had had a chance to simmer down. After the chaos below, finding the main concourse felt like stepping into a different world. A few people strolled along with the occasional shopping bag, last minute packing for the trip to Mars.

It was getting late and the bars were crowded with fans cheering for the Alabama vs Michigan State basketball game. Melissa caught just a glimpse of a single man in a military uniform hurrying by at a fast walk, his face grim, but other than that, the atmosphere was strangely relaxed. The faint scent of beer and pizza that the air filters hadn't managed to scrub made the place smell a little like the college party she and a few friends had snuck into once.

They were in a part of the ring station that Melissa didn't recognize, but the black block letters painted on the wall overhead called it, '-TT 250.220.0+'

"Why do these signs make no sense?" Devon muttered, his little sister fidgeting with a strand of hair beside him but not saying a word, as they tried to figure out which way to go next.

Melissa had no idea what the TT meant, but when they had started the second number was at 140 not 220, and if she was guessing… "I think we follow the minus sign," she suggested.

Devon thought about it for a few more seconds before tossing up his hands in frustration, "Whatever, I guess the whole station is a giant circle anyway."

As they set off, Melissa felt the urge to say… something… anything. Yet somehow she couldn't seem to fit together the words in her head to start. Thankfully the numbers began to tick down with a new sign every couple hundred feet. After maybe a quarter mile, they were back where it had all started '-TT 250.140.0+'.

"So… where's your room?" Devon asked.

Normally, Melissa would have laughed at a boy trying to escort her back to her door. She could take care of herself. She knew enough Taekwondo that she'd nearly been expelled when she used it on a boy who tried to kiss her a few years back. But now, after nearly dying, she wasn't about to turn down the gesture. "It's not far." She led off toward an elevator down the hall.

Stepping inside, Melissa promptly forgot to stand near the wall with the up arrow painted on it. She waited, staring at the floor, right until the elevator started moving, and the room felt like it shifted sideways. The twisting gravity sent them all stumbling to the side. "Stupid elevator," Devon muttered in frustration.

She completely agreed. After a few seconds, the lateral force stabilized to a constant shove gently pressing their backs against the up arrow wall. Melissa's gaze drifted towards him, "Devon, if they find us–"

"They aren't going to find us," Devon cut her off.

She shook her head. "If they do though, don't mention Evie. Just say you left her back in the cabin. I'll say the same thing. It's… better that way."

"Look, Kristina had a point. The cameras were probably off, and besides, if they weren't, there's no way they won't notice Evie when–"

"Just promise me, okay?"

Devon took a deep breath. "Fine, I promise."

Melissa's gaze fell to the young girl next to him. "You have to promise too, Evie. If anyone asks…"

Evie nodded, "Devon left me back in the room, and I took a nap."

"Good," Melissa allowed herself a satisfied look as gravity shifted back to normal, the elevator dinged, and the door slid open. "My room's down there." She pointed, "It's in the barracks so you can't come all the way, but..."

They walked a little way together, a part of Melissa dragging it out so she wouldn't have to be alone just yet. Eventually though, she saw a man with the stiff pose of a sentry waiting ahead, blocking the way into the military housing section of the station.

"I'm good from here." Melissa turned to say goodbye, then froze as she saw someone else hurrying up behind them with long, urgent strides. He was a tall, broad-shouldered man, wearing his blue camouflage uniform with a crisply shaven jaw and a close-cropped haircut that lent him a serious air.

Her dad.

"Melissa," he noticed and hurried to catch her with a relieved voice, "you're safe."

Melissa's heart nearly skipped a beat. Her dad couldn't know, could he? "Safe?" She probed with a straight face, "Is something wrong?"

"No just... nothing." Her dad quickly changed the subject, the way he always did whenever she asked about something sensitive.

"Who's this?" His eyes narrowed as he gave Devon the same terrifying look he reserved for any boy who got within ten feet of her. Like he was working out where best to place a bullet.

Melissa sighed, "Dad, this is Devon and his sister Evie. Devon, meet my dad."

"Hi..." Devon tried to put on a smile despite her father's withering glare. The only response he got was a noncommittal grunt.

There was a moment of awkward silence. "Evie and I probably ought to be going," Devon finally announced.

"Yes, probably," her father agreed in a low voice, his glare still fixed on the boy.

Melissa gave Evie a quick hug that finally brought a hint of a color to the young girl's cheeks. Looking up, she met Devon's reassuring brown eyes. "I'll let you know if I hear anything."

He nodded, and Melissa turned heading towards the barracks, trying to ignore the feeling of Dad's eyes boring into her neck. She waved her wrist near the entry scanner, eliciting an approving *beep* as the indicator light flashed green. Then it was straight back to her family's little cabin, her dad trailing uncomfortably close behind. Not talking.

Calling their room a cabin was being generous. It was more like a cold box with beds that left almost no floor space when they were pulled down. Her mom, Julia, was inside sitting on one of the cots. She was a short woman with sapphire blue eyes and smooth brunette hair that lacked Melissa's faint curls.

"Oh good, Melissa, you're back," her mom's face brightened. "I was just starting to worry. Did you hear that creaking sound?"

"Huh?"

"The noise half an hour ago, like the whole station shivered. Not sure what it was, but it was loud enough that I figured everyone heard it." Her mom cast a bemused glance at Dad as he followed her inside. "Your father ran straight off to headquarters when he heard." She put on a sly smile. "I don't suppose you can tell us what happened, Honey?"

Her dad shook his head. "Nothing important, just a... maintenance issue."

Melissa tore her gaze away from her parents and tried not to draw attention to herself. Mom always made an effort to pry every scrap of information she could out of her dad, a sort of strange game they played. At least Mom hadn't been paying enough attention to notice the scrape on her arm.

"Oh, Melissa, that reminds me," her mom quickly let the topic of the station shivering drop, "did you bring a dress?"

"Huh?" Whatever she'd been expecting, it hadn't been that. "I think I put one in my checked bag."

Her mother grimaced. "You didn't pack one in the carry-on you brought to Medea?"

Melissa shook her head. "It's in the bag that goes straight out to the Persephone. You said we just needed normal clothes for a few days," she added defensively.

Her mom opened her mouth to say something, probably to scold her, but the words died in her throat. "Your father has an event we need to attend tomorrow night. They're going to have a sendoff dinner with some of the other officers on the station and the ones going with us to Mars. They invited anyone over thirteen to attend, so your father RSVP'd for all of us."

Melissa stifled a sigh that she suspected would only get her in trouble. Of course her dad would have a dinner that she absolutely *had* to attend, and of course it was *her* fault for not anticipating it and packing a dress in her carry-on. She turned away so her parents wouldn't see the frustration that flashed across her face. "I'm sorry," she muttered.

"Well, I'm sure we can figure out something," her mom sighed, her voice still full of disapproval. "I suppose we can go shopping and buy a dress tomorrow."

Melissa tried not to read between the lines of that statement, but anymore it was almost automatic. Yes, they could probably find another dress somewhere on Medea Station. But, just like everything else up in space, it probably wouldn't be that nice, and no doubt atrociously expensive to boot. Certainly, more than her parents would feel comfortable spending. And of course, whatever Mom said, they all knew it was *her* fault for packing her dress in the wrong suitcase.

Combined with the chaos of earlier, the unfairness of it all was enough to make her want to stomp off to her room and scream into a pillow. But of course, she didn't have a room anymore either.

"Can I take a shower?" was all she could think to ask.

"Of course," her dad nodded. "Just, don't use too much water."

Melissa sighed and nodded – as if she needed any more reminders.

Barely an hour later, a freshly washed Melissa lay huddled beneath her covers in the pitch-black room. Her dad was always a stickler for getting to bed early, although given that it was basically four in the afternoon back home and he was supposed to be off duty tomorrow, she wasn't sure why it mattered. Regardless, between the time change, her dad keeping the thermostat at near arctic temperatures, and the fear tugging at the back of her mind that the station was going to be vaporized in a nuclear hellfire at any moment, Melissa couldn't sleep. Instead, she curled up under the sheets, her eyes transfixed on a dim little phone screen where she had typed out two simple words in a text to Devon. *"I'm scared."*

She didn't feel right sending it. You weren't supposed to tell boys when you were scared because… honestly, she wasn't quite sure. They would probably take advantage of it somehow. But even so, there was no one else she could talk to, and she *was* scared. After agonizing for a minute, she finally bit her lip and pressed send. Stupid, she told herself. Devon probably wasn't scared, and he probably didn't care anyway.

For a minute, she stared at the rectangular screen like the reply would appear instantly. That was dumb. He was probably busy. She was about to click off her phone and have another go at getting some rest when a reply silently popped up beneath hers, *"Me too."*

Chapter 6
A Lady of Many Talents

Devon slept surprisingly well that night. Sure, he was terrified out of his mind, but once he finally drifted off, he slept like a baby. Evie apparently didn't have such an easy time of things. When he woke sometime around eight in the morning station time, it was to Evie's soft sobs as she hid beneath her covers. His parents were already gone for their morning coffee, and after a moment Devon rolled out of bed. "Evie?" He walked over and took a seat on the corner of her mattress.

There was a sniffling beneath the covers. Finally, the lump that was his little sister shuffled around until her head peeked out, her soft brown eyes red from tears and her short locks a tangled mess.

"Are you okay, Evie?"

The young girl stared down at the covers for a long moment. "I'm sorry," she finally whispered.

Devon shifted closer and put an arm around the girl, "Evie, it's okay to cry. Did you have nightmares?"

"No," the miserable girl said. "Well, yes, but that wasn't..." her voice trailed off. "It's my necklace."

"Your necklace?" Devon blinked in confusion. "You didn't lose it again, did you?"

"When the bomb went off," she explained despondently, "I… I dropped it, then we had to run out and…"

Her voice broke off in tears, "I'm sorry, you went to all that effort to get it back and–"

"Hey, it's okay," Devon pulled her close. "It wasn't your fault, alright. None of this is."

"But if I hadn't–"

He shook his head and cut her off, "Evie, we couldn't have known there'd be a bomb. Okay? No one could have." He rubbed at her shoulder, "This isn't *your* fault. And so what if you dropped the necklace? I never liked it anyway." That finally brought a hint of a smile to his sister's face.

But while Evie sniffed and dried her tears, Devon ran through a more pressing problem. If the necklace was still there, would they be able to trace it back to Evie when they found it? It was drenched with sewage water, so there probably wouldn't be fingerprints, and a sewer was hardly the place to find DNA samples. Maybe it had gotten sucked out into space? Well, probably not. If his experience the prior night was anything to go on, stuff only got sucked out into space in movies, or if it was really close to the hole.

Still, that was yet another worry gnawing at the back of his mind. "Evie," he suddenly had an idea, "how about you stay in the room today."

"Why?"

"I want to look around a little more and try to figure out what's happening."

"You aren't going back down there, are you?"

"No, just umm… I have an idea. Can you stay here for a while and play a tablet game or something?"

She nodded. Flicking on his phone, Devon began a search. Even if the actual internet worked slower than a snail up on Medea, the local station directory worked fine. For once, that was exactly what he needed.

Melissa woke up sometime around 6 AM to the rustle of her dad rolling out of bed. Probably off for a morning jog with… whoever else was crazy enough to be up that early. She knew he was trying to be quiet, but given how small the room was, it was impossible *not* to hear him shuffling into his running clothes. When he cracked open the door to leave, an irritating slash of brightness spilled inside. Given the time change it felt like 3 in the morning, and Melissa pressed her face against the pillow to try and snatch another hour's sleep.

Unfortunately, with so many questions spinning through her head, she struggled just to lay still. Apparently, her mom was more used to this sort of napping, because after a few minutes laying there, Melissa could hear the long, even breaths as her mother drifted off.

The thought struck her that every morning for the next half a year was going to be *exactly* like this. Her dad *always* went running. If she ever complained, he'd just launch into some story about how he *never* slept back during the war, and still flew interceptor runs to kill recon satellites every morning. The possibility made her want to cry in frustration. Just because her parents felt obliged to only get six hours of sleep every night, shouldn't mean that she had to live on the same schedule.

For a good while she tried to doze off, but of course that never worked once she was already wide awake. By the time she gave up on going back to sleep, she was more alert than ever. Eventually, she grabbed her phone off the nightstand and started flicking through updates, only to quickly discover that the internet *still* didn't work, at least not very well. After waiting ten minutes for a single picture to load, she gave up and rolled out of bed to take another shower. There was no point after taking one the prior night. But it seemed that was the only thing to do on the station, that or go run. And running would just encourage Dad.

By the time she got out, Dad was back from his jog. He made sure to give her a scathing glare and mutter something about not wasting water when she stepped out of the bathroom. Melissa had to bite her tongue not to shout at him. Yes, okay, she knew about the hull breach in sewage treatment, and that the station was currently short on water. She just didn't care.

By the time her hair was dried and smoothed out it was nearly eight-thirty. Glancing in the mirror, Melissa pursed her lips when she saw that, despite her best efforts, her hair still curled at the ends. Yet another thing she couldn't fix.

"Do you want to go dress shopping this morning, sweetheart?" Her mom scooted in to share the single mirror above their bathroom sink.

Not with her mom, Melissa didn't. Every time they went shopping Mom used it as an excuse to put her in the most ridiculous outfits she could dig up, before always settling on something that looked like her grandma would have worn it back in the 2000's. That, and the stores they went to never had anything cute anyway.

"I suppose." Melissa swallowed back her frustration and crushed it all down until it was little more than a bee buzzing in the back of her head. "Can we get breakfast on the way?"

"Of course," her mother combed out her own silky brown hair as she spoke. "I think your father has something going on with work, so he won't be around much."

Melissa didn't ask what that meant. She already knew – her dad was going to spend the day hunting her, Devon, Evie, and Kristina. He just didn't know it yet.

Inside half an hour, Melissa and her mom had gotten bagels and coffee at some little shop she'd never heard of called Starbucks. For some reason her mom was in love with the place and kept talking about how hard they were to find anymore. After a quick and absurdly expensive breakfast, they found a map of the station that revealed there was basically one *real* dress store on Medea. Melissa recalled seeing it the prior evening, 'KA Dresses and Accessories'. There weren't many clothing stores in general – lots of restaurants, bars, a movie theater, a fair-sized commissary – but very few clothes.

Maybe it made sense. Except for a few days every couple of years, Medea was basically a military base. There couldn't be that much normal demand for overpriced dresses transported up into orbit. Not when anyone could just wait six months to rotate off the station back to a terrestrial duty post.

"Oh look, Melissa," her mom remarked when they found the dress shop, "it's that boy from yesterday."

"Huh?" She glanced around in bewilderment until she noticed Devon relaxing on a long bench stuck against the far wall. He was pretending to be busy with his phone, but from the way he kept looking up every two seconds, he was clearly watching something.

Melissa's eyes narrowed in a sharp glare. Why was Devon here? Her mom read her expression very differently though, "Did you want to go talk to him?"

"What?" Melissa felt her cheeks go hot. She did want to chat with Devon, just… not for any of the reasons Mom was thinking.

"Go on, sweetheart. I'll be inside."

Melissa's breath hissed between her teeth, but she still took the opportunity to see why Devon was spying on a dress store.

"Hello, Devon." She slid onto the bench next to him.

The boy gave an involuntary start, but he recovered himself quickly enough. "Hey there, Curls, fancy seeing you here."

"Don't call me that," her tone cooled. "What are you doing here?"

His voice was pure innocence, but Melissa noticed his hands fidgeting nervously. "It's a small station, can't a fellow sit on a bench?"

"Oh please, a five-year-old could see you're spying on someone." She paused with a sudden accusatory look, "Are you stalking me?"

"Are you kidding?" Devon stifled a laugh. "Not having met your dad, I'm not. If you must know, I'm stalking Kristina."

Melissa felt a chill run down her spine. "What? Where is she?"

"That's her store, right over there." He nodded towards the dress shop across the wide concourse where her mom had disappeared. "*KA Dresses and Accessories* stands for *Kristina Andrews Dresses and Accessories,*" he explained. "I believe she also runs the coffee shop next door. I guess she's sort of a big deal up here. Anyway, Evie was worried this morning, so I figured I could see what she was up to."

As much as she didn't want to admit it, Melissa was kind of impressed. "How did you figure all that out?"

"I looked her up in the station directory." His gaze shifted back towards the storefront, "Is that your mom?"

Melissa followed his eyes to see her mother waving her over. She could feel her face flush hot in embarrassment yet again, and wished she could just bury her head in her hands until this all went away. "I have to go," she said. "And Devon, be careful. If Kristina really is CIA, she isn't the sort of person you want to mess with."

She stood to head back and winced when she saw her mom admiring a frilly lace shawl in the storefront window. "Isn't this just the most gorgeous thing?" her mother asked as Melissa walked up.

It wasn't, quite the opposite in fact. Melissa was still working up a diplomatic way to say so, when Mom noticed the price tag and nearly choked. "That's a little steep," she stammered.

Of course it was. Melissa rolled her eyes. Everything on Medea Station was pricey. Why would the dresses be any different?

"What about that one?" Melissa used the opening to pick out a normal looking periwinkle blue dress, with a neckline that wouldn't instantly have her dad telling her to return it. She walked over and rubbed the smooth fabric between her fingers, leaving her mom to moon over some other absurd outfit.

"Excellent choice, Curls," Kristina's voice intruded.

Melissa half jumped and her head swiveled to see Kristina standing behind her, same wavy chestnut hair, but this time she was in a white embroidered top with blue jeans. "Kristina, I–"

"Shhh," Kristina whispered with a furtive wink as Melissa's mom walked over, "we don't know each other, remember?" Abruptly her voice shifted tone to sound more like a saleswoman. "So, what size are you, dear?"

A moment later her mom had introduced herself. Soon she and Kristina were in the midst of an animated, vaguely nonsensical discussion about dress theory. Melissa wasn't sure who was enjoying the experience more, her mom or the scary CIA lady. Eventually they picked out something that looked utterly ridiculous, and Kristina hustled her back into the dressing room.

Melissa was still working out how she was supposed to wriggle into the far too tight red gown when Kristina's voice interrupted from right outside. "So, Curls, maybe you can explain why your boyfriend is camped outside my shop like a bear watching a beehive."

Her throat tightened. Surely Mom wasn't still outside, right? "He's not my boyfriend," was all she could think to say.

"Of course not," she could hear the amusement in Kristina's voice. "But either way, that doesn't answer my question."

"He's worried," Melissa's voice broke off for a second as she had to jump a little to squirm into the bodice, "that's all."

"I don't suppose he could go be *worried* somewhere else?"

"Maybe you should go ask him yourself," she muttered.

"Oh, don't worry, I will. In the meantime though, since you and that boy insist on poking into my business, I have a proposition for you."

"What do you mean?" Melissa had the sinking feeling that whatever came next wouldn't be good.

"I believe the appropriate phrase is a *quid pro quo*, a trade of sorts." Melissa could well imagine the calculating grin on Kristina's face as she continued, "You see, I noticed the way your mother looks at all the price tags here. Since I don't care *that much* about turning a profit, I'm willing to do you a favor in exchange for some help."

"Help?" Melissa couldn't fathom what Kristina would need *her* help with.

"Oh don't worry, Curls, it's nothing dangerous, just a little acting gig."

Melissa froze at the word *acting*. Huh?

She understood what Kristina meant about the prices, it would be a nightmare for her parents to afford anything here, and… "What do I have to do?" the sullen words slipped out.

"Just go on a walk with me after this," Kristina said. "That's all."

Melissa was pretty darn sure that was not just *all*. But suddenly she didn't see any good options. She already felt bad enough about the dress and–

"Okay," she whispered.

"Promise?" Kristina asked with a sing-song cheer in her voice.

"Promise."

"And yet you sound so sad. It's not hard," Kristina reassured her. "Easiest three grand you'll ever make."

Melissa glanced at the price tag, "But this dress doesn't even cost—"

"Oh, don't fret," Kristina stifled a laugh. "*That* isn't your dress, that dress is just for mothers who like to torture their daughters. I already have something else picked out for you." Her voice abruptly switched back to that saleswoman tone, a sign her mom had returned. "Are you doing okay in there?"

Melissa gave one final tug to get the dress in place. "Just a second." She needed to figure out how to walk in this thing without falling over.

A moment later Melissa was outside, with both women cooing about how pretty she looked. Then of course, Kristina threw up her arms, declared that it was all completely wrong, and insisted she needed to try something different. Melissa found herself shoved right back into the dressing room with three more outfits and instructions to put on her very own quick-change magic act. She wouldn't have minded except that the dresses were utterly insane. There was a ballgown that looked like it had time-traveled from the 1900's, a miniskirt that her dad would have thrown out in an instant, and some weird specialty piece with Dalmatian puppies on it. Kristina had gotten one thing right, it was torture.

Kristina's evil plan wasn't hard to figure out either. She spent the entire time chatting with Mom, cheerfully vacuuming up every scrap of information she could. Melissa wanted to scream for her mom to just *stop talking*. But of course she couldn't, and as long as there was more to learn, Kristina could just keep her busy playing a never ending game of dress up.

After half an hour though, she got the feeling that things were almost over when Kristina handed her something more reasonable. A dark blue dress with a pleated skirt that hovered around her knees. A pattern of intricate silver embroidery cascaded down the front, and when she stepped into it, Melissa found it slipped right on. It was absolutely gorgeous. On a hunch she glanced at the price tag, and sure enough, $2999.99.

She walked out of the dressing room and after a few more admiring comments, Kristina finally declared the dress was perfect. She quickly threw in a matching belt, a pair of flats, and some cheap earrings. Before Melissa's mom could protest, she had them over at the checkout. Melissa saw her mom's eyes go wide as saucers when the total rang up to nearly four grand, and she heard a vague murmur about how things hadn't been so expensive before the war. Suddenly though, Kristina mentioned something about a military discount, and after a quick check of her mom's ID, she pressed a few more buttons and four thousand dollars became eight hundred.

Melissa's mouth nearly dropped open. Even back on Earth she couldn't buy a dress like this for eight hundred dollars, and now she was getting the whole outfit thrown in. Her first thought was that this was one of the nicest things anyone had ever done for her. Her second was the cold realization that Kristina now owned her, completely.

Her mom was shocked too, but Kristina waved it off with some comment about how she only gave the discount to people she liked and how much fun she had picking out dresses anyway. In a few minutes they were on their way out, having just gotten the sort of bargain they would have had to fight for on Black Friday.

As they strolled outside, Melissa's wristlet glowed a soft blue as a text came in. Checking her phone, her pulse nearly stopped when she saw:

Curls, I'll meet you and your boyfriend outside on the bench in a few minutes. Don't run off, (seriously, you WILL regret it) especially if you want answers. And since I'm guessing you're worried, don't be.

Had her mom not been three feet away Melissa would have cursed. *How did Kristina have her number?*

Her heart sank at the realization she didn't have much of a choice. Sure, she could always bail with her dress, but she had

the ominous feeling Kristina would have a plan for that and…
well, she was pretty sure the CIA lady's bad side wasn't a
remotely good place to be. Leaving the dress with mom, she
made a quick promise to be back before lunch, then doubled
back to where Devon was still failing miserably at his spy
routine. "Did you find out anything?" he asked eagerly.

Melissa nodded, frustrated. "Yes, but you aren't going to like
it." She showed him the text.

Chapter 7
Caught in the Web

She's going to murder us, isn't she?" Devon groaned.

Melissa's head tilted sideways in bewilderment. "Uh, that's not what it says *at all*."

"Well she's not going to say it up front."

Melissa opened her mouth but the words died in her throat, and she ended up shaking her head. "I don't think that's how this works. If Kristina wanted us dead, she would have just left us to suffocate last night. Besides, if you're so scared of her, why are you here in the first place?"

Devon shrugged, "I wanted to know what was going on."

"Right," she sighed. That was either incredibly brave or monumentally stupid, and trying to sort out which, Melissa eventually just settled for the conclusion that boys were apparently crazy. She changed the subject. "Is Evie doing okay, after... everything?"

"I mean, if nightmares qualify as okay, then sure." Devon's gaze drifted to the ground, his whole body seeming to deflate at the topic. "I just..."

Melissa bit her lip and laid a sympathetic hand on his wrist. "I'm sorry, I shouldn't have brought it up."

Devon shrugged, "Don't be, it's not your fault she can't sleep. I just don't know what I'm supposed to do about it." He swallowed and Melissa felt a shudder ripple through him.

"I… I could talk with her."

"Huh?"

"Evie, I could talk with her if you wanted," Melissa offered. "I remember what it was like to be her age. If you think it would help, I could try."

"Well, I wouldn't turn you down." Devon took a deep breath, then added, "Thanks."

"Sure." Melissa nodded, their eyes met, and her cheeks flushed with warmth, one hand brushing at her hair as she looked away.

The moment lasted for about three seconds. Then Melissa noticed Kristina strolling across the hall towards them. In an instant the color drained from her cheeks and her face darkened in a scowl.

"Hello there, Curls, Devon," Kristina nodded to each of them. It was all Melissa could do to keep her mouth from dropping open at Kristina's insistence on using that ridiculous name.

"What do you want?" Devon asked bluntly.

"Oh now, why must you be so forward?" Kristina's eyes glistened like a cat watching two mice. "That ruins the fun. If you must know, I have a sudden need for two troublesome looking children, and you both proved to be passable actors last night. Plus, you both seem dead set on butting into this espionage business, in which case it's better I keep an eye on you. I can't have you two bumbling into something that'll get you killed."

Melissa cocked an eye, "Oh please, what does it matter to you?"

Kristina actually had the nerve to look affronted, "Oh don't be like that, Curls. If you two die, that would let all my hard work saving your lives go completely to waste."

Right, like she actually cared. Melissa folded her arms and bit back a torrent of scathing remarks. "Okay, then, what do you need us to do?"

"The same as before," Kristina gave an infuriating smirk, "exactly what I tell you too." She gestured for them to get up. "Come on, I'll explain on the way." She wheeled and set off at a brisk walk.

"Wait," Devon had to jog a few feet to catch up. "Where are we going?"

"TT 250.10.0" Kristina answered.

"What does that even mean?"

Kristina wheeled on the teenagers with an incredulous look, like Devon had just admitted he couldn't add two plus two to make four. "You mean to tell me that you've both been wandering around the station without understanding basic directions?"

Melissa glanced toward Devon hoping for some support, only to find him looking right back, equally adrift. "Possibly," she said shamefaced. Just perfect, something else for Kristina to beat them over the head with.

Kristina shook her head and muttered something like '*du rocky.*'

"Okay," she explained as they walked, "directions up here are simple so long as you have two brain cells to rub together. I'm sure you can collectively manage that." She paused in front of another sign, '-TT 250.130.0+'"

"So, the TT is a structural reference, I believe it stands for Theta Oriented Truss or – something like that. It doesn't really matter for navigation. The important part is that the first number is up and down, the second number is degrees around the station, and the third number represents moving side to side. Follow the plus and the minus to increase or decrease the numbers. Does that make sense?"

There was a long pause until Devon gave a hesitant nod, "I guess."

Kristina shot him a glare like she strongly suspected he was lying. "Well, give it a few more days of getting lost and maybe it'll start to sink in. Anyway," she pointed up to the current sign, "in our case we need to get from 250.130.0 to 250.10.0 so the quickest way is to follow the ring around until we get to the 10 degree mark." She pointed off in the direction of the negative sign, "We want to decrease our angle, so we follow the minus. Simple."

Melissa wasn't sure 'simple' quite described it, but she did see Kristina's logic. Besides, it wasn't like they had a choice.

So, follow the minus sign it was. They set off again and sure enough the middle numbers consistently ticked down.

They were at 250.100.0 when she finally got up the courage to ask, "So what do we do when we get there?"

"Well, you two are going to play the same role you did last night, just instead of trespassers that I caught sneaking around the engineering spaces, you get to be teenagers I caught trying to shoplift. I'm personally dragging you both back for a long chat with your parents. So, try to look sad and scared, maybe cry a little. Act like you would if I had *actually* caught you shoplifting."

"Seriously?" Melissa narrowed her eyes. "Why do your plans always involve us being in trouble?"

"Don't complain, Curls," Kristina snapped back in a mock indignation. "All you have to do is play act. If someone asked you to go be a Disney star, you'd say yes in a heartbeat. This is just like that, except now you have to be convincing. Besides, I already have a reputation for this sort of thing. No one's going to question it." Kristina had an almost fond grin tugging at her lips as she added that last bit.

"This is dumb," Melissa muttered.

Amusement twinkled in the CIA lady's eyes. "Oh, just be glad I'm not asking you to put on a repeat performance of the last girl who tried to 'borrow' something from my shop. The name was Cara, if I recall. She was a lot like you, Curls, maybe a year older, some general's daughter who thought she was walking on top of the world and daddy would run along and save her. Anyway, she tried to be light-fingered, and by the time I was done with her, she was crying in front of the whole station." Kristina's smile widened into a wolfish grin, "Then, to top it all off, I made her scrub dishes for a few days. It was beautiful."

"You know, I even got the bracelet she was trying to take framed. If we get a chance, I'll show you."

Kristina chuckled, but Melissa's face turned a shade paler. "That's horrible."

"I prefer to think of it as *character development*," Kristina smirked. "I almost wish someone had done that to me when I was her age. I might have ended up in a more respectable profession. Regardless, the moral of the story is that you should look sad, because if you can't act well enough for my liking, things will get *much* worse."

Melissa shivered, not sure if she should be appalled or terrified. It wasn't hard to take Kristina's advice and begin blinking her eyes to work up some tears. No point testing the lady. In a moment she could feel a few trickles rolling down her cheeks, and when she wiped at one her hand came away smeared from the faint layer of blush she'd dusted on that morning. Oh well, at least it would add to the effect.

"That's more like it," Kristina nodded in approval and grabbed her arm like she was marching a prisoner around. Which, in a lot of ways, she was.

Devon wasn't so accommodating though. Despite a couple of swats on the head he stared sullenly at the floor. With their destination growing close, Kristina finally gave a low growl and steered them down a side hall and into a quiet room. Without any warning, she gave his arm a sharp squeeze right where the gash had been the prior night. Melissa had almost forgotten it was there, but Devon's mouth shot open in a voiceless scream and he desperately tried to twist his arm free.

"Stop it!" Melissa tried to struggle too, but Kristina's hand clamped down like a vise.

After a few seconds Kristina must have loosened her grip, because the agony on his face eased some. Devon winced and tears sprung unbidden to his eyes, "Owww... was that really necessary?"

"Yes," Kristina's eyes were hard, like twin sapphires. "This is serious, and if a few seconds of pain can drive that home, then consider yourself lucky. Now come on." She pushed them back towards the hallway.

"Are you okay?" Melissa whispered.

"I'll be fine," Devon nodded and tried to act like nothing was wrong. She could see the way he kept taking deep breaths and closing his eyes to fight off the pain though.

Up ahead she saw a sentry about fifty feet away, and Kristina steered them straight for him. "Remember," the CIA woman murmured, "look scared."

This time, Melissa didn't have to act.

"Miss Andrews," the sentry, standing stiffly at attention, nodded when Kristina stomped up with a scowl on her face and two teenagers with tear-stained faces.

"Serviceman Terrence, right?" She returned his nod.

"Yes, ma'am," his face brightened, "did you need something?"

Despite her taut, inflexible grip, Kristina's voice sounded perfectly at ease. "Well, you see, I caught these two being light-fingered in my store. I was hoping to run up and have a quick chat with their parents."

When she said that, the point of the whole elaborate ruse finally clicked with Melissa. Kristina was trying to bluff her way into the barracks. Normally, she could only do that if escorted by an adult with a military ID. Melissa had the ID part, a little proximity chip implant in her wrist, but she wasn't an adult. And of course, whatever Kristina was planning to do inside, the CIA lady wouldn't want Serviceman Terrence staring over her shoulder the whole time.

With all the people crowding onto Medea Station though, the barracks was packed full of strangers, soldiers much like Melissa's dad crammed into the rooms. Mom was probably up there right now, although thankfully, she would have gone a different way to get back to their room. Regardless, if Kristina could talk her way inside, a woman marching two teenagers around like she meant business probably wouldn't be questioned.

The sentry's eyes drifted towards Melissa and Devon with a sympathetic look. "I can call someone to fetch their parents if you like. It might take a while but–"

"Well, that's the thing," Kristina said. "You recall the situation with General Rosenfeld's daughter?" In response, a half-smile curled at the man's lips.

"Apparently, the general wasn't pleased with what happened and afterwards I was told to 'be a bit less public.' I was hoping to avoid making a scene this time. I'm sure you understand, no point antagonizing Colonel Perry."

Melissa could see the indecision in the serviceman's face. He wasn't supposed to let them through. Technically, he could get court-martialed for it, but Kristina was casually hovering the axe of the station commander's displeasure right above his head. The ruse wouldn't have worked for somewhere actually important, but a jam-packed barracks, where everyone locked their doors already, was hardly the most high security area. She felt Kristina give her arm a squeeze and despite the tiny part of her screaming not to, she summoned a quiet sob and let another burst of tears flow down her cheeks.

Her outburst seemed to be the final straw in his decision. "Well, I suppose as long as you're quick about it." The sentry stood aside, and waved them on through.

"Thank you," Kristina's mercenary smile made Melissa cringe as she pushed them inside the barracks housing. "And do come by the coffee shop later, Terrence. I'm having a half-off special this afternoon.

"Well, thank you, miss." He turned back to face the hallway, his expression brightening at the prospect, "I definitely will."

Neither he nor Kristina noticed the scowl on Melissa's face at that last exchange. Kristina was basically bribing E-4's with coffee. The thought made her *actually* want to cry. Why was everything on this station so completely screwed up?

At least the barracks seemed normal enough. A generically grey painted hallway with rows of identical doors and bright LED bulbs studded into the ceiling. It ran for at least two hundred feet, the corridor gradually arcing upwards along the curve of the station, until it appeared to merge into the ceiling. A few people were wandering the starkly lit halls, but it was midmorning so the place was largely quiet.

"What are we doing here?" Devon whispered, as Kristina led them over to a stairwell near the entrance.

"Looking for someone." Kristina's eyes constantly flashed back and forth as she spoke, like she was watching for anyone trailing her. "The person who, I suspect, brought a bunch of high explosives onto the station."

"Here?" Melissa nearly stumbled in shock. They were in a barracks, so if the person responsible for the explosions was here… "You think it was a traitor?"

"You're not very good at listening are you, Curls?" Kristina said. "I never said traitor, *fool* perhaps, and maybe even a criminal, but if I thought he was a traitor I wouldn't be trying to find him. I would have turned him in to Colonel Perry already."

Melissa didn't bother to stifle another scowled of disgust, but Devon's eyes glowed with curiosity. "What makes you so sure?"

"Because he doesn't fit the profile of a traitor very well," Kristina explained in a quiet voice as they headed up a level at the stairwell. "The man's name is William McGregor. He's a sergeant in charge of electrical subsystems or some-such. He's been in the service for… I think fifteen years. He even received a commendation for his part defending of Magong Airport during the Chinese landings on Penghu. He's a nice enough man – no wife, plenty of friends, always orders peach tea. He, unfortunately, also has a tendency to lose when he gambles and to gamble when he shouldn't. He isn't a likely traitor though, very loyal and proud of his service."

"If he is involved, I'd guess it's because he squandered all his money playing cards and now has a bunch of creditors knocking at his door. If that's the case, then it's an easy problem to fix. If not…" Her voice trailed off as she dipped a hand into her purse, pulled out her single shot stun pistol, and snapped open the chamber to load one of her dart rounds.

"That's a lot of really specific information," Devon questioned. "How do you…"

"You can learn a lot when you offer military discounts at a coffee shop. Especially if you keep your ears open. When everyone lives this close together, OpSec rules get a bit– *flexible*." Kristina dropped the gun back into her purse and grabbed his and Melissa's arms again to steer them wherever she was going. "Now stay close, both of you. Remember, same rule as before, if you want to stay alive and out of jail, do *exactly* what I tell you."

Chapter 8
A Knife in the Dark

Kristina needn't have worried about anyone running off. After the pain she'd put him through a few minutes before, Devon didn't like his odds to wrench his arm free, even if he wasn't already dizzy from walking upstairs. Melissa still had a sullen look, as though everything about the woman offended her, but Kristina clearly had some sort of leverage over her, because she went along meekly as well.

A few people passed by on their way through the halls, but no one seemed to pay any attention to a woman marching two mopey teenagers along like she had somewhere to be. He did hope that no one recognized him afterwards though. He had no idea how he was ever supposed to explain any of this.

Eventually, Kristina released their arms when they stopped outside a beige white door, the room number stenciled in precise black letters on the mantle. Complete with a black RFID-pad lock, it looked just like every other door they'd passed.

He opened his mouth to ask if this was it, but before a word could get out, Kristina shushed him with a finger to her lips. Glancing both ways, her hand searched back into her purse and emerged holding a thin pair of black leather gloves and a small flashlight, along with that pistol of hers.

"Another advantage of running a coffee shop," Kristina whispered as she slipped on the gloves, "if you're fast, you can clone people's access codes to your implant."

She hovered her wrist near the sensor pad, and there was a soft beep accompanied by a green blinking light as the door unlocked. "Wait here," she cautioned, "and if someone starts asking questions, just send them inside. I'll deal with them." Taking a deep breath and giving the handle a sharp twist, Kristina shoved the door inwards, raised her pistol and slid inside.

Devon tensed, expecting gunshots or at least shouts from within… but there was no sound besides the soft squeak of the hinges. He and Melissa waited, the door slowly swinging shut in front of them. Devon almost let it close.

Almost.

At the last second, he stuck his foot in the gap. It was still quiet, and if there was anyone waiting inside for them, Kristina would be the primary target anyway. A peek couldn't hurt.

Across from him Melissa's mouth dropped open and violently shook her head, *No*. He didn't pay her caution much mind. She hadn't really agreed with anything he'd tried thus far. Although, admittedly, things hadn't exactly been going fantastic of late.

Gently pushing the door open, Devon found himself in a short hallway with a sink and countertops to his left and an unadorned beige wall on the right. Ten feet ahead, the entry hall opened into a larger space. There he could make out some shelves, a row of closets and a desk, with a bed-frame barely poking into view.

Kristina was sliding down the hallway, her back to the wall. When she reached the main bed area, she drifted across the open space in a tight arc, scanning the room by slices. The lights were on and she didn't need the flashlight, but she still had it positioned beneath her gun. Devon stopped short, but there was no hiss of her dart gun being fired. Instead there was a brief pause, like she saw something, and he heard the woman mutter, '*bliad.*' Devon had no idea what that meant, but it didn't sound good. Ahead, Kristina kept moving and vanished from view.

Devon crept forwards. He had never been in a military barracks, but the room didn't seem too bad. Honestly it looked to be similar to his own, small and cramped. He took another step, but froze when he heard the distinctive *thwmp* of a door being thrown open, followed by Kristina's loud exclamation, "What the hell?"

Had Devon been thinking clearly, that would have been a sign to exit. Instead, he darted forwards and stopped dead when he saw what waited in the next room. Sprawled on a chair beside the bed, sat the lifeless corpse of a man with his throat cut, his eyes strangely empty as rivulets of blood laced down his neck. He heard more steps behind him, then a sharp gasp. Devon turned to see Melissa with a hand over her mouth like she was about to be sick.

Kristina reappeared through a small door in the back that looked like it led into a bathroom, her face creased in an exasperated frown and her eyes narrowed in a deep glare. "Do you two not pay attention to *anything* I say?"

She noticed the paleness of Melissa's cheeks. "Don't puke, Curls, or you'll be the one mopping it up." With a frustrated sigh, Kristina paused to fish two pairs of latex gloves out of her purse and toss them over. "As long as you two insist on ignoring my directions, take these and don't touch anything. The last thing we need is fingerprints everywhere."

She vanished back into the bathroom where Devon could hear sobs. It took a long moment to tear his eyes from the bloody corpse, but when he did, he followed after a shockingly calm Kristina.

Inside the bathroom they found something even stranger than a dead body. Curled up in the shower, not daring even to look up, was a sobbing, huddled ball of a woman, maybe twenty, her blonde hair hanging down like a curtain around her head. "Please… don't kill me."

"Valerie?" Kristina lowered her gun at the voice, and her gaze lingered on the girl in disbelief.

There was a sniffling as she glanced up at the CIA woman with a hunted terror etched on her face. "Miss Andrews? Wha… What are you…?"

"Shhh…" Kristina slid her weapon back into her purse. She knelt down next to the weeping young woman, whose panicked gaze darted between her and the teenagers crowding at the doorway. "It's okay, Valerie," Kristina said in a calm, soothing tone.

"Miss Andrews, how are you here?"

"Well, you were two hours late for your shift," Kristina wrapped a reassuring arm around her. "I was starting to worry."

Valerie's only response was a long shivering breath. "Miss Andrews, they… they killed him."

"I know," she nodded, "I know. Wait here for a second." She stood and went back out into the main room where the pull-down bed occupied most of the space.

Apparently, Kristina guessed the wave of questions piling up in Devon's throat, because she gave a curt explanation. "Valerie's been working as a barista at my coffee shop for the last six months or so. She liked to chat with William over there." Kristina nodded towards the corpse a few feet away. "I'm not sure if they were properly dating or just friends, but they did spend a lot of time together."

"Now, if you two insist on walking in on all this, you're going to help." She checked to make sure they had their gloves on. "First rule, don't take those off unless you fancy being charged with murder, and don't toss them in the trash either, I'll take them when you're done. Second, we can't afford to linger here long. I need you two to search the room for anything that might help us figure out what happened: computers, mysterious briefcases, a surveillance video would be nice." She paused expectantly, but the two teens kept staring at her, "Well…*GO*. Get moving already," she shooed them away. "I'll take care of Miss Inconsolable." She wheeled and paced off, muttering something that sounded like, "Chet-or-ski cat-a-strofa." Whatever that meant.

Devon's eyes roved across the room, lingering on the shelves and cabinets. At least this part wouldn't be too hard.

"Devon, this isn't right," Melissa whispered behind him, a tremble in her voice.

"You don't say," he dryly agreed, pacing over to the nearest cabinet and rummaging through it.

"Seriously?" Her face turned angry. "Does nothing about this strike you as wrong?"

"I don't know? Does the dead guy five feet behind us count?"

"Not that," she hissed, "I mean all of this. Why are we sneaking into a barracks, finding dead bodies, then sneaking out again? Doesn't that seem just a *little* screwed up?"

Devon took a deep breath and found himself rubbing his temple in frustration. "Look," his voice steeled to a hard whisper, "All of this is messed up, okay – getting dragged off to Mars, getting stuck on this station, almost getting blown up last night. By rights, I ought to be sitting back in Mr Fairview's algebra class with my friends right now, not trapped in a pressurized space box going through a dead dude's things. But at this point, it's not like we have a good alternative. Let's just do whatever Kristina says and hopefully all this will eventually blow over." He turned back to the cabinet, although he didn't imagine he would find much of anything.

Behind him, Melissa gave a displeased 'humph.' He didn't know what she wanted him to say. Yes, things were clearly bad, but standing at the scene of a murder was hardly the time to mope about it. Besides, the way Kristina was talking, the choices were work fast or go to jail, and he knew which one he preferred.

There were a bunch of odds and ends in the cabinet. An old-fashioned Dungeons and Dragons rulebook sat next to a flashlight, a cheap speaker, two bags that clinked with dice and a couple of decks of cards. Crammed at the very back sat an emergency decompression pack that Devon suspected should have been hung somewhere a bit more accessible. Nothing useful though, unless you were looking to kill goblins.

Melissa quietly rummaged through the cabinet next to him, all the while studiously pretending that he didn't exist. He nearly rolled his eyes – stupid girls and their stupid silent treatment. Either way, with Melissa going through the other cabinet, that left a bunch of drawers to search. The first one he opened held rows of neatly folded socks, nothing surprising. He quickly shuffled through everything until… there was a clink and a tiny flash drive dropped out of one of the socks.

Well, that was something. Picking up the diminutive black storage device he twisted it between his fingers for a moment. This was probably what Kristina was looking for, but… if he handed it over, he had a strong suspicion he'd never see it again. Behind him, Kristina was helping Valerie outside, the woman bursting back into tears when she saw the body sprawled out on the chair in front of her. It took Kristina a moment to lead Valerie over to a spot on the bed so that her back was to the gruesome scene.

With the seconds ticking away, Devon made a snap decision and plugged the drive into a little port on the side of his phone. A flick of his hand set the files to copy over, and in a few seconds, he tugged it back out and dropped the drive into his pocket. He hastily rummaged through the two remaining drawers, while Melissa finished up with the cabinets and checked the closet.

Kristina was just managing to get Valerie's whimpering under control, although now that she had stopped crying, her eyes just stared ahead with a blank emptiness.

"You two find anything?"

Melissa shook her head, and Devon handed over the drive, "Just this."

"Hmmm," Kristina regarded it for a moment before dropping it into her pocket, "passable work, I suppose." She went over to the body of the dead William McGregor and quickly patted him down, coming away with a phone for her troubles. "Odd that they'd leave this behind," she remarked, half to herself.

Together with the flash drive, that seemed to satisfy her and she took a seat on the bed next to Valerie, putting a comforting arm around the young woman. "Okay, Valerie," she said in an uncharacteristically reassuring, almost motherly voice. "You need to tell me what happened. Do you think you can do that?" There was a long pause but eventually Valerie gave a voiceless nod.

"Okay, then," Kristina began, "let's start with why you were up here."

"William," Valerie said with a sniff, "he invited me, said something about a surprise, about leaving Medea." Her voice broke off for a second like she didn't want to think about it. "Whenever he came in for coffee after his shift, we liked to talk… about all sorts of things. We both wanted to get off Medea, and I told him how I'd always dreamed about going to visit London. He wanted to go to Paris, even despite all the bombings. He always joked that he would be fine so long as he didn't take the subway."

She paused and swallowed, like that joke wasn't very funny anymore. "He took two weeks of leave in February," she continued in a halting voice. "When he came back last week, he started talking about how he was going to make it rich soon. He didn't say how, but he was thinking about retiring from the Space Force when his enlistment was up and going back to Utah with his parents. This morning, before work, he messaged me and asked me to meet him downstairs. We came up here, and he started talking about how he had come into a lot of money recently. He said his life was turning around and then…" Her voice broke off into a single haunted breath, and her hands covered her eyes to hide the tears that welled up in them.

"It's okay," Kristina whispered softly, "just take it one step at a time. What happened next?"

Valerie shuddered and reached into her pocket, her voice nearly breaking as she spoke. "He gave me this," she pulled out her phone and unlocked it to show Kristina, "a ticket to London." She paused and glanced at the older woman. "I know you paid to bring me up here to work, Miss Andrews, and I'm grateful for the opportunity, it's just… I miss the sky, and the birds, and breathing air that doesn't taste like it's been through a thousand other people's lungs. I just wanted to be back on Earth again." She paused like she was afraid she had gotten herself in trouble.

"I understand," Kristina nodded. "It's nothing to be ashamed of, Valerie."

"You do?" Valerie mumbled in surprise. "But–"

"But I'm a heartless witch?" Kristina supplied readily.

Valerie didn't answer, but she didn't deny it either.

"Don't worry, I get that from a lot of people. Now, what happened next?"

"Well," as Valerie spoke, the words seemed more and more to simply tumble out, "we talked about it for a while. I was just so excited at the chance. A little later I went to the restroom and while I was in there, I heard this sudden thump, then shouting. I couldn't tell what they were saying, but it sounded middle-eastern, maybe Arabic. I was so scared and... I could hear William trying to reason with them. He kept saying he hadn't told anyone, but he didn't say about what. Then they started talking to each other in the other language. There was this horrible gurgling noise and..." she shivered. "Eventually I heard them leave, and once I was sure they were gone, I peeked outside. When I saw William dead I... I didn't know what to do," she collapsed back into sobs on Kristina's shoulder.

Kristina gave her a moment to take a few deep breaths and regain control. "Could you tell how many people there were?"

"I only heard two voices," Valerie said, her green-grey eyes tinged red from tears. "But there could have been more."

"Okay then," Kristina glanced back at the body and shook her head, "here's how this is going to work, Valerie. You have two options, either stay on this station and end up in a lot of trouble, or do what I say, and I'll try and get you a job in London, back away from all this."

Valerie looked up in amazement, she opened her mouth but the words seemed to tangle coming out, "You... you would do that?" Valerie stammered. "How?"

"Best not to ask too many questions, but suffice to say I'm not completely heartless." Kristina patted her on the back. "You'll have to do the occasional favor," she added, "nothing complicated."

Valerie gave a grateful nod, and Kristina turned back to Devon and Melissa. "Okay, you two, we need to move fast. I assume you both were smart enough not to leave fingerprints anywhere except for the main door? You didn't touch anything else before I gave you those gloves?" They both shook their heads.

"Good, I'll clean up Valerie here, then we'll wipe down everything with prints on it and be long gone by the time the MP's show up. Those boys have no sense of humor."

Chapter 9
The Treacherous Heights

The door to the late William McGregor's room gently tapped shut and Devon promptly rubbed down the doorknob with a white cloth, taking a few seconds to make sure he was thorough about it. Kristina peered over his shoulder, and when he finished, she gave an approving nod.

A lot had happened in only a few minutes. Valerie's hair had been combed, and the makeup smudges on her face were gone. The only trace of the distraught young woman they'd found inside was the redness in her eyes and a few damp patches on her shirt. The inside was different too, although more subtly so. He and Melissa had quickly wiped down every surface that might have had prints on it to keep the military police from learning about Valerie before Kristina could shuffle her off station. He wasn't entirely sure why that was necessary, given that Kristina was CIA, but when he'd asked, she had just said something about not getting along well with military sorts. If the dark looks Melissa was giving her were anything to go off, that certainly had a grain of truth to it.

Kristina led off at a quick pace, and they were soon down at the main entrance. She sent Valerie out first, alone, so as not to arouse suspicion. Valerie had orders to head back to her room for an hour or two before taking the 'back way' into Kristina's office. With Valerie dispatched, that just left him, Kristina, and Melissa.

"Alright," Kristina took both their arms, but this time she wasn't quite as rough as before. "So, it's pretty much the same drill as before, except it seems you two lied to me about your parents being here. So now I'm hauling you both back to my shop for a more creative punishment. Understand?"

Devon's face tinged red in embarrassment, and Melissa didn't appear to be taking it much better. Neither put up a protest though. Devon just wanted to get away from that body upstairs. If the price was another ounce of his dignity, then so be it.

As it was, the guard didn't even bother to ask questions. He gave Kristina a curt nod as she left, and barely glanced at the two teenagers. A few seconds later, they were off down the hallway, no one the wiser.

"Where are we going now?" Devon asked after they were some distance away.

"Not much further. I just prefer to get well out of sight before I let you two run off, keep up appearances and all. The way the station curves up in the distance, it's far too easy to keep an eye on someone, even in a crowd."

"That's it?" Melissa asked in surprise. "We're free?"

"Well, if you tell anyone about this, you'll be dead. But for the moment, yes. Think of it as, your usefulness to me has expired."

"So, what are we supposed to do?" Devon asked.

"I don't know," she shrugged. "Go to a movie, make out in a corner, whatever it is children your age normally do." She paused, "Don't do drugs."

As they talked, Kristina steered them off to the side of the main concourse. "I think this should be far enough." She released her grip on their arms, "Curls, can I see your purse?"

Melissa held her bag a bit closer to her chest. "What for?"

"You have something of mine," Kristina sighed and gestured with a finger for her to hand it over. When Melissa finally did, Kristina slipped a hand inside and it re-emerged holding an intricate wristlet of twisted gold and silver bands.

Melissa's mouth dropped open at the sight, her eyes wide as cups, panic in her voice. "That's not… I didn't take…"

"Yes," Kristina said in a bored tone like they'd been over this before, "I'm quite aware you didn't steal it, Curls. It was just my little insurance policy, in case you decided to bail on our bargain."

Instantly Melissa's face went from worried to a mask of outrage, "You…"

Kristina didn't even give her a pause to vent. She just grinned, a patronizing look like she was about to pat them both on the head. "But look at you, all honorable and true to your word. I like it. We'll do this again sometime."

Kristina glanced around and exhaled a short breath. "Well, I think we're wrapped up here. You two go, have fun, enjoy Medea, and remember," her eyes narrowed to dangerous slits, "*not a word* about this."

"And what about the dead guy?" Devon demanded. "We still don't – Oww," Melissa jabbed a sharp elbow into his side. "What was that for?"

"Shut up," Melissa hissed beneath her breath.

Kristina bit back a laugh. "You know, I'm starting to like you two and your little 'cavalcade of stupidity'. Keep it up," she turned to leave, "and try not to die." Kristina strode off, leaving Devon and Melissa glaring at each other.

"Well, great," he threw up his arms, "now we have to find out how that guy died on our own."

"No, *actually*, we don't," Melissa snapped back in a foul temper. "How about we just steer clear before Kristina decides to ruin our lives some other way."

"You're not curious?"

"Of course I'm curious," she crossed her arms. "I'm also smart enough to know we should stay way."

"So what, we just sit tight and stick our heads in the sand until the station gets blasted apart beneath us?" Devon asked.

"No," Melissa fumed, "but…" her voice trailed off for a moment, uncertain, and when she did speak again her tone softened. "I don't know what *we're* supposed to do about it.

Besides, getting caught up with intelligence people is a quick road to bad things."

Devon shot her a confused look. "How would you know, it's not like it's happen before."

For a beat Melissa didn't answer, a stab of pain flickering across her face. "It has, actually," she finally answered, defensive, "and the last time I got involved with people like this, it ended up being really sad… for everyone."

That wasn't quite the answer Devon had been anticipating. The remorse in her voice was enough to give him pause. "Look, I'm sorry. Just… someone's murdering people and…"

Melissa sighed and bit at her lip, "Yeah, I know."

For a second the words hung in the air between them, like no one really knew what to do. Finally, Devon looked at her. "How about we go get food somewhere," he offered. "Figure out what we're going to do about all this."

Melissa's face flushed in embarrassment, "I ummm… I'm not sure anywhere on this station is really in my price range."

He shrugged, "Me neither. Fortunately, it's not a problem," he held up his phone with a grin. "My dad lets me use one of his cards."

"He doesn't mind?"

"Well, *technically* he doesn't know, so you have to keep it a secret."

"You stole it?" Melissa demanded, indignant.

"No need to start shouting," Devon cautioned. "And besides," his tone was that of a lawyer, "steal is such a simplistic term. We went on a field trip last year, and my dad authorized my phone to draw from his card so I could get lunch. Afterwards, I just… forgot to de-authorize it. No stealing."

Melissa didn't look terribly convinced.

"I try to be responsible," Devon added, "and dad hasn't cared in the last year, so I think we're fine. And, if you think about it, it's not even stealing. We can either *go get food*, or track down my parents and convince them to *go get food* for us. This way is easier for everyone."

Devon could see the wheels ticking in her head. Given all her objections to everything else, he probably should have guessed she was a 'follow the rules' type. Probably something to do with her dad. He hadn't seemed like a very fun person to disagree with. Devon could tell she was hungry though, and that tended to rebalance the scales of justice or morality or... whatever.

"Okay," Melissa nodded, although the effort brought a pained grimace to her face. "Where do you want to eat?"

"Well, given a choice, I'd choose Gino's," Devon remarked, half to himself.

"What's that?"

"Only the best deep-dish pizza ever." He saw the confusion on her face. "It's a Chicago thing. If we ever get back to Earth, I can show you."

"Yeah, *if.*" She shot him a sideways look, then her tone seemed to mellow some. "You know, there's a Seoul Express somewhere around here. I tried to convince my parents to go there last night, but we couldn't figure out where it was, and we ended up stopping at some bottom tier Tex-Mex place. It was TT 250.320.0, I believe."

Devon cocked an eyebrow. Out of the whole station, *that* was her choice? He eyed her a second, wondering if she was joking, but when she didn't laugh, he nodded. "Sure... I guess."

Kristina had dropped them off at -TT 250.40.0+ and from there it was just, face the letters painted on the wall, then go left to follow the minus sign back to 0 then 350, and soon enough, 320.

For a little while they walked in silence. Devon wasn't sure what he could say that wouldn't spark another fight. All he could really think to talk about was the fact that they had just seen a dead guy, but Melissa seemed hard set on ignoring that.

He wasn't sure why. Add that down as yet another thing he didn't understand about girls. It wasn't like not talking about it made it go away. Somewhere out there, two murderers were running loose. Even worse, they were probably the same people who had planted that bomb. Melissa might not want to talk about it, but if they waited too long, he suspected ignoring it might not be an option.

As though she was reading his mind, Melissa shook her head. "Why is this happening?" She glanced at him and Devon could see a faint mist clouding her eyes. "One day – *literally* twenty-four hours since we've been here – and we've been blown up, almost arrested, blackmailed by a crazy lady, and stuck in a room with a dead body. Thousands of people pass through Medea station, yet somehow we're the ones who have all the trouble."

Her voice trailed off like she had just had an idea. "Maybe you're the problem," her eyes narrowed on Devon. "You did just convince me to help commit bank fraud… against your parents."

"Okay, calling it bank fraud is a *little* extreme."

"Well, what would you call it?"

"Lunch," Devon paused for a second with a bemused expression. "Look, I don't disagree that this seems kind of unfair, but I'd say you're overthinking it, just a little."

Melissa glared and made a noise that somehow reminded Devon of an angry cat. Finally, she looked away. "It's just, I don't normally get in trouble, you know."

Devon shook his head and tried to hide a grin, "I never would have guessed."

It was close to noon now, and the halls were quickly filling up with people. With only one main corridor for the thousands of bodies crammed on Medea Station, it wasn't hard to see how traffic could get tangled up quickly. It was interesting too. He kept his eyes open for more teenagers his own age, the people he'd be spending the next six months getting to know. He didn't see many. They passed two older boys sitting in a restaurant, and a pack of girls about Melissa's age who wandered by going the other direction. He even saw a girl with aqua blue hair of all things, busy berating a boy about his own age in what sounded like… French?

There weren't many though, especially not compared to the number of adults they passed, and Devon was smart enough to run through the ratios in his head. Hundreds of adults compared to maybe ten kids, thirteen counting himself, Melissa and Evie. Scale that up to two thousand, and it was going to be a *very* small world on the Persephone.

At least the place they were looking for wasn't hard to find, a chain barbecue restaurant called Seoul Express. Devon had only been there once, when his family took a vacation down to

Florida. That it even existed was enough to convince him that southerners were completely crazy. Half the menu was a variation on Deep South soul food, mostly fried chicken and pulled pork. The other half was Korean BBQ. Basically, the bipolar step child of Bojangles and Panda Grill. Fortunately, it hadn't caught on in Chicago yet, although he couldn't fathom how one had ended up on Medea Station.

Melissa's face burst into a wide smile when she saw the sign looming up above the concourse, like she had just found an old friend. "Have you ever been here before?"

"Just once, a few years back. You come here a lot?"

"My friends and I used to go eat at the one back in Wichita Falls after school," she explained. "I suggest the Dak Galbi with fried okra and hushpuppies."

Frankly, that sounded… weird, also slightly unpronounceable. Devon found himself wishing for a good old hotdog as he stared at the menu and tried to remember what he had ordered the last time he'd been here. Thankfully, there was a line, which gave him a minute to work out his order.

"I used to drag my dad here whenever I could," Melissa added as they waited. "He hates the place, calls it 'an unholy fusion.' He grew up in rural Oklahoma though, so his perspective on good food is a bit of a mess."

"So, about your dad," Devon said, "I didn't get to ask after we bumped into him last night. I take it he's in the army or something?"

"The Space Force actually, *Lieutenant Colonel* Bryan Hale." The way she said it, Devon couldn't tell if it was pride or sarcasm in her voice. Perhaps she wasn't entirely sure herself.

"So, what does he do?"

"Whatever the Space Force says."

Definitely sarcasm that time.

"Hello there, can I take your order?" the man at the register interrupted.

"Yes," Melissa smiled and ordered her weird Dak Galbi dish, leaving him to make a more traditional choice of chicken strips and fries. At least they served *some* normal food. Devon had mentally prepared for the price, but he still swallowed when

$183 popped up. Back on Earth, he and Melissa could have gotten three meals for that. He didn't complain though, not in front of her. Instead he hovered his phone near the payment pad, and pressed the green 'Confirm' button when it popped up.

"Thanks," Melissa said as they got drinks and found a table, making sure to set a little stand with their order number so it was visible.

"Don't mention it." He took a sip of his fizzy Dr Pepper and shot her a side glance. "Seriously, *don't* mention it. It's not even my money.

"Still, thank you," she smiled, a soft grin that brought a rose tint to her cheeks.

Devon shifted the subject before he could embarrass himself too much. "So, you said your dad was a lieutenant colonel, what does that mean?"

"It means exactly that, he's O-5, a step above major and a step below colonel. I think he mostly specializes in Electronic Warfare and Countermeasures, if that's what you're asking. What about your parents?"

"Well, my mom used to be an elementary teacher back in Merrillville. She taught fourth grade, but she had to quit when the whole Mars thing came up. That's my dad's deal. He's a mining engineer with Mauldron Interplanetary Resources. He had a cool office in the Hancock Building and everything, but they wanted him to go out and help with some big project in the Tharsis Mountains, so… here we are. My mom's going to try and get a new job on Mars. Supposedly it's pretty easy to find work there. I was even thinking of trying to get a job myself. It'd be cool to have some of my own money for once, and I hear they pay really well."

"Assuming we survive to get there," Melissa said dryly.

"Yes, there is that," Devon's voice trailed off for a moment, and he became more serious. "Melissa, since we're in this together there's umm… something you deserve to know."

She must have seen the hesitance in his eyes, "Oh no, Devon, what did you do?"

"It's nothing bad," he raised his hands to mollify her. "You remember that flash drive I found?"

Her eyebrows rose like she guessed what was coming next. "What about it?"

"Well, I might have, sort of, cloned the data to my phone before I handed it over."

"You what?" Melissa's hands clenched in frustration. "Why would you do that?"

"Curiosity...?"

"Devon," she unconsciously massaged her temples as she spoke, "you do realize these people are *not* to be screwed with? Right?"

He shrugged, "I don't think we have to worry about Kristina coming–"

"It's not that," Melissa looked like she wanted to tear out her hair in frustration. "Look, regardless of what Kristina thinks about this whole screwball mess, the further we are from her, the safer we are. Her sort always run towards trouble, and if we wander too close, we'll get dragged along. If you aren't careful your curiosity is going to get us both killed... or worse, arrested." She glanced up and abruptly fell quiet as a waitress walked up with their food.

"Enjoy your meal." The woman set two aluminum trays in front of them.

"Thanks," Devon muttered. He waited until she left, then his brown eyes honed straight back in on Melissa, "You were saying?"

"That you're going to get us killed," the girl met his gaze with an insistent frown. She laced together her fingers and set them on the cool steel table. "You still don't believe me, do you?"

"I just think you're overreacting," he said, levelly. "Yes, this is dangerous, but I don't see how we can just go back to our lives after all this."

Melissa didn't respond, not right away at least. Instead, she turned to her tray and hungrily popped something into her mouth that resembled an overdone tater-tot, except with a hint of green inside. Probably the fried okra. Watching her, Devon felt his own stomach grumbling in a demand to be fed, and he tentatively tasted one of his chicken strips. It was actually edible, a little spicy for his tastes, but everything from the south was spicy. After his awful burger the night before, he rated it as a pleasant surprised.

He took a few more bites, while Melissa stared at him with a thoughtful look, quietly nibbling on a hushpuppy. "Did you mean what you said earlier? About us being in this together?"

"Of course."

She regarded him for a long moment, her gaze reminding Devon very much of the way Kristina had looked at him, like she could peer straight into his soul. "Okay then," Melissa said, her face turning grim, "in that case, you deserve to know what you're getting into." She paused for a second, as though she was working up her nerve. "I don't normally talk about this, but have you ever heard of Frankfurt?"

In point of fact Devon hadn't, but he could make an educated guess. "Is that German?"

She nodded, "It's a city in south Germany, not far from Ramstein Air Force Base. The Space Force shares some facilities with the Air Force, and my dad was stationed there for a year and a half before he got reassigned back to Wichita Falls. Anyway, do you recall about two and a half years ago, there was a bombing at the Zeilgalerie?"

"The what?"

"It's a shopping mall with really abstract, fancy architecture."

That did jog his memory a little, "Oh yeah, I remember something like that. That was the one where the American girl got killed, right?"

"Yes," Melissa's voice was strangely quiet.

Devon nodded, "Yeah, it was all over the news back home for about a week. I guess Germany is kind of messed up with all the terrorist bombings and everything. What was her name anyway, it was something like Audrey or…?"

"Amy."

"That's the one. But…" He noticed the mist in Melissa's eyes, his voice faltering as he understood. "You knew her?"

Melissa stared at the table and brushed away the tear that rolled down her cheek. "She was my friend. My best friend." Her voice broke, and she took a long shuddering breath. "That's not what I wanted to talk about though, what matters is what happened next.”

“I had another friend there too, a German girl named Fatima. Her parents were going to Frankfurt for the day and Amy and I convinced them to take us along for a shopping trip. Her dad was really strict about her going outside without an escort and all, so we ended up saddled with her older brother, Ahmed. It was still fun though, up until…” She bit at her lip a second, “We were in a perfume shop when the bomb went off. Fatima’s brother hated it there. He’d just dragged her outside. Said it was *improper* for a girl. She was furious, shouting at him. Honestly, I think she was more embarrassed than anything else, but without realizing it, he saved her life.”

Melissa shuddered like there was a part of the story she didn’t want to recall, but finally she continued. “The last thing I remember is the paramedics giving me a sedative, then I woke up in a hospital bed. My parents were there and it was… bad. After a while they told me there were some *people* outside who needed to ask me a few ‘questions.’

“They were with the *Bundes-nach-richten-dienst*, the BND, it’s… it’s like the German version of the FBI, and they were *just* like Kristina. On the outside they were friendly, all sympathetic smiles and condolences. But if you pushed just an inch beneath the surface, they were the sort of people who would stick a knife between their friend’s ribs if they had to and claim it was all just business. When Kristina said we could go because our *usefulness* had expired, I don’t think she was lying. In fact, it was probably the only true thing she’s told us.”

“Anyway, the BND people seemed nice enough. They asked what happened, and my parents told me to just tell the truth… so I did. I was thirteen and I had just watched…” her voice broke off with a tiny shake of her head. “I didn’t understand how things looked. When I got to the part about Ahmed and Fatima, and how he had pulled her outside right beforehand, they were suddenly all ears.”

“They started asking me these questions about Ahmed. Had he ever seemed overly religious? Did he ever get angry? What were his friends like?”

"It was just question after question," she shook her head. "I didn't like Ahmed. I thought he treated Fatima like dirt, and frankly, he was pretty religious… and not in a good way. So I told them that. They asked if I knew about his 'subversive' activities online. That was when my mom figured out they were looking for someone to blame. She got super-pissed, told them to leave right then."

"Dad though, he takes the whole duty thing really seriously, and he said they should stay. Looked me right in the eye, and told me to tell them the truth, whatever it was."

My dad was a major back then and my mom was just – my mom, so they stayed. At the time I was so angry about what had happened to Amy, and when they started hinting at terrorism… well, I said some things I wish I could take back."

Melissa sighed, and Devon noticed she was unconsciously chasing her food around her plate with a fork. "The Germans call it *Krieg der Schatten,*" she continued, "the War of Shadows. After the Chancellery bombing in Berlin, German policy was to just expel anyone with ties to *Radikal Islam*, even if they weren't convicted of a specific crime. It was guilt by association."

"After the BND people left, my parents had an awful fight right outside my room. They barely spoke to one another for a week, and I was stuck lying in a hospital bed terrified that they were going to be divorced by the time I got home. The first few days I was there, Fatima came to visit at least, but then she stopped, didn't answer my texts. It was like she dropped off the face of the earth."

"When I got out of the hospital a week and a half later, I wanted to go see her. But Mom kept telling me no. She wouldn't say why, so the next Friday, I put on a headscarf and snuck out to Fatima's apartment. It probably wasn't the best idea, but I caught a DriveMe into Kaiserslautern. I got to Fatima's place, and when she answered the door I looked in her eyes and…" Melissa's eyes pressed shut as she spoke, like she was trying to hide from the memory. "It was like she knew."

"They'd taken Ahmed a few days earlier, given him what they called *Die endgültige entscheidung*, 'the final decision.' Ankara or Tehran, Sunni or Shiite. They were the only places that would take radical westerners that no one else wanted. I might not have liked him, and maybe Ahmed was mixed up in some bad things, but he didn't deserve that." Melissa's voice fell quiet, like she wasn't sure what else she could say.

"You don't think he planted the bomb?" Devon asked.

Melissa shook her head, "I've been over it a thousand times in my head, he was never in the right part of the store. Besides, if he had, he would have been arrested and thrown in jail, not expelled." She shook her head with a painful remorse. "That part was all thanks to me."

Devon nodded, one finger nervously tapping on the table. After a moment, he offered, "I'm sorry."

Melissa tore her focus away from the table and met his gaze with a strange fire in her eyes. "I didn't tell you the story to ask for your pity, I've got plenty enough of that on my own. My point is that all it took was ten minutes of talking with people like Kristina. Ten minutes of me *not* being careful, and I lost my friend, I nearly lost my parents, and Fatima's family was ruined. All because I couldn't shut up. And Devon, if we aren't very careful, if we treat this like a game, that is *exactly* what will happen to us too."

Devon didn't know what to say to that. After a moment Melissa turned back to her meal. He barely touched his food. "So what do you suggest we do with the files from the flash drive? Delete them?"

"I don't know. Maybe?" Her middle finger drummed on the table. "I will admit, I'm curious, but like I said, curiosity can get us killed."

Melissa paused to take another bite of her fried okra, and suddenly her lips curled in a mournful smile. "I've ruined lunch, haven't I?" She shook her head and Devon couldn't separate the amusement from the sadness in her voice. "All this talk of death and despair when we're supposed to be enjoying a meal."

"It's okay," Devon took a deep breath, "you're not wrong, not entirely."

"Not entirely?" Melissa cocked her head to one side. That was definitely amusement in her voice now. "Well, I suppose that's progress."

Chapter 10
Working the Other End

Lieutenant Colonel Bryan Hale wasn't having the best day. The layover on Medea station was supposed to be relaxing. At least that was how his previous CO had described it when he saw the transfer orders, 'Enjoy your space vacation.'

That vacation had lasted all of three hours, right up until someone decided to do some explosives testing down in sewage treatment. Now, ten thousand gallons of water and more than three hundred thousand SCF of air had been lost to the vacuum of space. Meanwhile, sewage treatment was undergoing emergency repairs to get it functional before the station ran through its two-day water reserves. His life was right back in crisis mode. Even if he wasn't technically part of the station garrison, he was currently the third most senior officer on Medea, and so he had been swept up in the investigation, regardless of if it was 'vacation' or not.

"Let me understand this," Colonel Hale was sitting across from Staff Sergeant Tiffany Bell with a severe expression, "the last thing you remember is going to sleep the night before last. Then you woke up, no uniform, lying on the floor in engineering, and no memory of anything?"

The woman stared at the table in obvious humiliation, "Yes, sir... I'm sorry."

Colonel Hale wanted to punch the table in frustration. "Nothing else?"

She shook her head.

He tried not to be angry that she couldn't remember. It wasn't her fault, and Tiffany wasn't the only one with the exact same story. A *substance inhibiting long-term memory formation* was how the doctor had explained it. Shaking his head, the Lieutenant Colonel stood and walked out of the interrogation room, rubbing his forehead. Outside, a woman in military uniform with short cropped brown hair stood waiting for him, next to a man in casual civilian clothes.

Colonel Hale nodded to the woman. "Any luck, Major?"

She shook her head. "I'm sorry, sir. I've had them try every trick I know. Any surveillance footage from last night is gone."

"Can you tell if it was deleted, or did someone just turn the cameras off?"

I suspect they were off, sir," Major Sophie Tannenhill wet her lips. "The database has a file with the correct timestamp written to it, but it's a two-kilobyte header file. It seems the system tried to log the data, but there was nothing to log."

"And no one who was watching noticed two hours of blank screens?"

"We suspect whoever infiltrated the system looped prior footage. One file from earlier yesterday was accessed around the time in question, that could have been fed to the monitor's screens while the actual feeds logged nothing. Whoever did this was very good, sir."

"Or they had access to our systems," the man in civilian clothes remarked suggestively.

Colonel Hale and Major Tannenhill both glanced at him in irritation. "Yes, *obviously* we were hacked," Sophie remarked contemptuously. "We were just saying that."

"You misunderstand, Major," the other man said smoothly. "I was referring to the source of the infiltration. Perhaps it was so effective because it came from *closer* to home."

Sophie's look turned very nasty when she realized what he was hinting at. "Perhaps it would be best for you to keep your *theories* to yourself, Mr Banks," she hissed. "Especially if you're going to make insinuations about my command."

"Major," Bryan caught the edge in Sophie's voice, "Banks is just trying to help."

Sophie stiffened a little at the implied reprimand, "Apologies sir, I was just offering him some advice… for his own safety."

Bryan Hale couldn't help but grin. "Of course, why don't you head back and see if you can dig up anything else on the other surveillance cameras. Banks and I have other business to attend to." He paused, "And, Major, I trust you will be very serious about Mr. Banks' *safety*."

"Yes, sir." Sophie forced a fake smile and snapped to attention for a quick salute.

Bryan matched the salute and Sophie wheeled to leave.

"Touchy woman." Evan Banks' brown eyes glared after her.

"No," Colonel Hale declared levelly, "touchy subject. I don't know if this foolishness is normal for you CIA sorts, Banks, but if our places were switched, I might keep my insinuations of treason to a minimum. Especially when on a station surrounded by the very soldiers you're accusing."

"Of course," Banks' eyes glimmered in irritation, but he didn't raise his voice.

"Now, what was it you wanted? Unless pissing off Major Tannenhill was your goal for the day."

"Just a bonus," Evan Banks remarked disdainfully. "While you two were busy playing with computers and interrogating amnesia patients, I asked around and found something far more interesting. One of your sentries had a very strange experience last night. I couldn't get the whole story, but it sounds like a woman snuck out of engineering with several teenagers in tow. Odd, wouldn't you say?"

Bryan's brow furled in confusion. "He didn't report it this morning?"

"He claimed he didn't think it was important. But I got the feeling he assumed he would be in trouble." Banks shrugged, "I don't know how all that works, so I figured he might be more talkative with a senior officer sitting across from him."

Bryan Hale regarded the lean CIA officer for a moment. Thus far, Banks hadn't shown much talent for anything besides irritating everyone he came within twenty feet of with his smug sarcasm. He also suspected that Banks had a notebook somewhere where he was keeping a precise tally of all the help offered and planning exactly what leverage he was going to get out of it later. That said, the Colonel couldn't afford to let a lead go cold, especially not when everyone else was drawing blanks. They needed to know who was trying to sabotage the station before it happened again. He gestured the CIA man forward, "Lead on."

***

By the time Devon and Melissa were finishing their lunch, they still hadn't figured out what to do. Devon didn't want to fight about it, and the only thing they could agree on was that they'd at least look at the files, and figure out what to do afterwards. It was one of those 'plan to make a plan' sorts of plans.

In the meantime, he needed to think. He tried not to show it, but Melissa's story had him a little rattled. Ever since meeting Kristina, he hadn't really thought of her as dangerous. Granted, she was *functionally* dangerous – he had seen her tranquilize people on a snap decision. But she was dangerous the way a gun or a sword was dangerous. She was targeted, controlled.

Maybe it was something about Kristina's demeanor, the casual sense of calm that seemed to radiate out around her, but some part of Devon's brain insisted that a person like that wouldn't just turn on them. Melissa treated her like a wild dog that might bite them at any second, but he wasn't so sure. Kristina could be scary, but she was playing a very specific game, and he and Melissa weren't her targets. In a way, Kristina was very predictable. She had a goal – save Medea Station – and she could be depended on to do exactly that.

Except… if she wasn't telling the whole truth, then it was like playing chess without knowing the rules. Melissa's point – that Kristina was only reliably honest about the fact that she was

100

using them – rang truer than Devon cared to admit. And that upset the game.

He shook his head to try and brush away the worrisome thought. At least lunch was good. Despite his misgivings, Devon enjoyed the Seoul Express. His chicken was surprisingly crisp and crunchy, and the whole restaurant was flooded with the spicy scent of sirloin marinated in ginger, garlic and sesame oil. Behind it all he heard the soft humming of fans feeding smoky air from the kitchen into the CO2 scrubbers. Maybe it was just that he was growing used to the bland staleness of his cabin, but the strange menagerie of scents was a genuine pleasure. Anything was better than recycled air and the overpowering odor of bleach whenever he used a bathroom.

"I wonder how they got all this up here?" Melissa finished the last bites of her lunch and tilted her head to one side, staring at the steel table with a half-frown. "I'm not allowed to put more than fifty pounds in a suitcase, but somehow they can get steel tables and metal trays shipped up here."

"Shipped *down* actually," Devon answered between bites as he munched on a spicy French fry. "My dad was explaining it to me last night. Most of the metal they used to build Medea isn't from down on Earth. A few decades ago they captured some asteroid called Apophis and mined the whole thing out. I guess it was a big deal at the time, almost kicked off a war over who got it."

"So, this is all from outer space?" Melissa regarded her tray with a newfound respect. "I suppose that's cool, they just drop it from way up in orbit and catch it down here."

"Actually, you can't *just* drop it," Devon explained. "They use ion tugs to drag it down to a lower orbit. Since there isn't air resistance, it takes work to move down to a lower orbit, same as moving up to a higher one. It's just more efficient to go down, because you can use lower thrust ion engines instead of chemical rockets for the transfer burn."

He paused, realizing Melissa was watching him like some sort of strange specimen she'd stumbled onto. "Huh, interesting," she finally said in a voice like it clearly wasn't

Suddenly Devon wanted to kick himself.

For a moment he chewed on his lower lip, trying to think of anything else to discuss. Finally he said, "So, do you know somewhere private we can go to look through the files?"

Melissa fidgeted with her hair, twirling a few strands around her finger. "Your cabin doesn't work?"

"I'd rather not get Evie involved in this any more than she already is. What about your room?"

Melissa shook her head. "Trust me, you don't want my parents finding us there."

Devon mulled it over for a moment, her dad *was* pretty scary. "Where do people go to make out around here?"

"What?" Melissa's face curled in a scandalized glower.

He sighed, yet another mistake on his part. "I don't mean like that, it's just…logically that should be an isolated spot."

"Except for all the other people with the same idea," she muttered coldly. "How about we just walk around for a while until we find somewhere. Kristina seems to have hidey holes all over the station, I'm sure we can find one."

Devon nearly snickered at her use of the phrase 'hidey hole.' That was very country bumpkin-ish of her. Not the time though.

His phone beeped and he glanced at the message. "Actually, maybe we can use my room after all. My parents are taking Evie out for lunch." There was another beep and this time Devon winced. "And mom's angry that I left Evie alone. Great."

***

Lieutenant Colonel Hale sat next to Evan Banks, the two examining the short list of names on the tablet in front of them. "This is supposed to be everyone that matches the description your man gave?"

"Not exactly," Banks explained, "A woman in her late-twenties and two teenagers are probably impossible to narrow down. But a ten-year-old leaving engineering with them is… irregular. I can't imagine why she would be there if she wasn't somehow related to one of them. This is a list of every teenager on the station with a younger sister ages 8-12. There are only three, which limits our search significantly.

102

Bryan Hale found himself massaging his temples again in frustration. This was idiotic. Where would a ten-year-old girl get her hands on high explosives, and what saboteur with a brain would drag a child along on a mission to blast a hole in Medea Station? Unfortunately, it was also the only lead he had, so it was either this or stare over Major Tannenhill's shoulder as she wasted the day trying to recover surveillance files that simply weren't there.

"I say we should just run down the list and interview everyone," Banks continued, ignoring the Colonel's obvious displeasure. "If we can find the girl, then maybe we can start unraveling this mess."

Bryan scanned through the names, and one jumped out at him, 'Devon Northrop' younger sister, 'Evie Northrop.' That was the boy he'd seen Melissa with yesterday evening, wasn't it. That probably excluded him from the list of suspects. Melissa knew better than to hang around with terrorists, but it was an opportunity of sorts. Let the boy know he was being watched… closely.

"Let's start with this one," he pointed to Devon's name. It was last on the list but Banks didn't protest.

***

Melissa was surprised when she walked into Devon's cabin. She shouldn't have been. It looked pretty much like her own, except a little bigger to accommodate an extra bed. For some subconscious reason, she had been expecting something nicer. Maybe it was just the ingrained jealousy of civilians she'd been nurturing since before she could remember.

She found a seat at the foot of one of the beds. The sheets were still in a wadded-up mess, so this was probably Devon's. On a whim she gave it an experimental bounce. Yep, the mattress felt the same as hers also.

"Sorry, the bed's not made." Devon swung the door shut behind them and dropped down next to her. "I was busy this morning."

"Is it ever?" Melissa made a cheeky guess.

103

"Ummm..." his cheeks tinged scarlet with a guilty expression. "So, those files." He dug out his phone and set it on the floor in front of them. A quick flick of his hand brought up the semi-transparent holographic display, and a second enlarged it to the size of a full sixty-inch screen. "This is going to be murder on the battery," he muttered.

Melissa had never seen a full-sized holographic screen except in commercials. "How does it work?" She reached out and suddenly the whole screen blinked and scrambled up.

"Careful," Devon waved his hands to get everything back to where it was, "the gesture recognition is still a little touchy. I've only had it a few weeks and I haven't had the time to work out how to make it less sensitive yet."

Melissa took the hint and put her hands firmly in her lap as Devon flicked his way through the various screens until he pulled up a folder. "So, this is it."

He popped open the folder and inside found two files. The first was one of those weird 1 KB files that computers seemed to spit out for no reason. The other was a video file labeled 'Insurance.'

"Well, here goes." Devon pressed play.

The camera shook and wobbled, like the holder couldn't figure out what angle he wanted to use. The room looked familiar though, very much like the apartment where they had found the dead William McGregor. Suddenly, it flipped around, held at arm's length and focused in on an oversized version of the visibly nervous man's face. "Hello, this is Technical Sergeant William McGregor, United States Space Force. Today is February 28, 2067," the man announced to the camera, a little cautious at first but gaining confidence as he spoke. "If you find this video, either I'm dead and you're investigating why, or something went wrong with what's about to happen and I turned this recording over to the authorities. In the event that I'm uhh..." he swallowed, "dead, there's a box back in my quarters labeled 'to my parents' that I request be sent to them."

"In a few minutes, I am going to deliver this—" the camera spun around and looked down on an open suitcase, filled with large squat bars in green saran wrap. "I don't know what these are, but someone is paying an awful lot for them. I'm videoing the swap as insurance and leverage in case anything goes wrong," he paused for a second.

"Umm… also, I suppose if I am dead, I might as well say that the suitcase was smuggled aboard with the spare parts on my shuttle up. I assume whoever's watching will want to fix the hole in security. Anyway, it's time to go."

What followed was a good minute of the camera bouncing wildly enough to give Melissa a motion sickness overload. They were treated to a string of awkward grunts and uncomfortably loud breaths as McGregor tried to hide the camera on his body. Eventually he finished. And stooping to pick up the case, McGregor headed outside. The walk down to the exchange point was long, and the way the camera bounced with each step was enough to set her head back to throbbing. They didn't skip forwards though, on the chance that he would say something else. Unfortunately, the only things they heard were passing snippets of conversations as he went.

After five minutes, he turned down a side hall, headed down a flight of stairs, then made a quick series of twists and turns that left Melissa completely lost. Finally, he stopped in a dim, empty corridor that ran about ten feet before dead ending, as though the designer had built half a hall then got bored and quit. "They should be here," McGregor's voice murmured anxiously.

He waited a moment until there was the sound of footsteps in the hall. It grew ever louder until a woman in military uniform rounded the corner. "Major," the camera jerked as McGregor snapped to attention.

"Sergeant," she saluted, "fancy running into you down here. What's in the case?"

"Personal things, ma'am." McGregor's answer was curt.

"Excellent." The major gave a wolfish grin. "Leave it there."

There was a pregnant pause, like McGregor was trying to figure out exactly what was going on. Behind the major, two slim but tough looking men rounded the corner as well, their hands down around their waists like they were bodyguards. That was enough to make up Melissa's mind about what was going on. On the video McGregor made up his in almost the same instant.

"Of course, ma'am," he set the case against the wall and gave a nod as he strolled away. "You have a good day, Major."

"Oh, don't worry Sergeant, I will."

The recording cut out about thirty seconds later, and a flick of Devon's hand had the huge holographic screen vanish like a puff of mist, leaving just his phone lying at their feet.

"If that was C-4B in that case…" Melissa bit her lip, eyes fixated on the phone in front of her.

"It was a lot," Devon finished for her. There was an expectant pause. "Do you know that major lady?"

"No," Melissa shook her head, "but I can probably find out." She'd been hoping this wouldn't happen, that they would check the files and discover it was a collection of funny cat videos. Instead, it was a pretty clear indicator that someone had some deeply unpleasant plans for Medea Station. Melissa was still busy moaning to herself why this had to happen to her when there was a knock at the door… and her life got infinitely worse.

Chapter 11
Busted

Devon snatched his phone off the floor when he heard the knock. "Evie probably left something behind. Just be cool, okay?"

Melissa nodded as Devon went to get the door. He got it about halfway open before his mouth fell open and he froze.

"Devon, what is it?" Melissa followed, and when she saw who was waiting outside, she also froze, her voice shaky. "Hey… dad."

Her father's only reply was a dark scowl. Melissa tried to put on her most innocent face, but she knew this looked bad. Really, *really* bad. She tried not to wince, but she could see it in his face. Her dad was going to ground her, forever. She paused as an even worse thought occurred to her. He was going to kill Devon, like, actually murder him. She had to say something.

"So, umm," she forced a smile, "what brings you here?"

His ice-cold glare flashed from her to Devon and back again. "You better have a good explanation for this young lady."

Melissa opened her mouth to try and talk her way out of things. The innocent princess trick normally worked with her father. Except, most of the things she would usually say would be immediately misinterpreted as something worse. The only excuse that leapt to mind was, "We were watching funny cat videos?" She could barely meet his eyes and ended up staring at the floor and trying not to shudder. That was a horrible excuse.

She could feel her dad's glare honing in on her like a laser guided missile, but eventually he switched targets to Devon, who was shuffling his feet uneasily. "Can we come in?"

"Yes," Devon hastily swung the door open. "What's going on… sir?"

"This is Mr Banks." Colonel Hale gestured to the man in jeans and a relaxed, button-up polo. "We have a few questions."

"Questions about what?" Melissa asked.

Her dad wheeled on her, his face creased in an immovable glower. "I don't want to hear another word out of you, young lady," he warned. "And when we get back to the room, we are going to have a *very* long discussion about all this. You understand?"

Melissa hadn't seen her dad this angry in a long time, not since she'd been seven and nearly lit their apartment on fire with a candle. She stared at the floor and tried not to tremble. "Yes."

"Yes, who?" he repeated with a low growl.

"Yes… sir." She wanted to burst into tears. Fine, he was angry, but he didn't have to humiliate her like this.

"If she can't ask questions, then I will," Devon intruded angrily. "What's this about?"

Melissa's dad acted like he hadn't even spoken. "Sit down. Both of you."

His gaze followed them, and Melissa saw her dad's expression ice over when she and Devon picked spots right next to one another.

When they did, Banks stepped closer. "So, it's Devon, correct?" He regarded the boy with a penetrating gaze but a much more pleasant demeanor than her father. "We just had a few questions about last night."

Melissa felt the bed shift a little as Devon tensed and one of his fingers nervously tapped on his leg. He kept his voice calm though. "Specifically?"

"Where were you yesterday evening around 8:00 PM?"

Devon's eyes flickered over to her dad for a moment. "I was with Melissa," he declared finally.

"Doing what?" her father demanded.

"None of your business."

"Now you listen here," Bryan Hale growled, "you're going–"

"Colonel," Banks held up a hand, "remember, we're all friends here."

Melissa was surprised to see her dad close his mouth. The guy was just a civilian, why would he...?

Ohhh, the truth hit her like a tank. He was CIA, wasn't he. That would explain the casual clothes contrasted with the commanding presence. It would also explain why he was working with Dad in the first place. But if he was CIA, why hadn't he talked with Kristina? She would have told him all about what had happened, wouldn't she? Unless, maybe there was a more complicated game going on here.

Either way, Melissa knew that no good would come from answering any more questions. She breathed a silent prayer that Devon had learned something from her story. "Devon, don't talk to him, he's CIA."

"Melissa, quiet," her father hissed.

Melissa knew she would pay for that later, but she could see in Devon's eyes that he understood the danger, and he understood what to do. "Get out," Devon declared quietly.

"Now, Devon," Banks was still all smiles, "there's no need for that. We just want to talk."

"Well, I don't, so go." His foot was nervously tapping on the floor, but he put on a brave face. "Besides, if you're here to question me about something, shouldn't I have a parent present?"

Banks' expression transformed to a dark scowl that made Melissa shiver. "Very well," he rose with a nod, "maybe we can continue this conversation down in an interrogation room later... with your parents, of course."

The two adults made for the door and Melissa didn't have to be told that she was going with them. The only way her dad would leave her and Devon alone was if Devon was dead... probably not then either. "Devon, I'll umm..."

"I'll see you later, Melissa," he said with a thankful smile. "Let me know how it goes." She gave a grim nod and followed her father outside, the door swinging shut behind her with a click as it locked.

"Obviously, he's hiding something," Banks was saying.

"It's not him." Her father shook his head as Melissa waited quietly a few feet away. "My daughter has had some bad experiences with intelligence sorts in the past."

"And how did she know?" Banks' gaze shifted to Melissa. "Hmm, young lady?"

"Civilian clothes, smug expression, an inflated sense of self-importance buried beneath a fake smile?" Melissa gave a disdainful shrug. "Not hard to notice a snake when you know what to look for."

Banks' expression cooled, but Melissa almost caught a trace of a smile on Dad's face... almost. "Feisty little lady you have there, Colonel." Banks' glare honed in on her. "The thought occurs to me that she might just be our third culprit. A girl, a boy and a younger girl? Rather matches the description of your daughter and her disagreeable friend back there."

"Now you listen here, Banks," her father took a few steps closer, his tone becoming dangerous. "You can say whatever you want about that boy, but if I hear you making insinuations about my daughter again, I'll tell Major Tannenhill to ignore that order about keeping you safe. We wouldn't want that, now would we?"

Banks sneered, "Of course not." Despite the cosmically disastrous trouble she was in, Melissa felt a hint of a gloating grin. Today was just not going well for the CIA fellow, delightful.

All traces of amusement vanished though as her father wheeled back to her. "Melissa, we're going."

***

When Melissa closed the door behind her, Devon could still dimly hear voices out in the hall for a few moments. His heart was pounding, and when he grabbed his phone, his hand shook slightly. Had he made the wrong call? Maybe telling the CIA guy to go shove off hadn't been the best idea. Banks hadn't seemed very friendly beneath his veneer of sociability, and Devon couldn't escape the feeling that the man would be back. Still, Melissa had a point. No reason sitting around and letting Banks pick apart their story like a cat clawing up a sweater.

He needed time to think – about what to do next, about the video, about what Kristina was really playing at. Dropping his phone on the charging pad by his bed, Devon did two things. First, he keyed up a search for '*dusha.*' It wasn't much, but if he could find out more about those weird bullets Kristina used, at least that would be something. Given the internet speed, that might take a few minutes to finish. In the meantime, he started up the video again, this time pausing to take in every detail. If he wanted answers, that was as good a start as any.

***

By the time Melissa's father dragged her back to her room, she was ready to weep in frustration. The only reason she didn't was to avoid giving her dad the satisfaction of knowing he had won. It was just so unfair. She hadn't done anything wrong. And seriously, of thousands of cabins on Medea Station, her dad *happened* to show up at Devon's? Really?

She just wanted to go home. She didn't even care where – Sheppard, Wright-Patterson, Ramstein – she'd settle for a satellite control bunker up in Alaska just as long as it was back on Earth and away from this miserable metal deathtrap.

Her mom was already in their room, sprawled out on the bed and flicking through a book on her tablet. When the door swung open, Melissa caught Mom's gaze for only a second, before looking away and wiping the first traces of tears from her eyes.

"Dear, what's going on?" Mom clicked off her tablet.

"Our daughter," Dad answered curtly, his face permanently stuck in a scowl.

"And you caught her… what? Doing drugs?"

"I caught her with that boy. Alone. In his room."

"Ohhhh." Melissa glanced up and saw her mom give an understanding nod, but for some reason she didn't get the sense that mom was angry with her. "Did she have her clothes on?"

Melissa blushed, but her father just tapped his foot in irritation. "Well, yes."

"And were they kissing?"

"Not that I saw."

"And… what exactly were *you* doing there?"

"Official business. That boy is the subject of a terrorism inquiry."

"Of course he is," her mom gave a nonplussed nod. "Dearest," she continued levelly, "I think what you have discovered is that your daughter has *friends*. At her age that's perfectly normal. Except, she might not have *friends* anymore after all this."

"It is not *normal* to find our daughter alone in a room with a boy."

"Yes, much better to sneak off into the forest together, now isn't it," her mom added suggestively.

Her dad's face went red in indignation, "Julia, that has nothing to do with any of this."

"Doesn't it though? Don't you think dragging your own daughter back here in tears is a bit excessive?" Her sapphire blue eyes flicked across to Melissa, her tone softening. "Sweetheart, what were you doing?"

"Watching a video on Devon's phone," Melissa murmured.

Her mom leaned back with a frustrated expression. "Now Bryan, doesn't that make more sense?"

"Doesn't explain why they were alone in his room."

"Would you have preferred to find them hiding in the air ducts? Where else are they supposed to be alone with the station packed full of people? Besides, Bryan, we spoke about this and you promised you were going to give her space."

"Not like that."

"Like *what*, you said yourself they weren't doing anything wrong."

"Not *yet*."

Melissa unconsciously slid toward the corner, her cheeks burning as she desperately wished a hatch would pop open and vent her to space already.

Mom at least noticed, and thankfully seemed to register how awkward this conversation must be. "Melissa, maybe you should go back down to the shops for a bit."

"Absolutely not," Dad interjected before she could take more than a step toward the door. Melissa ground to a halt as he added, "she'll go straight back to that boy."

"Well, do you trust her?"

Surprisingly, that question seemed to catch her dad off guard, "I… yes, but I don't see how…"

Before Dad could clarify his opinion, Mom turned to her and said, "Melissa, you understand we have rules in the family about how to behave around young men?"

Melissa would have chosen almost anything over having this conversation with her parents, but somehow she managed a mumbled "Yes, Mom."

"And you understand, regardless of the intent, it's not prudent to be alone with a young man in his room?"

"Yes."

"And you promise that you weren't doing anything inappropriate with this boy?"

"No," Melissa shook her head, red-faced. Nothing inappropriate, at least not with Devon, Kristina was another story.

Mom forced a smile, "Well, Bryan, if you trust her, I don't see the problem."

Dad shot her a dark glower, like he'd prefer nothing more than locking her in the cabin for the next few months, but finally growled, "If I catch you back in his room—"

He left the rest unsaid, but she could imagine several terrible and horrifying punishments to fill in the gaps, "Yes, Dad." She nodded, then before he could change his mind, she slid toward the door and darted outside.

Out in the hallway she slumped against the wall, letting out a sigh of relief. She'd been certain she was about to be grounded, and from inside she caught snippets, her parents' voices rising.

Bryan you should be glad. She made a friend on the first day I don't see how that's such a bad thing—

Not with a boy. It'd be one thing if it—

But I told you this might happen, and you said you were okay with it. We agreed.

For a few heartbeats, she hesitated not sure where to go now, mainly just grateful that she wasn't still trapped in the cabin.

Then her wrist band glowed a soft blue.

***

Devon hadn't been able to find a bench, so instead he put his back to the corridor wall and took a seat on the floor as he waited. He was certain he'd found something, and somehow Melissa had gone from, 'going to be grounded forever' to 'be there in five minutes.'

He was still mentally rehearsing what to say when Melissa appeared in the corridor. "Hey, Devon."

"Still alive, I see."

"Yeah," Melissa seemed a little surprised herself, "I'm not sure what even happened. Normally my parents just shout at me for a while and it always ends with 'go to your room, young lady.' But my mom – she saved me. Like… I can't even explain it."

She dropped down next to him. "What's so urgent?"

"Something's wrong," Devon said.

"You're just now realizing?"

"Well…this time though it's more specific." He pulled out his phone and glanced around. "Is that CIA guy still stalking us?"

Melissa shook her head, "I doubt it. He made some accusations out in the hall, and Dad basically told him to shut up or bad things would happen. What's the problem?"

"I was re-watching McGregor's video and something jumped out at me." Devon unlocked his phone, but the first thing to pop up was a weird picture from earlier, a bunch of screaming teens with a creepy bluish thing hovering behind them.

"What's that?"

"Nothing," Devon shook his head and flicked past to the video. "I was trying to look up what Kristina's **Dusha** bullet was. Apparently, they're a poorly reviewed Russian ghost film from ten years ago."

"Anyway, the bigger issue is this." He didn't turn on the hologram this time. Instead, he skimmed through the clip until they got to the part where the major's two bodyguards, one a burly white guy, and the other a stocky black man came into view. Devon paused, "These two are wrong."

"And you know this because…?"

"Because of what Valerie said." Devon handed her the phone as he explained. "She said the two men who killed McGregor sounded Middle Eastern. These guys don't look Middle Eastern *at all*."

"So what?" Melissa shrugged. "It was probably different people."

Devon shook his head. "Was it? Think about it. McGregor was so worried about his delivery that he made a video in case he got killed. Then, a few days later, he actually *does* get killed. Good odds it's related."

"And?" Melissa seemed unconvinced. "Kristina said he gambled, maybe the guys who killed him were from a debt collector."

"Up here? Tell me, where does one go to find a loan shark on Medea Station?" That elicited a glare from Melissa, which Devon ignored. "Besides, if you want someone to pay up, you don't kill them, you threaten them. At most you break an arm. And McGregor insinuated that he was getting paid plenty of money for his smuggling, if the alternative is death why not just cut a deal? That doesn't make any sense."

"Well, maybe that major lady behind all this is just an equal opportunity employer. Just because she's trying to blow up Medea Station doesn't mean she only employs *these two guys*."

"And where is she supposed to find goons up here who speak Arabic? I could understand if they just *looked* Middle Eastern, but that's a pretty specific language skill. Maybe there's a translator with all the military people, but that's still a lot of effort to recruit one very specific person, let alone two. Besides, unless they knew Valerie was listening, why not just speak English?"

Melissa rolled her eyes. "Okay, I think that's a stretch, but you clearly have a theory, so let's hear it."

He grinned, "Valerie was lying."

She threw up her hands in exasperation. "Okay, do you hear yourself? Her boyfriend was just murdered in front of her. Why would she lie?"

Devon hadn't actually thought that far ahead. He'd gotten excited upon concluding that Valerie was lying, and his mental train had ground to a halt at that station. In fairness, Melissa did have a point. There wasn't an obvious motive. It wasn't as though Valerie gained anything by lying.

Or did she? He thought back to the scene of the murder. There was McGregor, dead. The blood wasn't fully dried, so he had been killed very recently. What else? He still had a phone on him. Kristina had seemed excited to find that, so why hadn't the assassins taken it? For that matter, why hadn't they gone looking through his things? Kristina had ordered him and Melissa to search through his stuff straight away, and it wasn't as if the flash drive was spectacularly well hidden. Heck, the Space Force probably would have found it when they eventually investigated.

If the people who had killed McGregor were spies too, why hadn't they checked for any of that? Either they were really sloppy, bordering on incompetent, or…

Or there was some other reason. The only one he could think of was that they were in a hurry, but why? They couldn't have known Kristina was coming.

And how had they even gotten into the barracks? Kristina had needed to use him and Melissa, but he doubted many people were crazy enough to bluff their way past the guards. That couldn't work very often. Maybe one of the killers was a soldier, but that circled back to the issue from before, why go to the effort of recruiting the one or two soldiers on the station who *possibly* spoke Arabic just to go murder someone.

Devon shook his head, trying to shove away all the competing theories for a second. This was getting too complicated. What was the simple explanation? The simple explanation was that McGregor had been killed for what he knew. He still had his phone because the killers had been in a hurry. The killers had taken an obvious route into the barracks. They hadn't spoken Arabic–

He paused as one overriding thought echoed in his head. Why would Valerie lie?

And then he understood.

"She killed him," he whispered. "No one snuck into the barracks. There were no middle-eastern assassins. The phone was still there because we interrupted her right afterwards."

"What are you talking about?" Melissa gave him a skeptical look and Devon realized he had been sitting there for about a minute, lost in thought.

"Valerie," he explained, "she killed William McGregor."

"Okay," Melissa nodded with a sarcastic smile "that's fricking crazy." She folded her arms. "Did you *see* Valerie? I doubt she could kill me, let alone a sergeant."

"And if you didn't know better, you'd probably say the same thing about Kristina, now wouldn't you?"

Melissa tried to reply, but no words came out in answer. Ha, Devon smirked to himself, score one.

Chapter 12
Three Minutes

Ten minutes later the two stood at the entrance to Kristina's dress shop. A young, slim woman at the counter eyed them as they came in. "Can I help you?" She focused so that the *you* seemed directed at Devon, like she wasn't sure what to make of him here.

"Yes," Melissa strolled up to the counter, "we're looking for Kristina."

"I'm sorry, but Miss Andrews isn't available at the moment." The woman's eyes finally flickered towards Melissa, her voice bored, like she was ready for her shift to end. "Can I help *you* find something?"

"She'll make time for us," Melissa said confidently.

"Of course she will," the woman gave a patronizing nod. Then lapsed into sarcasm, "Who do you two think you are, royalty? Miss Andrews said she wasn't to be disturbed, so she won't be."

"We just need a few minutes."

"And the answer is still *no*."

Devon took a step forward, his voice hardening, "Look, we need to talk to Kristina, *right now*. It is genuinely urgent. Now if she wants to get angry and scream at us, then fine, you can just say we snuck past, it's on us. But if she doesn't... well, it'll be a good thing you let us in."

The woman regarded him for a moment, as if she were weighing the possible outcomes. Finally, she flicked her hand for them to go on. "Fine, whatever. She's back there past the break room. Go get yourselves in trouble, but when Kristina decides to tan both your hides, don't say I didn't warn you."

The two were past almost before the woman finished. There was a short hallway leading to the back of the store where they found a black painted steel door. The two paused for a second, listening... but they couldn't hear anything from within. Eventually, Devon pushed it open.

Melissa's eyes swept across the room beyond, and instantly she could tell something was wrong. On her right several racks of dresses crowded in front of a door to something like a giant closet, to the left a steel spartan door led... somewhere. And against the far wall sat a plush couch, and right next to it, Kristina's purse was lying discarded on the floor, like it had just been dropped.

Kristina might be a lot of questionable things, but Melissa was pretty sure she wasn't the sort of woman to leave her purse on the floor. Across the room sat a door with 'Kristina Andrews' on the placard, and Melissa froze as she caught sharp, distorted sounds like shouts inside.

"Something's wrong," she whispered.

Devon nodded and, together they crept across the room, the air thick with the earthy rich scent of coffee. For once Melissa was grateful for the ubiquitous steel construction of the station that wouldn't creak or give them away. Pressing close to the door, she finally caught the voices more clearly.

"I want answers, Kristina, what are you doing up on Medea?" Maybe it was just listening through the door, but Valerie's voice sounded much stronger and harsher than Melissa remembered.

"Isn't it obvious?" Kristina's retort was heavy with sarcasm. "I run a dress shop. Oh, and by the way, Valerie, you're fired."

There was a foreboding pause inside, then a shriek of pain from Kristina. "Tell me who you work for!"

"Well, you won't believe me, but it's a guy called Marty, he's from the future. Mostly he pays me in sports betting tips."

"What?" Valerie's voice rose to an outraged roar. "Tell me you witch, who do you work for – the CIA, MI6, Interpol, Mossad, the Iranians?"

"Well, if I'm a witch then, Hogwarts maybe?"

"Kristina, if you keep screwing with me, I swear I'll kill you."

"And here I thought you wanted answers. I notice you didn't mention the MSS, Chinese State Security… now why would that be I wonder?"

"Shut up," there was a loud slap. "Now tell me who you work for."

"Well, now I'm confused, do you want me to shut up, or tell you?"

Melissa stopped listening. This was bad. She had been okay with stopping by to give Kristina a heads up, but this was wandering right back into the lion's den. Next to her Devon muttered a quiet curse. "We have to do something," he whispered.

"Such as?" Both their gazes drifted over to Kristina's purse lying on the floor. Oh right, that.

Frankly, Melissa had zero interest in rummaging through Kristina's stuff. The C-4 could still be stuck in there for all she knew. Devon had it open in a flash though. After a moment, his hands reappeared holding Kristina's gun and one of her darts.

"What are you doing?" she hissed.

"This'll be easy," Devon fumbled with the pistol trying to snap it open to load the dart. "We just knock open the door and shoot Valerie."

Melissa wanted to shout at him but she gritted her teeth and kept her voice low. "No, that's not how it works. What if there are two of them? What if she has an *actual* gun? There are a billion things that could go wrong when you open that door. Let's just call station security."

Another scream rang inside, followed by a string of indecipherable curses from Kristina.

Devon shot her a side glance. "You really think she's going to last that long?"

Melissa grimaced. Why couldn't she just let Kristina die? It would solve so many problems. She couldn't bring herself to walk away though, even if she absolutely knew she was going to regret saving the woman later.

"Do you even know what you're doing?" Her eyes stuck on Devon as he tried to twist Kristina's weapon open.

"Ummm…"

Melissa shook her head in exasperation. "Give me that." She snatched the gun away, popped it open, slid in a round, and snapped it shut. Then she dug into the purse until she found a fresh pressurized air cartridge and deftly screwed it in.

"Okay, here's how this is going to work," Melissa whispered, trying not to feel the way her chest clenched in terror. "You get the door and fling it open." She positioned Devon on the side near the knob while she took up a spot on the other. "Once you do that, get out of the doorway, I'll swing in and fire. If there are two of them in there, we run. Otherwise, the primary goal is to disarm Valerie."

Melissa looked at Devon, "Do you have any martial arts training?"

"Not really."

"Okay, when the taser hits her, hopefully Valerie drops whatever she's holding. Kick it away from her. If it's a gun, grab it. I'm sure she'll have a round chambered, so point it at her and shout 'hands up.' If she charges you, pull the trigger until the gun stops firing. If she's fighting me though, *please* try not to shoot me. Understood?

Devon gave a hesitant nod, his voice hushed. "And what are you going to do?"

Melissa bit her lip and tried to fight off the knot of fear in her stomach. "We should have the element of surprise, so maybe I can buy you a few seconds. Hopefully the drug in the dart kicks in fast."

Melissa paused for a moment to try and remember if she'd forgotten anything important. Suddenly she was extremely grateful for all those weekends her dad had taken her out to shoot guns or play paintball. At the time she'd hated it, but now skills like the proper way to breach a room and how to handle an airgun were about to be pretty handy. She tried to run through a few scenarios in her head, but they all got jumbled up when she tried to think about anything beyond shooting Valerie.

Finally, Melissa took a deep breath to calm herself. She closed her eyes, prayed a quick prayer, then she looked at Devon. "On the count of three." She pressed her back against the wall, put both hands on the pistol, and lowered it down to around her waist, both arms straight as steel bars, just like Dad had shown her.

"One"

"Two"

"Three"

Devon twisted the handle and flung open the door. As he did, Melissa rotated into the doorway, snapped the gun up to firing position, and it was like the world slowed to a crawl.

The office within was large enough to give her space to maneuver, couch to the left, flex-screen on the right and a work desk as the centerpiece. Valerie had her back to the door, and Melissa could make out a knife in one hand, clear as day. Behind her, Kristina's hands and feet were tied to her own desk chair with an obvious bruise on her forehead and the trace of a reddish handprint on her cheek. Most critically though, Valerie was alone, and they had absolute surprise, which meant their odds of surviving had just jumped by an order of magnitude.

In front of her, Valerie began to wheel in confusion. For laser focused Melissa, there wasn't even a hint of indecision.

She fired.

There was a soft *pfft* of air as the gas cylinder discharged, the quiet hiss of the dart as it lanced across the room, then a *thunk* as it struck Valerie right above her hip. The woman barely seemed to notice the dart, but an eyeblink later the taser electrodes hit and their clicking discharges began.

Melissa bulled into the room as Valerie convulsed and her knife clattered to the floor. "Devon, the knife!" Melissa shouted, right before she threw herself at the woman. She probably only had a few seconds before the taser stopped working, but that was enough time to land at least one good kick. Almost without thinking, Melissa took a fighting stance and roundhouse kicked Valerie dead in the stomach.

The combination of the taser and a blow to the stomach sent Valerie to her knees. Somewhere nearby there was a clatter as Devon kicked the knife away. Melissa's strike managed to dislodge one of the taser electrodes though, and when the clicking sound stopped, she knew things were about to get a whole lot worse. She kicked again and caught Valerie in the side, sending the woman sprawling on the floor.

Valerie was fast though. She rolled and got her arms around to block a third kick. Melissa kept up the attack, but Valerie scrambled back to her feet, a few wild jabs from her longer arms driving Melissa backwards.

The two broke apart, and Melissa caught a quick glance of Devon in the corner. He had snatched up Valerie's knife and was moving to help, but she waved him off with a shake of her head. Hopefully he understood what that meant. Even if he had the knife, if Valerie knew what she was doing, she could easily grab it back and leave him dead on the floor.

Valerie jerked the empty syringe out of her leg. "What is this?" she snarled.

"You'll see soon enough."

Valerie didn't bother with a reply, she charged.

Melissa already suspected she couldn't win. Even injured, Valerie had a good thirty pounds and two inches on her. That, and if she *was* a spy, she would have actual hand-to-hand training. Melissa had four years of Taekwondo in her corner, which was at least something, but unfortunately, Valerie's martial arts system would be designed for efficiently killing people, and Melissa knew hers wasn't.

As Valerie barreled in, Melissa backpedaled, snapping quick kicks and barely keeping out of range, a single question thundering in her head.

When would the drug kick in?

She knocked aside a jab from Valerie and tried to remember how long it had been since she fired. A minute? Thirty seconds? She had no idea.

It didn't matter anyway. The drug might take ten minutes to knock Valerie out. Every time Kristina had used it, she'd physically incapacitated the person before the effects began to show.

The two circled, and Melissa's foot snapped towards the larger woman, catching Valerie in the side. The woman gasped, and flailed at her with one hand, but a quick step back put Melissa out of range. Valerie rushed forward and Melissa connected another kick straight to her gut. But Valerie was close now and a wild fist slammed into Melissa's side.

The shock knocked the breath from her. Valerie was strong, but the adrenaline kept the pain as little more than a shadow in the back of her mind. She countered with a hail of blows right into the woman's stomach. Valerie stepped backwards and struck with an open palm at Melissa's throat.

Melissa batted aside what could have been a killing blow. That was low, trying to crush her windpipe. In a fury she sent her next kick slamming right up between the woman's legs. Valerie wasn't a guy, so connecting there wasn't a winning shot or anything, but Melissa knew from experience it would still hurt… a lot.

Valerie jumped, and with a pained yelp, the woman stumbled backwards in surprise. Idiot, Melissa thought, she should have had a proper stance.

As Valerie circled back, Melissa suddenly realized that maybe she did have a chance. Valerie wasn't looking too good, and when she stumbled, some of that dizziness seemed like more than just getting nailed between the legs.

That thought lasted all of three seconds.

Then Valerie rushed her.

This time there were no tactics. Valerie grabbed at her, and her momentum slammed Melissa against the cold steel wall. The woman slugged her so hard she gasped for air. Not even the adrenaline could keep down the wave of agony that surged up, and tears sprung to Melissa's eyes. She tried to punch back, but caught up in a primal fury, Valerie didn't so much as flinch. Crushed against the wall, Melissa felt a cold terror as Valerie's hands clamped around her throat.

Valerie squeezed.

From somewhere far away she heard Devon shouting, and suddenly the boy slammed into Valerie, tackling her to the ground like a football player. The hands crushing the life out of her vanished, and Melissa slumped to the floor, gasping for breath while Devon tried to wrestle Valerie into submission.

Devon wasn't doing well. He was closer to Valerie's weight class and a guy, but even though he was fighting hard, she deftly shoved him off her. Struggling to her feet, Valerie lashed him across the face hard enough to split his lip. Devon stumbled backwards, stunned and a second kick sent him sprawling to the ground.

Through her tears, Melissa saw that Valerie seemed shakier than before. The drug was working, but not fast enough. Valerie turned back to her, unrestrained fury on her face. Melissa's whole body tensed as it registered that she was about to die. She just hoped Dad wasn't the one to find her body, he didn't deserve that. Even worse, the last thing they had done was to fight… she hadn't had a chance to tell him she was sorry.

Valerie towered over her with a sneer. "You're going to pay you little–"

"Valerie!" Kristina's voice echoed in the room. Melissa's eyes rose to see Kristina, the last ropes sliced around her feet. She stood, knife in hand.

A grimace crossed Valerie's face along with something else… fear, maybe. She spun around to face Kristina. Her eyes drifting to the knife with a taunting, "I see you don't fight fair, Kristina?"

Kristina's lips curled in a vicious grin. "It's Miss Andrews to you. And no, I don't."

Valerie stumbled, and charged Kristina with a scream. Melissa could swear Kristina was laughing as she ducked beneath the swing, only to pop up with Valerie horribly off balance. Kristina reversed the dagger and deftly cracked her ex-employee on the head with the pommel. There was a horrible *thunk*, and Valerie crashed to the floor.

She didn't move.

Chapter 13
The Den of Secrets

Huddled on the floor, Melissa could feel her entire body shivering. She only dimly registered as a few feet away, Kristina tapped Valerie with her foot, then glanced at Devon, sprawled out gasping on the ground. "You okay?"

Devon said something, but Melissa barely heard. She was staring at her hand, it wouldn't stop shaking and—

"Hey," Kristina's voice sounded close, and Melissa looked up as the woman knelt down right in front of her, serious faced, "Are you hurt?"

Honestly, it felt like everything hurt, her hand was shaking like mad and she couldn't seem to blink back the tears pooling in her eyes. "Yes," her voice came out hoarse and raspy when she spoke.

Kristina nodded, her voice softening, "Shhh, *tikhi milaya*. It sounds like she had you hard around the throat. You'll be alright, but try not to speak for a bit." Melissa nodded, pressing her lips together as her gaze lingered on the floor.

"I saw she got you right in the chest too, can you breathe?"

Melissa nodded.

Kristina took a seat beside her, the feeling of the older woman at her shoulder strangely reassuring.

Melissa sniffed and tried to wipe away the first tears rolling down her cheeks. She didn't even know why she was crying.

The pain where Valerie had punched her was receding, and outside of her raspy breath, her throat didn't feel that bad. Yet it was like this swirl of terror and regret and relief was all bottled up inside her and…

"It's okay to cry," Kristina said quietly.

"What?" she murmured

"Crying's nothing to be ashamed of, it's natural. All that adrenaline, it dams up everything else, the fear, the anger, the regret. When it's over, the dam bursts and everything floods in all at once. It can be overwhelming."

Kristina paused, like she was trying to think what else she could say. "The first time I fought someone – for real – I thought it would be like a sparring match, a dance. Then she pulled a knife, and it was like I forgot everything I'd learned. There was just this surge of rage and desperation and the only thing that mattered was that I had to win."

"When I umm… when I beat her, there was this moment of exhilaration, like I'd won the Olympics or something. Then I took a breath, and ten seconds later I was on the floor in tears. I didn't know if I should be happy that I survived or hate myself. It'll pass though, your emotions just need a few minutes to untangle themselves."

Melissa hugged her legs close to her chest and shivered, but Kristina was right. The mess of emotions was starting to drain away. "Is she dead?"

"Valerie? She'll be out for a few hours, but I think she'll survive. Her head's pretty hard. Although, after being drugged, I'm not sure she'll remember anything from today. Too bad I suppose. Might have been useful."

Kristina rose from her spot next to Melissa and walked over to Valerie's motionless from, dropping down and doing a quick check of her pulse. "So, not to question whatever strange fortune landed you two in my office… but, what are you two doing in my office?"

Melissa wasn't in the mood to talk about much of anything, so she left that part to Devon.

***

127

Devon slowly forced himself up to sitting, carefully rubbing his arm where the wound from yesterday was aching again after being thrown around.

"We were coming to warn you about Valerie," he explained, wiping at his stinging lip, and seeing his fingers come away red with blood. "We… well, *I* copied the files off that flash drive we found. It's just a video of McGregor delivering the bomb to someone, but it was enough to start poking holes in Valerie's story." He gave a brief summary of his logic, and by the time he was done, Kristina's eyes were regarding them both with a new light.

"I must say, I'm impressed. You two did some good work. When I saw you talking to Stephanie up front, I was a little worried. But you seemed to have pulled a few surprising rabbits out of your collective hats."

"Huh? What do you mean, *you saw us*?"

In answer Kristina nodded to the wall behind them. Devon's head swiveled to see a flex-screen mounted towards the ceiling near the door. On it he noted a dozen windowed camera feeds, most showing images from within Kristina's shops, and even one that he recognized as the break room. The monitor was positioned so Kristina could make out what was going on from her desk, but if someone walked inside, they wouldn't notice unless they specifically looked.

"Why do you think I was being so rude to Valerie? I assure you, that's not what you're supposed to do. I couldn't have her looking back and noticing you two though. Turns out I made a good wager."

"And if we hadn't barged in?"

"Well, I needed to interrogate her somehow," Kristina shrugged. "I suppose getting her angry was as good a way as any. At least at this point, I think we can be reasonably certain she works for the Chinese. That's a promising start."

She focused back on Devon, offering him a hand up and leaning close to peer at his bloody lip. "And you… you just keep getting yourself busted up." Kristina took his chin, tilting it up a second, before stepping back. "At least it's not too bad. It should heal up fine, but it'll be hard to hide. If you want, I can see if some lip gloss and make-up will keep it disguised, but that won't survive forever. And I have no intention of playing makeup artist for you until it heals. I doubt Curls does either."

"I can just say I got it in a fight," Devon waved her off. "It's basically the truth, I just won't say with whom. That, or maybe tell my parents I bumped into a door."

Kristina shrugged, "So long as you can keep your story straight." She paced over to Valerie's unconscious figure on the floor, her brunette hair splayed out in a mess around her head. "Now, the next problem is Little Miss Secret Agent here." Kristina puffed out a sigh, "Are you feeling well enough to give me a hand with her?"

Devon nodded, and a moment later he found himself struggling to hold up Valerie's ankles, and feeling dimly like some sort of serial killer. The limp woman was shockingly heavy. Watching as Kristina grabbed her arms, the entire situation felt bizarrely surreal. How had they ended up here?

"On three." Kristina said, pulling in an anticipatory breath "One, two… three."

Devon lifted and together the two stumbled over to one of the chairs in front of Kristina's desk letting her body slump back to the floor. "Alright, help me get her up," Kristina gestured for him to drop her legs. Grabbing one arm, while Kristina took the other, they half lifted, half drug Valerie into the chair, and dropped her slumbering figure into the seat.

Kristina let out a relieved breath, "Excellent."

Yeeeeah, not the word he would have picked. Devon sighed, well, at least she wasn't dead, he wasn't sure how he would have handled that. While he stared, Kristina stepped behind her desk.

"I think you'll need this, Devon." He looked up as Kristina tossed him a square of blue cloth that looked kind of like a handkerchief.

"For what?"

"Your lip," Kristina raised her eyes as though he were a moron. "Unless you prefer it all bloody."

"You don't have Kleenex?"

"Not up here. It's more weight and space efficient to have real cloth and just wash it. Tissues just clog up the plumbing and costs a fortune to ferry up. One of those things you'll have to get used to if you're headed to Mars."

Same as the toilets then, Devon sighed. That had been a rude shock, discovering the bathrooms in space didn't stock things like toilet paper. Instead, they were all those advanced Japanese toilets that like… did it for you.

Gingerly dabbing at his split lip, Devon stepped around the desk to see Kristina rapid-fire flicking her way through the oversized dial lock that secured her bottom drawer. With a final sharp twist, the lock clinked open. Devon nearly choked as Kristina slid it out an extra deep file drawer packed to the brim with… all the spy things.

Whatever she was looking for must have been at the bottom, because in a flash she'd pulled out a little box that clinked with silvery air gun cylinders, that she promptly piled on the floor Then came a pair of brown-glass chemical bottles, with dangerous looking pictograms on the labels. Followed by a miniature pressurized gas bottle complete with a regulator valve.

Devon watched her like a car crash that he couldn't tear his eyes away from. And he'd thought her purse was scary.

"Where is…" Kristina pulled out a clear plastic case in which Devon could see several more of her special darts sitting next to a pair of syringes. "…there it is."

She pulled out a pack of heavy-duty zip ties and glanced over at Devon, her lips twitching in amusement. "You ever tied someone up before?"

"I, umm…" Devon stumbled over the answer. What sort of a question was that anyway?

"Well, come on." Kristina said, deadpan. "Might as well learn to do it the right way."

Devon could feel his face heating in embarrassment, as Kristina stood and walked around to Valerie's unconscious figure. "Zip ties are great for this sort of thing. You can chain them together to be just about any length, and no one questions…"

Devon didn't really hear her. For a second, he hesitated, kneeling down to peer at Kristina's strewn out little arsenal, and fighting back a worry nipping at the back of his head. At first glance, he'd assumed the dial lock was just paranoia, but... she sure seemed prepared for a serious fight.

That wasn't even all of it either. A couple little boxes that looked vaguely medical in nature were neatly stacked inside. There was also a bigger cardboard box wedged in the back corner, that he really didn't want to touch. And down at the bottom... a little picture frame?

Nothing special, just a digital frame, the touch-screen, battery sort that would play a slideshow. Mom had few around the house that she stuck all the vacation pictures on. Maybe it was just the oddity of seeing something so mundane, but Devon reached down to touch it, the frame flashed on... and he saw Kristina.

Except not the Kristina he knew.

She was maybe five years younger, her hair trimmed short, and wearing forest-green military cameo. It was a shot of her and a dozen other girls all in similar uniforms, grinning and flipping hand signs as they crammed together for the picture. And in the background, rose the bulbous, multicolored spires of the Kremlin?

What was...

Almost without thinking, Devon's hand flicked right on the touchscreen. And he saw Kristina again. This time with her arms looped around two other girls, all of them beaming, with delicate blue and white soccer-balls painted on their cheeks. And all of them wearing similar, sky-blue jerseys scrawled on the front with that unreadable mix of scrambled blockish English letters, backwards R's, and N's that he recognized from the movies... it was Russian.

Why would she be at–

"Whatever happened to *Don't touch*?" Devon started, looking up to see Kristina right across from him, hands planted firmly on the desk, and her eyes like laser cutters.

Devon scrambled to put the frame back. "I'm sorry," he stammered, "I just... I thought..."

"You just thought you could go snooping through my things?" She snapped, her voice acrid.

He backed away as Kristina stalked around her desk. Her eyes lingering for just an instant on the open drawer. Then she *clanked* it shut, and when she looked up, Devon saw anger written on her face. Anger... but also traced with a hint of fear.

Why was she scared?

And suddenly it clicked in his head.

Something so simple he didn't know how he'd missed it. Kristina wasn't with the CIA was she?

She was russian.

Devon blinked as all the puzzle pieces dropped right into place. Kristina's *Dusha* bullets; he'd assumed he'd hit a dead end at finding that *Dusha* was just the name of a ghost movie. But in a flash he understood, the word was Russian– a *Ghost* bullet. All the weird curse words she dropped? Russian.

The fact that she seemed so eager to dodge the military? That she hadn't just flashed a badge to walk into the barracks that morning? That the actual CIA guy, Banks, hadn't had a clue what was going on? Well of course, she was a spy.

And above all, there was the fact that she was scared. Why would she be scared of him seeing her pictures? Unless, of course, they were *exactly* what they looked like.

The revelation hit like a freight train, and Devon swallowed back a sudden rush of panic, as he glimpsed everything in a new light. Kristina was a Russian spy. His eyes flashed towards the door that led outside, suddenly seeming very far away, then to Melissa, huddled on the couch and fidgeting with her hair, completely oblivious.

Frick.

He had to warn her.

Kristina loomed up in front of him, her voice arctic cold, "Next time try not to poke the dangerous stuff, alright. And stay out of my vacation pictures."

Oh, *that's* what they were? If anything, that absurdly pedantic explanation solidified in his mind that he was dead right.

"I'm sorry." Devon backpedaled, not meeting her gaze for fear his eyes would give him away. "I just…"

"Sit down." Kristina flicked him toward the couch, "There's a lot we need to discuss."

Devon was relieved for any excuse to step around her.

Maybe she didn't know.

For a moment, Kristina knelt behind her desk, the drawer *clanking* back open, and Devon heard the glassy *clink* of her shuffling her chemicals.

He beelined over to Melissa on the couch, shivering as he tried to bottle up his nerves. Dropping down on the couch, he nudged Melissa, then urgently thumbed towards the door. They needed to run– now.

Except… Melissa just cocked him a look like he'd lost it, raising both palms and mouthing a voiceless, "*What.*"

Devon could feel the budding urgency in the back of his mind. And with hand signs not working, he finally leaned close hoping Kristina couldn't hear as he whispered, "We need to go. Kristina's a russian."

Melissa had a truly bewildered expression, as she murmured, "Devon, what are you talking about?"

"*Kristina is a Russian spy.*" Now that he saw it, Devon felt like her identity was patently obvious. Yet when he tried to work out a way to explain it, there wasn't time and, "Come on." He grabbed at Melissa's hand, half standing to pull her.

The girl's tone turned to a hiss, "Devon, stop. Kristina's not a–"

"Actually, Curls, I am." Kristina popped up from behind her desk, a needle tipped syringe in one hand. And rushed them.

Devon froze, paralyzed in panic as Kristina smashed into him and his world went sideways. His gut exploded in blinding pain, and everything blurred. When his brain finally caught up Kristina had him pinned to the couch, basically sitting on his lap and Melissa was screaming.

"KRISTINA, WAIT– NO!"

Devon frantically tried to shove the woman off, but her arms were like steel and with her free hand she deftly jammed the syringe into his thigh.

Amid the tsunami of adrenaline, Devon only dimly felt the needle, but he knew exactly what it meant. He wrestled for Kristina's other hand, while next to him a frantic Melissa grappled with her. A second later, he felt a sharp jerk in his thigh, as he managed to jerk the now empty syringe popped loose, and send it skittered across the floor.

Kristina swore.

An instant later the crushing weight of the woman was off him as Kristina stood. That just left just a stinging pain in his gut and a stunned horror like daggers in his chest as Devon stared at his thigh. What had Kristina done?

***

As Kristina stood, Melissa still desperately clutched onto her, but the woman felt impossibly strong. Kristina gave one sharp jerk, Melissa's fingers slipped, and she crashed to the floor on her bottom.

"Curls, stop it!" Kristina snapped, patronizing.

"The hell is wrong with you?" she frantically glanced at Devon, "We just saved you!"

"And, I'm very grateful for that." The woman agreed, even as she calmly strolled towards the office door, blocking them in. "But you should have stopped your boyfriend from prying into places he doesn't belong."

She swallowed back the cold betrayal as she scrambled to her feet, "So you *are* a Russian spy?"

"I prefer *officer*, but yes." Kristina remarked, surprisingly nonchalant, given the last twenty seconds. "GRU, military intelligence. Now *sit down.*"

"Why?" Devon demanded, one hand clutching his gut as he stumbled up off the couch, and faced her down from the middle of the room. "So you can kill us?"

Melissa scrambled to her feet next to him, and Kristina let out an exasperated hiss, "Devon, we've been over this before. I'm not a heartless witch. I just gave you something to make the last hour or so... hazy. You'll take a nap, and when you wake up, you won't remember any of this." As she spoke, Kristina stepped

134

outside, vanishing for a heartbeat then reappearing, having grabbed her purse off the break room floor. Digging inside, she pulled out one of her syringe darts.

Melissa's blood turned to ice in her veins, her mind racing.

That was for her. And Kristina was blocking the only way out.

"I'm sorry, but there *are* rules about this sort of thing," Kristina added, almost sympathetic. "Try to think of it as a favor. You can forget about almost getting killed by Valerie. Trust me, it won't be a great memory."

Next to her, Devon audibly gulped, whispering, "Melissa, you have to run."

"But how do we get past..."

She glanced over at Devon, and her voice died in her throat as she saw the brave determination on his face...

He wasn't coming, she realized numbly. He was staying to distract Kristina. That was how *she* got past. Suddenly Melissa felt sick at the prospect of just abandoning him, even as Kristina took a calculating step closer.

"No, Devon you can't–"

"Don't waste it." Devon murmured, his tone razor focused, like he didn't hear her at all. "And help me remember... when it's all over."

Kristina took another step closer, and in a single insane heartbeat, Melissa didn't see another way out. This was happening, she was leaving him and–

She turned and gave him a swift kiss on the cheek, along with a promise, "I will."

She saw his face redden, then he rushed straight at Kristina, "RUN!"

Melissa bolted, dimly catching the two struggling as she pelted for the door. One of Kristina's hands swiped towards her wrist, but she danced around it, and suddenly she was in the break room. Devon shouted in pain behind her, but Melissa charged for the door leading out to the rest of the store and didn't look back. If she could just... the lock gave an ominous click. Melissa grabbed at the handle and pulled it as hard as she could, but the door wouldn't budge. No, no, no...

"Curls, get back here." She spun to see Kristina standing at her desk with an un-amused expression, one finger pressing what must have been a hidden button. Meanwhile Devon was laid out on the floor between them, gasping in pain.

Melissa shook her head, "Don't touch me."

"Please, this will all go a lot easier if you just come back and sit down. I promise it won't hurt."

"How would you know?"

"Because I've tried it before," Kristina answered bluntly, pacing towards her with the dart still clenched in one fist. "I can't remember much, but my friends said I didn't seem to mind. Just come back and—"

"Melissa, RUN!" Down at Kristina's feet, Devon made one last effort. Surging forward, he tackled her around the legs like a football player, sending her crashing to the floor.

"GET OFF!" Kristina screamed, trying to shake the boy free. "RUN!"

Melissa gulped, her panic meter spiking up to eleven and her eyes darting across the room. Yeah, run, but where?

With the main door locked she needed – she needed a back door. In a flash she remembered Kristina telling Valerie to use the back way into her office. Right, that was her way out, she just had to find it. With storerooms to the left and racks of dresses to the right, Melissa guessed and went left.

Left was Kristina's coffee shop. It must have had a rear entrance to bring in food. Right? Darting into the room while Kristina's enraged shouts echoed behind her, Melissa's eyes searched for an exit. All she saw was a second storeroom in the back. Fortunately, the baristas were all up front and the rooms were both deserted. Searching further back, she found tall racks piled with dozens of mugs and bags of coffee beans. And at the very rear, waiting for her like a pair of steel sentinels, was a set of wide, double doors with a trolley parked nearby. Melissa fumbled with the knob for a beat, but finally it turned. The door swung open to reveal a narrow hall that curved away in the distance, probably running behind most of the shops in the station.

She cast a quick glance backwards to make sure Kristina wasn't close, but there was no sign of the woman. She felt horrible just abandoning her friend but...

"I'm sorry, Devon," she whispered. Then she shut the door behind her and took off at a run to get as far away as she could.

Melissa wasn't really sure how far she ran. For a while, the only sound was her shoes pounding against the heavy steel floor as a thick numbness gripped her heart. Eventually, she found a turn that spilled out onto the main concourse. At two in the afternoon it was jammed with people. Melissa grimly slipped into the crowd, letting it sweep her away while she tried not to think about what had just happened. At first she just focused on putting one foot in front of the other, but if she did that for too long she'd follow the huge ring all the way around and end up right back at Kristina's. When she saw a small side hall with an empty bench, Melissa slipped out of the crowd and quietly sat down.

She almost wished she hadn't. With nothing to do, her mind raced through everything – the fight with Valerie, just how close she had come to having the life choked out of her, Kristina's betrayal, the way she had left Devon there with Kristina's drug slowly chipping away at his memories. She knew there was nothing she could have done... but that didn't make it right.

Nothing was right. Even through the numbness that gripped her, Melissa could still feel cold tendrils of panic smothering her. She was a traitor, she dimly realized, with a feeling like a cold knife in her chest. It felt weird to even think that, but Kristina was a Russian spy, and Melissa had helped the woman break into the barracks earlier. She'd covered Kristina by lying about the bomb going off last night. She'd given aid to an enemy of the United States. That was the definition.

She should have just told her father the truth. He would have been angry, but he would have understood. Now though... now she didn't know what to do. She had lied to the actual CIA, lied to her parents, the Chinese were planning to do something terrible to Medea, and the one person she and Devon had trusted had turned on them in the blink of an eye. She was all alone. And she didn't know how to fix any of this.

Melissa didn't try to stop the tears that trickled down her cheeks.

Chapter 14
Gabrielle

You are not well? *Non*?"

Melissa started at the strong French accent. She glanced up through tear-stained eyes to see a girl about her own age with bright, aquablue-dyed hair, and a sympathetic expression. She tried to answer, but nothing came out except for a muttered, "I'm fine."

The girl, wearing a white shirt beneath an olive cardigan, regarded her for a moment, "Hmmm, why do I not believe you?" She took a spot next to Melissa on the bench. "Do you want to talk about it? It helps to have someone to listen, I think."

"Please," Melissa sighed and shook her head, "you seem like a nice person, but I… I don't want anyone else to get hurt."

"Well then, we are both in luck," the other girl declared in an intrigued voice. "It does not usually hurt to tell a story or to listen to one."

Melissa didn't answer; maybe if she didn't say anything the girl would leave her alone. For a moment there was silence, but then…

"Is it about Mars? *Non*?"

Melissa bit her lip. "I just… I'm in trouble. Okay?"

"Parent trouble or boy trouble?" the girl guessed.

"Both, I suppose."

The girl nodded. "That is the worst combination," she agreed. "He is here, or back on *la planète*? The boy?"

Melissa sniffled and rubbed her cheeks to brush away the tears. "He's up here."

"*Oui,*" the girl nodded sympathetically, "I have heard this story before."

Melissa cocked her head to one side, lost. "Ummm… you have?"

"Of course, it is *évident,*" she said readily. "*Vous* – I mean, you, you like the boy, but your parents do not approve, so you see him in secret. They find out and suddenly you are trapped between the person you care for, and the ones who care for you. It is uhh… I think you say, a pickle, that you have found yourself in. *Oui?*"

"Well," Melissa tried to work out how to respond to that, "you aren't entirely wrong. I guess I should have said I have two problems."

"You have a bigger problem than love?"

"Yeah, actually," Melissa stared at the floor. "Trust me, you don't want to hear about it. It's safer if you just stay away from me."

The other girl leaned in with a fascinated expression. "*Non, non,*" she insisted with a wave of her hands, "you must tell, I am curious now, and there is nothing else to do anyway. My name is Gabrielle, by the way."

"Melissa," she offered the French girl her hand, "and thank you… but you really don't want to get involved in all this. It's really bad."

"*Absurdité,*" Gabrielle maintained with an impish grin. "Whatever *problèmes* you have, they cannot be so bad that you cannot share them with someone else. Besides," she added cheerfully, "they cannot be so bad as my own. I have, *une prime sur la tête…* you would say, I think, a bounty on my head. Not the rest of me, just the head. I do not think it gets worse than that."

"Huh?" Melissa snapped out of her daze of self-pity. "Did you just say–?"

"*Oui*," Gabrielle nodded eagerly. "Now, I have shared a little, so you must tell me about your *curieux problèmes.*"

Melissa stared at the French girl for a moment. What the hell?

The thought crossed her mind, maybe Gabrielle was a spy for that CIA fellow, Banks. Maybe he figured she would admit something to someone her own age… but then, why would he pick a peppy French girl with blue hair and give her such a weird story to tell? At the least he could have found someone who spoke proper English.

For a moment her thoughts drifted. Maybe it was also possible that the two most screwed up people on Medea Station had just stumbled into each other. Call it fate, God, dumb luck, the way things had been going Melissa wouldn't be that surprised. And maybe it didn't matter either way. She needed someone to talk to and if Gabrielle would listen…

She took a deep breath, "Promise me you won't repeat this to anyone."

"*Oui*," she nodded and made a show of crossing her heart, "*Je promets.*"

Whatever, that sounded vaguely promising. "Okay," Melissa winced at what she was about to do and then plunged right in, "basically, a crazy woman kidnapped my friend and everyone else thinks I'm a terrorist."

Gabrielle's face went white, "Oh, *merde.*" She paused, "You are not actually a terrorist, *non*?"

Melissa slumped against the wall and her eyes drifted towards the ceiling. "Anymore, I'm not really sure. I didn't used to be one."

Gabrielle tilted her head to one side, the color returning to her cheeks. "So… I do not need to be running away quite yet?"

"I wouldn't be offended if you did." She glanced at the French girl with a wry expression. "I told you I have problems."

Gabrielle's dark brown eyes studied her for a moment. Melissa couldn't help but feel it was the same sort of look the girl would give a stray dog she wasn't quite sure about. After maybe twenty seconds Gabrielle leaned forward, her mind apparently made up. "There is more to this story, *oui*? The friend of yours with the crazy woman?"

Melissa grimaced, "His name's Devon, we met yesterday on the shuttle up and he invited me to hang out with him afterwards. Since then we've somehow got caught up in this giant fight between a Russian spy, Chinese saboteurs, and the CIA. Although it's a little confusing who's actually on what side."

"Until half an hour ago, I thought we were helping a CIA agent named Kristina, but it turns out she's actually a Russian agent named Kristina. I guess we aren't supposed to know that though, because she got really pissed and drugged Devon to make him forget everything. She would have done the same to me except that I got away and ended up here."

Gabrielle paused for a moment, like she was trying to piece all that together. "You swear, you are not making this up?" Melissa shook her head. "So then, whose side are you on?" the French girl asked with a confused expression.

"Honestly, I have no idea," Melissa answered, despondent. "At this point, Devon is trapped with the Russian lady who wants me to forget that she's a Russian lady. The only *actual* CIA person I've run into hates me. I'm fairly sure the Chinese would just shoot me on the spot. Meanwhile my dad's angry because I've been spending too much time with Devon, and I'm fairly sure my mom only let me out of the room to spite him. So, it… it's just me."

"I must admit," Gabrielle bit her lip with a thoughtful look, "this was not what I was expecting. Do you have a plan?"

Melissa didn't, but apparently her phone felt like beating her to the answer, because it picked that moment to vibrate and her wristlet flashed blue. She flicked on the screen to see:

Curls, get back here NOW if you want to see your friend again. And if you're thinking of running to the MP's, don't. It won't end well for either of you.

"Perfect," Melissa shook her head in despair, "just perfect."

Gabrielle leaned over, eagerly skimming the text, then she glanced at Melissa. "You are being sarcastic, *non*?"

"Frick, I don't know. I mean what am I supposed to do?" Melissa threw up her hands. "She has Devon, I can't fight her…"

she sighed, and swallowed. "Maybe I should just go back and get it over with."

Gabrielle frowned, "*Ne pas, qu'elle aille se faire voir…* I mean… well it does not translate. The point is, she does not even respect you enough to call you by your proper name and you want to surrender? What is wrong with you? You are *Américain.* 'Go, fight, win' that is your national motto. Right? At least on Sunday afternoons. Do that."

"How?" Melissa demanded. "Even with Devon's help, she just rolled right over us. If we couldn't beat her together, how am I supposed to do it alone?"

Gabrielle nibbled at her lip for a moment in thought. "And, if you were not alone?"

It took Melissa a second to realize what the French girl was suggesting, but when she did, she emphatically shook her head no. "Gabrielle, thank you, but you don't want to–"

"*Oui, Oui*, I know," Gabrielle waved a hand as if to brush away her objections. "You have made it quite clear that you have *grave problèmes* and you do not want other people to be involved. Well, you know what? I do not care."

"You should care," Melissa crossed her arms. "This is dangerous and–"

"And the worst that happens is that your Russian CIA *putain* will try to make me forget as well. And you know what?" She waved a finger in front of Melissa. "*I do not care.*"

"If she wants to steal my memories… fine. Today has been boring, and maybe she can take away the last year while she is at it. I would not miss it very much."

Melissa wanted to scream in frustration. The logical part of her brain was shouting that this was a disaster waiting to happen, which it clearly was. Gabrielle sounded just like Devon had when she'd run into him the prior day, all eager and excited to have an adventure. Now he was having his memory of the last few hours pharmaceutically chiseled away. Gabrielle didn't understand just how dangerous Kristina was. She was treating it like a game, where if you lost you got to forget that you ever played. Melissa would have bet money this was a colossal mistake.

Unfortunately, she was also desperate. She felt like someone hanging off the edge of a cliff grabbing at tufts of grass, even when she knew they wouldn't hold her weight. The truth was, she needed help to deal with Kristina, and if Gabrielle really did want to help…

"You're absolutely sure you want to do this, because… trust me, you really don't."

Gabrielle arched her eyebrows. "And you are so convinced things will go better if you are alone? Besides, you cannot tell a strange story about spies and *espionnage* and expect me to go back about my life."

"Fine." Melissa shook her head and resigned herself to whatever came next. "I suppose I could use the help."

"*Excellente.*" Gabrielle grinned. "So, tell me more about this crazy lady we are going after."

Melissa shook her head. The strange French girl was acting like she had a mad death wish. Then an even scarier thought hit Melissa – maybe she did.

Chapter 15
La Grande Contre-attaque

You did not tell me we were going after the dress store lady," Gabrielle remarked as she and Melissa peered down the main concourse towards the 'KA Dresses and Accessories' storefront. They were a substantial distance from the store, several hundred feet at least, but the way the station curved up in the distance it was possible to see it over the crowds of people filling the concourse at three in the afternoon.

"Wait, you know Kristina?" Melissa wheeled on Gabrielle in sudden suspicion.

"*Oui*," the French girl remarked in an unconcerned voice. "I was bored yesterday and so I went... *shopping*? Is that an English word also?"

"Yes," Melissa suppressed a low growl. "You didn't think to mention that you knew Kristina earlier?"

"That is making it out to be more than it is. I talked with her for ten minutes and we discussed my waist size. She has an excellent *sens de la mode*. I would never have guessed she is a spy though, or a Russian."

"So," Gabrielle glanced at Melissa, "you have a plan? *Oui*?"

"*Non*," Melissa retorted in a sarcastic mocking French accent, "I still don't, same as the last two times you asked."

"You do not have to be *une putain*," the French girl muttered in a hurt voice.

"What does that even mean?"

"Uhhh… you will not like me if I tell you," Gabrielle cautioned. "Anyway, where exactly is your friend? That is a good place to start."

"I don't know for sure," Melissa said. "If I was guessing, he's probably still in Kristina's office." She paused, weighing their options. Somehow they needed to get Devon out of there, but he was probably still half drugged. It wouldn't be quite as easy as charging in and telling him to run for it.

Then there was the Kristina problem, Melissa had no idea how to deal with that. The woman would no doubt be waiting. And in an even fight, Melissa had no illusions. Kristina would crush them both. So, how could she tilt the field in her favor?

"Gabrielle, you said you ran into Kristina yesterday. If you were to return for a second visit, would that be weird?"

"*Non,*" the girl nodded like she guessed Melissa's plan. "You want me to keep her busy."

"Yeah," Melissa slowly nodded. We need a distraction."

***

Kristina sat in her office with a deep scowl creasing her face. Her eyes flickered between the two unconscious figures – Devon slumped on the couch and Valerie tightly bound to a chair. Both of them, problems.

Her focus lingered on Valerie for a moment, and Kristina couldn't stop a smirk that tugged at her lips. She was going to be awfully stiff when she woke up. No more than she deserved though. Kristina still couldn't understand how the woman had been spying under her very nose. She'd hired Valerie six months ago, and from the way the girl handled herself, Kristina had the sneaking suspicion that she had been in the espionage game a lot longer than that.

Had whoever sent Valerie known about her little operation as well? Kristina mulled over the possibility. Probably not. Back at the room, Valerie had seemed genuinely shocked to see her. Besides, if they'd known all along, why suddenly try to kill her now?

Maybe Valerie had just tried to get a job at the coffee shop for the exact same reason that Kristina ran it in the first place. It was an excellent place to get information. They had both likely been running similar operations without even realizing it, just for different employers.

Putting the pieces together wasn't enough to stop Kristina's worrying though. It stung her pride that she'd been duped. She hadn't suspected a thing when that snake of a woman had showed up looking all contrite and teary-eyed. Yet, the moment her back was turned, Valerie had slammed a dagger pommel into her head. Ungrateful *suka*.

Kristina shook her head, she needed to stop doing that. People back at the GRU had been telling her for years that cursing in Russian was a bad idea. She hadn't expected Devon and Curls to be the ones to notice though. Those two were cleverer than she had originally credited them. And a lot more trouble.

Kristina sighed, this whole thing was idiotic. She was ought to be keeping the Chinese from getting their hands on the world's most valuable orbital asset, but instead she was playing nanny… again. Maybe she should have just let Devon and Melissa walk away when they found out who she was. They were clearly scared and they might not have talked but… no, she couldn't do that. There were very clear rules about things like this. In the back of her mind, her old mentor's voice echoed his favorite line, "*Tolko adin mojet imet sekret.*" Only one can have a secret.

Besides, Curls was one of those self-righteous, duty first sorts, and her father was a military officer for goodness sake. If that wasn't a recipe for trouble, Kristina didn't know what was.

She let out an unbidden sigh. The picture frame from earlier was laid on her desk, and she spent a moment just flicking through the faces of her old friends. Usually it relaxed her, having a few glimpses of home. But today she ended up feeling more anxious than ever.

She needed to find Curls. The longer the girl kept running, the harder this all became. If she had just stayed put and taken her medicine, she and Devon could have fallen asleep and been gone in an hour or two, none the wiser.

Every minute Melissa was gone though, it became harder to take away her memories. And of course, if the girl decided to take a nap, that would royally wreck things. Sleep would trigger the transfer of her short-term memories to long-term ones and the inhibitor in Scopolamine that normally blocked exactly that process wouldn't matter. Then Melissa's memories couldn't be erased, and things would get… complicated.

Kristina's gaze drifted across her desk, and her eyes fell on the flash drive from earlier. She hadn't had the time to look at the video, but according to Devon, it had answers. Since she wasn't close to finding Curls anyway, she figured it wouldn't hurt to take a peek. Maybe she could sort out what all this murder and subterfuge was about.

Plugging in the drive, Kristina skimmed past the part at the beginning. She might watch it later, but she didn't have infinite time to waste, and with McGregor dead, his motivations didn't really matter. Skipping ahead to the part where he made the handoff, Kristina paused the video when she saw the major appear on screen. *"Suka cin,"* she muttered.

The woman on screen was none other than Major Sophie Tannenhill, head of station surveillance and electronic warfare. That raised a lot of questions about what was going on… none of them pleasant. *"Der'mo."*

"Miss Andrews?" There was a voice from outside and a knock on her door.

Kristina glanced down at her phone on the desk. She'd told Steph to give her an hour alone, but according to the clock it was already ten minutes past. Time sure flew when you were having fun, she mused without a trace of humor. "What is it?"

"There's a girl up front to see you."

So, Melissa was back. Glancing up at the surveillance videos Kristina didn't immediately see her, but she couldn't imagine who else would want to talk with her. Melissa might just be avoiding the cameras since she knew they were there. "Tell her I'll be up front in a minute, Steph!"

With a sigh, Kristina pushed her chair back from the desk and rose to leave. Fortunately, Valerie wouldn't be waking up anytime soon, and Devon was still in a lethargic, drug-induced stupor. Maybe with a little time they could work out some sort of deal, or maybe Curls was going to try something stupid. She debated grabbing the gun from her purse but decided not to. It might raise too many questions.

***

Melissa, in point of fact, was not up front waiting for Kristina. She was standing at the rear of the store, near the service door she had originally used for her escape, with her phone tucked in her pocket and one earbud in. In the military they used radios, but who really needed those when you had wifi? Before they had split up, she had called Gabrielle's phone and left the line open. Gabrielle had hers muted, but this way Melissa could hear everything going on inside. Particularly, Gabrielle could warn her if Kristina decided to head into the back.

Listening close, she tried to filter out the soft swishing sound of Gabrielle's anxious pacing. "She is coming? *Non*?"

"She'll be up front in a minute," answered a muffled woman's voice.

Good, if Kristina was coming up front, then she could probably… Melissa tried to turn the door handle and her heart sank as she realized it was locked. Not good.

Why hadn't she thought of that? Melissa gave herself a mental kick. It was probably one of those doors that only opened from the inside. Of course it made sense that Kristina left her back door locked, that was Shopkeeping 101.

Melissa fought at the handle and bit back a despairing curse when it didn't budge. No, no, no!

Her heart turned to ice as she realized it was too late to call off Gabrielle. They were only going to get one shot at this, and she'd just ruined it because of a door.

149

Right, she took a deep breath and got a hold of herself. What to do? She couldn't get in the back, and she couldn't go in through the dress store, so that just left the coffee shop.

Setting off at a run, Melissa dashed down the hall and circled around toward the front, praying that she wasn't going to be too late.

***

Gabrielle wasn't worried… much. She kept telling herself it was the same as when she'd come in the previous day. Except it wasn't.

Before, she hadn't known she was dealing with a Russian spy. That made things a tad different. She tried her best not to let it show. If there was one thing she was good at anymore, it was taking problems and squashing them down until even she started to forget it was there. She put on what she had heard the *Américains* at school quietly call a 'Resting Bitch Face,' whatever that meant. It was just her normal expression. She shook her head. Strange *Américains*.

"Hello," she saw Kristina walking up with a confused look. "Where is she?"

"You mean *moi?*" Gabrielle raised her hand a tad and tried to put on as thick an accent as she could to sell the act.

"Oh…" Kristina stared at her in surprise, "it's Gabrielle, right?"

"You were expecting someone else?"

"No, it was nothing." Kristina waved a hand dismissively. "What brings you here?"

"Well," Gabrielle launched into her prepared story with a smile, "I was hoping you might be able to help *moi.* You see I am uhhh… looking for something to wear when I get to Mars, and you seemed so well versed in all the latest fashions. I was thinking you might be able to help me find something that feels nice but is not too casual. Something I could both wear to parties and also just out with friends?"

"Well, I think Stephanie here could probably help you," Kristina gestured to her assistant.

150

"*Non, non, non,*" Gabrielle shook her head, layering on the compliments and hopefully not being too obvious. "I do not mean offense to your *assistant, mademoiselle* but when we talked yesterday, I felt that you have a *sens exquis,* an elegant taste for these sorts of things. It would be a shame not to get your thoughts."

"Well," Kristina appeared more than a little flattered, "I suppose I could give you a hand. I do have some other things I'm working on so I may have to leave, but I'm sure Stephanie and I can help you out."

***

"Hello there," Melissa tried to walk slowly enough so as not to be too suspicious when she strolled up to the coffee shop counter. Even so, she was painfully aware of how many precious seconds she had just wasted.

"What do you want?" A young lady, maybe twenty or twenty-five, strode down the counter to her.

"I umm… I have an interview… thingy… with Kristina?"

The other woman regarded her for a very long moment, and Melissa couldn't escape the painful awareness that she wasn't in remotely appropriate clothes for a job interview. She also probably looked a little young to be applying at all.

Melissa was certain she was about to get run off. Eventually, though, coffee woman's face twisted in an amused grin. She shook her head, like she kind of suspected something was off, but she wasn't paid enough to deal with it. Maybe she also wanted to see the fireworks when it blew up. "Well, whatever, I guess you can have fun with that," she shrugged. "And, by the way, if you don't want to get run out of here in a hurry, I suggest you call her *Miss Andrews.*"

Melissa gave an eager nod and grinned, "I'll do that, thanks."

"Her office is right this way." The barista led her back to the storage room holding the heavy that Melissa recalled from earlier, before pointing her towards the waiting room outside Kristina's office. "Take a seat in there. She'll be out when she wants you. And unless you want to get screamed off the station,

151

DO NOT go inside her office unless she asks you too, understand? Miss Andrews is very particular about that rule."

"Okay, thanks." Melissa made a show of nervously biting her lip then plopping down on the oversized couch near the door.

She waited a few seconds for the barista to give her one final nod and turn to leave. As soon as she was out of sight, Melissa was up off the couch. She grabbed for the handle to Kristina's door and… it wouldn't turn.

No. Melissa suppressed a frustrated groan. Why did Kristina have to be so particular with her security all of a sudden? The door had been unlocked earlier. Granted, that was probably because Kristina had been inside, but it still felt unfair. How was she supposed to pick a lock?

Melissa knew she was running out of time. She popped in an earbud and thankfully heard Kristina and Gabrielle discussing what colors went best with her aqua shaded hair. That gave her a few more minutes at least.

She tried to think. In the movies, people always used a bobby pin or something like that to pick locks. Worth a shot. Digging one out of the small purse looped across her shoulder, Melissa jammed it into the lock, jiggling it around but to no avail. It always looked easy when people did it on TV, but when jiggling the pin accomplished nothing, an awful sinking sensation clawed at her.

She desperately tried to make something… anything happen, but thirty seconds later she still hadn't made an ounce of progress and in a burst of impatience she jerked the pin so hard it bent in the lock.

Great… now that was useless too. In a surge of anger, she hurled the worthless bobby pin across the room where it made an unsatisfying *ting* against the wall. She followed it up with a sharp kick to the door that only resulted in a loud bang and left her toes smarting in pain.

Muttering a curse beneath her breath, the girl tried to keep back the tears of frustration. How was she supposed to do this? She couldn't pick a lock, she wasn't strong enough to knock down the door, and time was running out like water from a bowl. Why couldn't something just work right for once?

Praying for a miracle, Melissa dug out a second pin. It was stupid, but she couldn't think of anything else to do. She slid it into the lock, and this time she probed around for a moment until…

"Who's there?" a voice echoed nearby.

Great, now she was hearing Devon's voice in her head.

"Hello? Who's there?"

Or… maybe it wasn't in her head. "Devon?" She pressed her ear close to the door, "Is that you? Open the door."

For a moment there was no response, but finally there was a click and the door swung open. Behind it she found Devon watching her through bleary, defocused eyes, his posture loose and woozy, like he was about to tumble over. "Melissa?" he mumbled.

"Devon… are you okay?" She looped an arm around him to make sure he didn't fall.

Slurring the words like he was drunk, he murmured, "What's happening?"

"Kristina, she drugged you. Look, we have to go before–"

"Hello, Curls."

Melissa whirled around to see Kristina standing across the room with an amused smirk.

Chapter 16
Trapped

You know," Kristina continued, as though she was savoring the moment, "I really did appreciate your strategy, sending that charming French girl as a distraction. I think she overplayed her role a bit. But still, excellent effort given what you had to work with."

Melissa winced, and Kristina added, "Now, given your situation, are you willing to accept your fate with a bit of dignity?"

Melissa sure as hell wasn't. Unfortunately, there was only one way to go. She shoved Devon back inside the room, and dashed in herself, slamming the door behind her with a bang, and making sure to lock it from the inside.

"Seriously, Curls?" Kristina was almost laughing from the other side of the door. "You want to lock yourself in *my* office? You realize I can still get inside, right?"

"Screw you, Kristina!"

Kristina burst into laughter, but Melissa's brain kicked into high gear. "Devon, sit there! Don't move!" She helped him stumble over to the couch, then immediately darted toward Kristina's desk and began digging through her purse.

All she needed was... ahhh Kristina's gun. Okay, she chambered a dart, this could work, it would be just like fighting

Valerie. She needed to get off one good shot, then hold Kristina back for a few minutes.

That hadn't worked at all though, had it? Valerie had nearly killed her. Without even realizing it, Melissa's free hand massaged her throat, the memory of Valerie's steely grip on her neck still seared into her mind.

Okay, maybe she needed a backup plan. Melissa's eyes drifted across the small room for a moment until they fell on Valerie's knife from earlier, still lying on Kristina's desk. That could work. She had no idea how to actually fight with a knife, but it couldn't be that hard – just use the pointy end.

Leaving the knife on the desk beside her, Melissa took a firm stance in the middle of the room, put both hands on the pistol grip and raised the barrel. Over by the door there came scratching noises like Kristina was actually picking the lock. Probably with a bobby pin, Melissa thought with a twinge of irritated resentment.

With precious little time, Melissa nerved herself for the fight, but no matter what she did, she couldn't get the lurking sense out of her head that Kristina was going to win. The frustrating fact was that Kristina seemed to be better than her... at everything. She made plans, Kristina saw straight through them. She couldn't pick a lock, Kristina could. She lost a fight to Valerie, Kristina didn't. She was scared...

And Kristina wasn't.

Melissa shook her head. She couldn't beat that. Deep down she knew she couldn't. She'd already run away once, because of exactly that. But, she swallowed, she also owed it to Devon to try. And it wasn't like there was anywhere left to go.

Fifteen feet away the office door swung open, and there was Kristina, regarding her with that same infuriating smugness. Melissa's finger tugged back on the trigger, the gun fired – and missed.

For a horrible instant Melissa couldn't believe it. One second, there was Kristina, arrogantly posed in the doorway. Then she twisted her whole body to one side and ducked out of view. But Melissa had already pulled the trigger and sent the dart harmlessly slicing through the empty space.

There was a metallic *ting* as it hit the back wall. Then, almost like she had never moved, Kristina was right back in the doorway.

"Again with the predictability, Curls." Kristina sighed and shook her head like she was lecturing a student who had missed a math problem. "Don't get me wrong," she added in a conversational voice, even as she strolled closer. "It's a good plan, probably what I would have done in your situation, but you panicked and fired early. Newbie mistake. And you really ought to have stood *behind* the desk instead of in front of it." She paused for a second and gave Melissa a calculating look.

"Still though, you have potential." Kristina's face lit up in a hawkish grin. "You want a job?" she asked out of the blue. "If you were willing to do a few favors I might forget all this ever happened."

Melissa knew she was being serious, but if anything that just strengthened her resolve. "I'm not a traitor," she hissed.

"Oh, well… too bad." The Russian lady gave a regretful '*tsk*'. Then she struck.

It was so fast, Melissa almost missed it. One second Kristina was ten feet away, slowly circling like a cat eying a mouse, and the next, the bigger woman was barreling forward. Melissa barely snatched up the knife in time to make a wild slash and keep Kristina back. The lady slipped right away from her though, and resumed her slow calculating circle… but closer now.

Melissa gripped the knife hilt so hard her hands turned white, making sure to keep it leveled at Kristina. "Just let me take Devon and leave."

"Sweetie," Kristina cocked her eyebrows, "you know I can't do that. And by the way, stop holding that knife like a pistol. You're embarrassing yourself; it doesn't shoot people."

Melissa's cheeks turned hot, although she wasn't sure if it was embarrassment or anger. "Am I supposed to believe you're helping me?"

"Curls, I don't care if you believe I'm Alisa Selezneva and I'm here from the future, let alone if you *believe* I'm helping you." She paused with a sigh and shook her head. "You probably don't even get that reference, do you? Look, I admire that you had the courage to come back for your friend, but this is over. Sit down and take your medicine, or I'll make you."

Melissa didn't move, and finally Kristina gave her a regretful frown. "Then, I'm sorry."

And just like that, Kristina attacked. Melissa tried to keep the small blade between her and the woman, but Kristina batted it away and landed a sharp punch to her side that sent the girl staggering backwards. Melissa tried to recover and keep the knife up, but Kristina was too fast. Before she knew what was happening, the woman slammed her back against the wall, her arms and the knife trapped at her side. Their faces pressed close together as Kristina calmly plucked the knife from Melissa's helpless hands and tossed it back towards the door.

Melissa sucked in a frantic breath. Recovering from the shock of being smashed across the room, she jerked her knee up and caught Kristina right in the gut. The woman's grip loosened just a hair and Melissa broke free. She shoved Kristina away and landed a quick kick to her side. Kristina stumbled backwards in surprise with a pained grimace.

Kristina growled, and for the first time she seemed… angry. She threw herself at Melissa and instinctively the girl kicked out, hitting her straight in the chest. Despite a grunt of pain, Kristina caught her foot, and a quick twist sent Melissa sprawling to the floor. She tried to get up, but Kristina pinned her arms down, and all Melissa could manage was to knee furiously at the woman straddled atop her.

Kristina grunted when one knee finally did connect, and wriggling an arm free, Melissa punched her as hard as she could, grazing Kristina's jaw. The bigger woman rolled off her then up to standing, a trickle of blood coming from her lip. Melissa scrambled to her feet.

"*Suka cin,*" Kristina muttered through gritted teeth as she wiped away the blood. "I'm trying not to hurt you, Curls, but you're making that difficult."

"Well, bring it on," Melissa taunted, gaining a little confidence for a change. She stepped in and jabbed a quick punch at Kristina. Then everything went wrong.

Kristina caught her wrist in midair and immediately retaliated with a blow straight to the solar plexus. She didn't even hit that hard, but somehow Melissa's whole chest felt like it was on fire. She wanted to scream in agony… except she couldn't breathe.

She couldn't breathe.

For what felt like forever, her whole world was consumed by desperate panic. Her lungs screaming for air

She crashed hard on the floor, and finally gulped down a frantic breath, only to find she was laying on her back with Kristina pinning her.

Melissa desperately tried to knock the woman off like before, but Kristina hadn't made the same mistake twice. Melissa's knee found nothing but empty air. Behind Kristina she could just barely glimpse the door to the outside, so agonizingly close, yet so terribly distant.

"Don't make me do that again, Curls," Kristina warned, shifting and putting a smothering pressure on her chest. "I'd rather not have to explain how you ended up with a broken sternum."

Melissa gasped for air, so much she could barely whisper. She tried to squirm loose, but she couldn't. Even now she could barely force her chest to rise with Kristina's weight piled on. And that feeling – when Kristina had punched her, the searing pain and the gripping fear that she was about to die – she couldn't take that again.

Her murmur was so soft even she could barely hear it. She'd tried to come back for him, but now… "I'm sorry, Devon."

"What was that, Curls?"

The tears welled in Melissa's eyes, and she had to choke down another gasp. "You win, Kristina. You win."

Whatever strength Melissa had left drained from her arms with those words. It was replaced by flowing tears of rage, frustration, and utter helplessness as the horror of what would happen next sunk in.

Then, from back towards the door, Melissa heard the strangest, most beautiful thing.

"Ne Pas! Bon nuit putain!" There was an audible 'thunk' Kristina's eyes abruptly rolled up in her head and the woman

tumbled off her, sprawled out on the floor beside Melissa. Her face was replaced by Gabrielle's glowing grin. *"Bonjour,* Melissa, you are okay? *Non?"*

"Gabrielle?" Melissa gasped down a few shocked breaths, "What are you…?"

"I think she was on to us," the French girl readily explained, her hands fidgeting nervously with the knife hilt she had used to knock out Kristina. "Your Russian friend, she dodged off after a few minutes. I figured you might be in some trouble, so I said I had to use the *toilette.* Then I came back here and, well… you know the rest."

Gabrielle knelt down next to her, "You are okay?"

In reply, Melissa reached up and gripped the girl in a fierce hug. "Thank you," she whispered.

If it was possible, Gabrielle's smile widened. "It was my pleasure. To be honest, this is the most fun I have had all week. I do not usually get to go around knocking people on the head."

"Melissa," Devon's slurred voice murmured from where he was struggling to keep his eyes from slipping shut over on the couch. "What's going on? Who's the blue-hair chick?"

Now that she could breathe again and the fire in her chest was dying away, Melissa struggled to her feet. "Devon, did Kristina hurt you?"

"Why would she do that?"

"Right," Melissa frowned, "you don't remember, do you?"

"Remember what?"

"So, this is your boyfriend?" Gabrielle tilted her head a little with a skeptical expression.

Melissa's face went red at the offhand remark. "Gabrielle, this is Devon," she stammered. "Devon, meet Gabrielle."

Devon tried to raise his hand in reply but only got it a shaky halfway into the air. Even with the drug hopefully starting to wear off, Melissa suspected his mind was still foggy…at best. She was probably going to have to explain everything all over again afterwards.

"We can talk later. Right now, we need to go before Kristina wakes up," Melissa said. "She's going to be extremely pissed."

"Uhhh…sure," Devon murmured groggily.

Melissa helped him up, and together they staggered to the door. "Come on," she waved Gabrielle to follow and shut the door to Kristina's office behind them. "We'll take the back way out."

Leaving Kristina sprawled out unconscious on the floor, Melissa, Gabrielle, and Devon stumbled their way out the back entrance to Kristina's shop and into the long empty hallway that wound its way around the station. For a little while no one said much, as Melissa focused solely on getting as far from Kristina as possible. Once the door had dropped out of sight from the curvature of the station though, she allowed herself to breathe a sigh of relief. The walking had apparently been good for Devon too. He was still staggering, but not as badly.

"Melissa," Devon leaned close, his whisper much less woozy now, "that girl, Gabrielle, how much does she know?"

Nearby, Gabrielle shot him an irritated glance. "*That girl* knows you are not so good at whispering," she retorted.

"Don't worry, you can trust her," Melissa assured him. "What about you, what's the last thing you remember?"

"I guess we had lunch, and... did we go watch that video? Everything after lunch is fuzzy, then it just sort of goes blank until your banging at the door woke me up." He paused in realization, "Kristina drugged me, didn't she?"

"Not with a full dose, but yes."

"Well, what the heck did I ever do to her?"

"You figured out she was a Russian spy."

"What...?" His voice died away, "That..."

"There's a lot to catch up on," Melissa said. She spent the next few minutes filling him in on all the details since lunch – the video, Valerie, the whole Kristina was a spy thing.

In retrospect she was shocked at how much they had done in the last four hours. She tried to keep her promise though and explain everything. She even gave him the credit for working out who Valerie was, although a part of her knew he would probably be insufferable for it later. A promise was a promise.

The only thing she didn't mention was the kiss... that memory... that was her secret. Devon wouldn't understand what it meant, and in truth Melissa didn't quite know herself. There was no point in complicating things. Plus, Gabrielle was listening intently a few feet away and the French girl would… well, Melissa blushed, she didn't really know what Gabrielle would do, probably something weird.

Chapter 17
Touching the Light

By the time they were finally back at Devon's room, he was much improved from the groggy mess that Melissa had dragged out of Kristina's office. He kept rubbing his temples like he had a pounding headache, but at least he was walking straight. She had been briefly worried that Devon's parents would think she had gotten him drunk… or high. She wasn't sure which would be worse.

"You are sure you do not want to go to my *chambre?*" Gabrielle asked for the second time. "It is not far. My parents are at *un film* and I do not think my brothers would object."

"Thanks, but I'll be okay," Devon nodded and glanced at his phone. "Besides, my parents keep texting me and asking if I want to go to dinner. I should probably put in an appearance before they get worried and call the cops."

Melissa shuddered at that remark. That would be a disaster, although likely not for the reasons Devon suspected. Her dad would probably hear about it one way or another, and if he started prying into the events of the last couple hours… well, not even her mom would be able to save her then.

"You're sure you're going to be okay?" Melissa asked, concerned. "Are you really up for dinner after… all that."

"Don't worry," he managed a pained half smile. "I'll just tell them all the artificial lights are getting to me and I need to lie down for a little while. Mom will probably buy that."

He paused and looked her straight in the eye. "And thank you, Melissa…for everything." Devon leaned in like he was about to kiss her, and for a half second Melissa's heart jumped into her throat.

Devon didn't though, he grabbed her in a tight hug, and Melissa was happy to hug him right back. When they finally pulled apart, Melissa had a coquettish grin. He should have tried for the kiss, she thought to herself.

"Tell Evie I said hi," she added in parting.

"I will, and let me know if anything else comes up." He nodded to both the girls then swung open the door. "Hey, mom, I'm back."

The door closed with a 'thunk' and it was just Gabrielle and Melissa out in the otherwise empty hall.

After a second Gabrielle turned to Melissa with the sly smile of a gossiping girl. "So, you never did tell me, Devon is your *copain* or *petit ami?*"

"Gabrielle, you realize I don't speak French. Right?"

The girl struggled for a second, grasping at the air as though she could pull out the correct phrase. "It is not my fault," she finally declared in embarrassment. "English does not have all the words right. When people just say boyfriend, it is *ambigu* what they mean. Is he a boyfriend that you kiss, or a boyfriend that you play board games with? In French we have two words, *copain et ami.* It is very simple." Her voice broke off for a second as though she thought better of whatever she was going to say next. "Well, actually I suppose it is very complicated. But you like him? *Non?*"

Melissa felt herself blush at Gabrielle's question. "Devon's just a friend."

Gabrielle grinned, "Of course."

Melissa blushed even more, but the French girl seemed not to notice. "You want to go find more trouble?" she asked cheerfully. "Maybe of a *différent* type?"

"I actually have a thing. There's a party later I have to attend."

"A party?" Suddenly Gabrielle was all ears.

"Not like… it's a military party."

Gabrielle frowned and cocked her head to one side. "You seem a little young to be in the military."

"It's for my dad," Melissa suppressed a chuckle. "Like I said though, I need to get home or my parents are going to scream at me. Well, they'll probably scream at me anyway, but…" She sighed. "I'll see you around?"

"*Oui*, I suppose we will have plenty of time to catch up on the way to Mars."

Suddenly Gabrielle leaned in *way* too close, so her cheek was right next to Melissa's, and she made a quick kissing sound. Melissa froze, not really sure what to do, but Gabrielle just gave her a second kiss on the other cheek. Finally she pulled back and noticed the stunned expression on Melissa's face. "Oh right, I forget sometimes, you *Américains* do not kiss, do you? The cold, heartless people that you are." She stepped back with a bemused grin. "*Au revoir,* Melissa. Enjoy your party."

"Umm, okay…" was all the stunned girl could manage for a goodbye.

By the time Melissa got back to her room it was close to six. Her dad was nowhere to be found, but mom was already busy dusting a coat of blush on her cheeks.

"You know, Melissa," she didn't look away from the mirror when the door opened, "When I said you could leave earlier, I didn't mean for you to run off for five hours."

"Sorry, mom, I kept getting distracted and…"

"Too distracted to answer your phone?"

Melissa winced. She had put it on silent for the whole Kristina thing, which meant her bracelet wouldn't have lit up either. Pulling her phone out she found a screen full of message notifications.

"I'm sorry," she murmured in an abashed voice. "I guess I forgot."

"Well, you had better hope your father wasn't trying to find you either because I don't..." Mom turned around and her voice trailed off in concern. "Melissa, what happened?"

"Huh?" Sure, she'd been in a few fights, but Melissa didn't think she looked *that* bad.

"Your throat, it's all red and puffy."

Oh crap. Melissa had just put that whole 'being choked to death' episode out of her head. Obviously, she should have realized something like that might have left a mark. Instantly her hand shot to massage her throat as though she could hide it. "Umm... it was nothing, I just uhh... well, it's kind of embarrassing. My hand got in some cleaner and I guess I touched my neck without realizing. Anyway, it was kind of itchy afterwards and I think I scratched it too much."

"Well, do you want to see a doctor, sweetheart?" Her mom came closer, makeup brushes forgotten. "It looks horrible."

"It's fine." Melissa swiftly maneuvered towards the bathroom door. "I can put a little concealer on and no one will notice."

"Sweetheart, are you sure you—"

Melissa didn't hear the rest as she snapped the bathroom door closed behind her. A quick glance in the mirror confirmed her worst fears. Her neck looked like... well, like someone had tried to murder her. She shook her head in despair. How was she supposed to hide *this*?

Some concealer might work for the night, but give it a day or two and she would probably have splotchy purple bruises on her neck. Melissa didn't care how good a liar she was, her mom wasn't an idiot. With a dejected sigh she dusted a heavy layer of beige makeup onto her neck until the swollen redness beneath was more or less covered over.

By the time she was done, there were tears of frustration welling in her eyes. She honestly didn't know what to do. Kristina was probably just waking up and no doubt plotting something nasty. There was still that Major... whoever she was, that was planning to do something terrible to Medea Station. She was quickly digging herself into a *very* deep hole with all these lies to her parents, and currently her only friends were an over-the-top French girl, and Devon, who was busy sleeping off an involuntary drug overdose.

She brushed the first tear away. 'No' she told herself. She had already been crying too much today and it hadn't fixed anything. That, and it would smear her makeup if she wasn't careful. Melissa allowed herself one last sniffle, then she took a deep breath and headed back out of the cramped bathroom.

"There you are." Her mom was seated on the bed waiting for her with a worried look. "Melissa, is everything alright?"

No, it wasn't. Melissa bit her lip and tried to stop her face giving her away, but inside she felt a shudder of sheer terror as she lied. "I'm fine. Like I said, just a little too much scratching. Nothing a bit of makeup won't fix."

"Sweetheart, I know I said we wanted to give you some space, but you run off with that boy and come back looking like…" Her mom shook her head. "If there's something going on, you can tell me, whatever it is. I can help."

Melissa almost did. She came within a hairsbreadth of spilling everything – but she couldn't. No matter what mom said, she couldn't help with the fact that the Chinese were trying to destroy the station, nor could she stop Kristina. But Melissa knew her mom, she would try, and if she got in the way…

She shook her head and forced herself to lie, this time with a smile. "There's nothing, mom. I just… I just wish we could be back in Texas, that's all."

"And that boy?"

Of course her mom would ask about that. "Trust me, mom, you don't have to worry about Devon. He's probably the nicest person I've met on the whole station."

That comment finally seemed to break the ice between them, and her mom broke into a good-natured grin. "I wouldn't mention that around your father."

"Is he still mad?" she asked apprehensively.

"He'll be okay," her mom spoke as though there was a lot more to that statement that she wasn't saying. "But you need to be on your best behavior tonight. That would go a long way towards smoothing things over. And maybe for the next few days, try not to spend every moment with your new boyfriend."

"He's not my boyfriend."

"Of course not, sweetheart," her mom gave an unconvinced nod. "You'll have to persuade your father of that though, or Devon's liable to find himself tossed out an airlock midtrip."

Melissa figured that was a joke…right? Either way, Mom didn't give her the time to decide. "Now you need to get dressed. We leave at seven and you barely have a half hour to get ready."

"Right." Grabbing the backpack with the rest of her clothes, Melissa scurried off the bed and over to the narrow closet where her dress still hung in the plastic sheath from the store. Delicately taking it off the hook, she headed back into the bathroom, and for a moment she found herself staring at the thing. It really was pretty, beautiful even, a knee length field of dark blue crisscrossed with silver strands that wove into intricate patterns around the waistline. But when she looked at it, she couldn't reconcile the woman who had picked out something so utterly gorgeous for her, with the woman who had tried to drug her six hours later.

She shook her head and Kristina's words echoed through her mind. "Easiest three thousand dollars you'll ever make." Melissa almost laughed at the absurdity. She had nearly died… for a dress. Next time she'd just pay the list price, thank you very much.

Slipping into the wavy silken fabric, Melissa paused for a moment to admire herself in the mirror. She did look gorgeous… but it wasn't worth it. In that instant her mind snapped to a decision, she couldn't keep lying like this. It was getting to the point where even *she* couldn't keep her story straight, and anyone who bothered digging more than a few inches would discover that pretty quickly. She had to tell someone what was going on, but it had to be someone who could both help and who would listen to her. Unfortunately, there was only one person who fit those criteria – her dad.

And he was going to be *soooo* pissed. Probably ground her for the rest of her natural life. *But* she also knew that he wouldn't arrest her and maybe he could keep that Banks fellow from tossing her in a secret CIA prison. Melissa gulped nervously. She couldn't tell him quite yet. She needed to get the video from

Devon as proof that she wasn't just making things up, and if she could identify the woman in it at dinner later, that couldn't hurt either. She could probably grab the video file from Devon tomorrow morning and tell her dad then.

A lump formed in her stomach at the thought of waiting that long. Maybe she should just do it tonight. It wasn't like waiting would make Dad *less* angry with her. She could just find out who the major in the video was, pull her dad aside, and tell him straight away. If he wanted to see the video... well, maybe her dad wouldn't be so hard on Devon if he knew what had really happened. Fingers crossed.

With her mind made up, Melissa reached around the back of her dress, and after a little wiggling and some acrobatics she managed to zip it up. By the time she finished donning the shoes, belt, and earrings Kristina had thrown in with the dress, the lump of fear and trepidation in her stomach hadn't gone away, but it felt... better somehow. She couldn't explain it, but it was like all the secrets had been slowly suffocating her and just the chance to make them go away was like a breath of fresh air to a drowning person.

As the swirl of thoughts danced through her head, Melissa almost unconsciously combed out her hair and dusted a hint of rosy blush onto her cheeks. She had to keep her hand from trembling when she put on a layer of pinkish lipstick though, and she didn't even bother trying to apply a coat of eyeliner with her eyes still misty.

"Are you almost done?" Her mom tapped at the bathroom door.

"Just a second." Melissa did one last check in the mirror, making extra sure that the swollen redness around her neck wasn't too visible. At least she wouldn't look like a complete fool... hopefully.

Sliding back outside, mom gave an appreciative murmur. "Sweetheart, you look beautiful."

"Thanks." At least someone thought she looked nice. Melissa certainly didn't feel that way. "Where's dad anyway?"

"Same place he always is," her mother remarked caustically. "He told us to meet him down at dinner."

Melissa bit at her lip, nervous. She had been to a lot of semi-formal parties and dances growing up, but this was probably the most formal. Her mom had been a little unclear about it, but from the way she was dressed, this was going to be close to a full-on military ball. Teenagers didn't typically get invited to those, so this fell into some grey area in between. Probably because being stationed on Mars was a bit unusual, even by military standards.

"Would you like to borrow a bracelet for the night?" her mom interrupted.

"Sure… I guess." Trust mom to always have a jewelry box. Holding out her hand, Melissa felt the cool sterling silver links lace around her wrist, each nestling a polished, sky-blue topaz. Her mom had a good eye for jewelry and it matched her dress beautifully. It all matched beautifully. The shoes and the belt and the earrings Kristina had thrown into her *bribe* fit perfectly with the dress, and the bracelet was just the finishing touch. One last glance in the mirror confirmed that she looked stunning, perhaps the best she ever had, yet somehow it all made her feel even more like a lie.

"Well, I think that's everything." Her mom grinned as she clipped on a pearl necklace for herself. "Are you ready to go?"

"Yeah." Down at her side, Melissa's hands nervously fidgeted with her dress pleats. She met her mom's eyes though, "I'm ready."

Chapter 18
Dancing with Wolves

When we get there, just stick close to your father and I," Mom explained as they hurried through the press of people crowding the main concourse. Melissa tried to pay attention as they walked, but with the sound of the crowd already reaching a dull roar it was hard to hear everything. The constant need to dodge around people while making sure her dress stayed straight wasn't helping either.

"And whatever you do, try not to run off. We'll be meeting a lot of people tonight. When your father introduces you, you'll need to look them straight in the eye and shake their hands. Don't try and interrupt either, especially when someone else is talking."

Melissa's mind drifted as her mom droned on. She got the general idea – keep close, look pretty, stay quiet, and above all, *don't embarrass your father*. It was the same as always, just more serious this time. She started paying a little more attention when her mom got to the part about how one of the punch bowls would have alcohol and she was *absolutely not* supposed to drink out of that one. Other than that though, it was fairly standard.

A sentry stood guarding the post entrance. They were being picky tonight, asking to double check physical ID cards instead of the usual implant scans, which was... stupid. Unfortunately, since Melissa's dress didn't have pockets, it took her a few seconds of digging through her purse to find her military ID. A quick glance was enough for the man to wave her and mom on by, and they found her dad in his dress uniform, waiting for them outside the Mess Hall.

"Julia." He gave mom a curt nod, and Melissa got little more than a glance of acknowledgement. Oh well, probably better than being shouted at.

"So, how are you, dear?" Somehow her mom managed to put on a pleasant face as though nothing at all was wrong.

"Busy."

"Still investigating that terrorist boy, are you?"

"I…" his face creased in a dark frown, and suddenly Melissa wished she could just go curl up in a hole somewhere. "I can't really talk about it," he muttered.

"Did I hear someone mention terrorists?" A smooth faced, middle-aged woman with the golden crescent moon insignia of a major turned towards them, and Melissa's throat tightened at the sight. That was her… the woman from the video. The one who was trying to destroy the station.

For a brief instant, she had the strange hope that her dad would suddenly tackle the woman to the ground and arrest her right then and there. That illusion was promptly shattered when dad offered the woman a courteous half smile

"Julia, I suppose I should introduce you to Major Sophie Tannenhill. She runs surveillance, communications, radar, ladar, infrared – a whole EM spectrum worth of systems. We've been working together on some… issues that cropped up yesterday."

"Always a pleasure." At least Mom had a hint of veiled hostility in her voice, although probably for different reasons.

Her dad didn't seem to notice, "Major, may I introduce you to my wife Julia, and my daughter Melissa."

"How wonderful to meet you." Sophie offered a broad smile and shook both their hands.

Melissa tried to act perfectly normal, but she couldn't erase the fear flickering in the back of her eyes, or the paleness that tinged her cheeks. She knew she was probably safe. There was no way Sophie could know who she was.Right? But when the woman met her gaze, Melissa couldn't escape the creeping sensation that Sophie was reading the secrets written in her eyes.

"So, what had you all talking about terrorists?" Sophie asked with the polite interest of someone who might as well have been mentioning the weather.

"Oh, it was nothing," her dad waved off the topic, "just a discussion from earlier."

That momentarily killed the conversation, until Melissa's mom nodded to the slim gold ring on Sophie's finger. "You're married? Is your husband here?"

A flash of pain crossed the major's features. "I umm… I *was* married," she said quietly.

Julia's breath caught in her throat. "I'm sorry. I didn't mean to…"

"It's fine," Sophie tried to smile but couldn't hide the way her eyes clouded over. "If I didn't want to remember, I wouldn't still wear the ring. Besides, Timothy wouldn't approve of me being sad. He was always the cheerful one. He passed away last year… a training accident off the California coast, a mechanical failure."

Sophie stared at the floor for a moment and Melissa saw her mom's face turn pale, like just the thought of that happening terrified her. "I'm so sorry."

"Like I said, it's fine." Sophie took a deep breath, forcing a smile. "But enough about all that. We're here for a party. How have you all been enjoying Medea? Some people find the transition to space a bit unnerving." She glanced at Melissa and the girl bit her lip nervously. "What about you, honey? They say kids have an easier time adjusting."

"Oh she's been having all sorts of fun," her father remarked in a disgruntled voice. "Found herself a boyfriend in all of two days."

"Dad, Devon's not my boyfriend."

Sophie appeared amused at her protest, the flash of sorrow replaced by a probing smile, "Well, isn't that sweet."

"Hardly the phrase I would use," her dad muttered.

"She needs something to keep her occupied on the trip to Mars," Sophie pointed out. "From what I hear it gets pretty boring after the first few weeks on the ship. People start to pick up odd-ball hobbies just to keep busy. A boyfriend is hardly the worst option. Have you ever heard of space diving?"

"Of what?"

Sophie had a fiendish grin. "The way I understand it, there was this guy a few years back who went insane out of boredom. But instead of knitting like a normal person, he had a friend grab a shuttle and come alongside the ship. Then he flushed himself out the airlock without a space suit. I think he was trying to jump into the shuttle and repressurize before he died of vacuum exposure."

"Who flushed himself out an airlock?" A uniformed man a little younger than her dad, accompanied by a wife and two boys about Melissa's age, broke into their conversation.

"Oh, just your run-of-the-mill madman." Sophie offered him her hand with a smile, "Major Sophie Tannenhill."

"Major Stephen Garcia."

What followed was a long round of introductions that involved Melissa shaking a lot of hands. There was the major's wife Maria, and his twin sons, Matthew and Mark. Apparently they were also going to Mars and, in fact, Major Garcia was going to be a part of her dad's new command. While all the adults chatted on and laughed at Sophie retelling a few of the more ridiculous stories she had heard about Mars, Melissa found herself staring awkwardly at the two boys.

"Sooooo, how are you doing?" one of them finally asked. She wanted to say it was Matthew, but they both looked eerily alike.

"Fine. You?"

"We'll be better when we find the punch bowl with the alcohol."

"Oh… that's nice. I guess."

"You want to join us?" Mark offered. "It'll take the edge off, and besides, you look like you could use some cheering up."

"Ummm…" Melissa couldn't quite believe what she was hearing. "I'm already in enough trouble, so thanks, but no thanks."

"Suit yourself." Mark cocked his head to one side, "What'd you do to get in trouble?"

"Nothing really," she answered in a melancholy voice. "There was just a misunderstanding, a *big* misunderstanding."

"And you're sure you don't want a drink? That's exactly the sort of problem those are good at making you forget."

"I'll manage."

Next to them the adults all burst into laughter, and Melissa glanced over to see Sophie staring right back at her. The major's eyes tried to dart away like it was nothing. But for a tenth of a second their eyes locked, and the message that flashed between the both of them was crystal clear. *I know.*

Instantly the lump of fear in Melissa's chest that she'd almost managed to forget was back. Despite being surrounded by friends, the fear that surged up in her was so palpable that it was hard to breathe. She turned back toward the two boys, feeling like she was about to be sick. "Is there a restroom around here?"

"A little way down the hall there," Matthew pointed to a door across the room. "Are you okay?"

"Yeah, I just umm…" Melissa chanced another look at Sophie, and saw this time the woman wasn't watching her. "I need a minute."

She ducked away before there could be any more questions and dodged off down the hall, searching for a few seconds alone. In a moment she found herself in the deserted restroom staring at the mirror. Melissa kept telling herself to calm down. There was no way Sophie could know about her. She was probably being paranoid and imagining things. She figured nearly dying twice in two days could do that to you.

In an effort to calm herself, Melissa pulled her phone out of her purse and started tapping out a text to Devon. If she was going to tell her dad everything, Devon probably deserved to know about it before a bunch of MPs busted down his door demanding a video. She tried to keep it short, but it was one of those messages that kept getting longer and longer as she went on explaining herself. Eventually, she ended up with something several times wordier than she had planned, but Melissa didn't have the patience to scroll back through. After a half second of hesitation, she pressed send.

Somehow, that simple act solidified things in her mind. Before, she had been able to turn back, but in a way she couldn't quite explain, telling Devon committed her. She was about to walk back outside, find her dad and spill everything, when she caught a squeak from the bathroom door. An amused feminine voice shattered the quiet. "So, it's *Curls*? Right?"

Melissa started and wheeled to find Sophie casually leaning against the wall by the bathroom door, watching her with hawkish eyes. "Interesting," Sophie mused as though Melissa's reaction had told her everything she needed to know. "So tell me, how did you end up with a name like Curls, your hair isn't even that curly?

"What do you want?"

"Oh now, Melissa… don't go pretending you don't know. It wastes everyone's time, and I'm on a bit of a schedule."

As she spoke, Sophie drifted across the restroom, quickly checking to ensure the stalls were empty. Melissa almost made a run for it, but the way Sophie's eyes always snapped right back to her kept her rooted to the spot. She wouldn't get far.

"I will admit, I was a bit surprised." Sophie finished her sweep and found a spot right between Melissa and the door. "I suppose you match Valerie's description – teenage girl, brown hair, brown eyes, goes by Curls, but doesn't have curly hair. Tags along with a boy named Devon and Kristina Andrews of all people. Still though, I never would have guessed you were Bryan's daughter."

"I… I think you have the wrong person." Melissa tried to back away but bumped up against the sink countertop.

"Now, what was it I just said about pretending?" Sophie chided her like an elementary school teacher. "I don't have time to waste playing charades with you, so come on."

"Fine then," Melissa frowned darkly and met Sophie's glare. "The truth is, I'm not going anywhere with a filthy traitor like you, and if you try anything, I'll scream."

"Now, that's more like it." Melissa's blatant defiance only brought a perverse grin to Major Tannenhill's face, and Sophie took a few menacing steps nearer. "And since we're being completely honest, I should probably tell you, you aren't going to enjoy what happens next."

"Don't come any closer," Melissa warned as she took a frantic step backwards, her back bumping against a wall.

"Or you'll scream?" Sophie taunted. "You honestly think they're going to hear you through a steel door, down the hall and through another door? While they're having a party? There's no daddy dearest to save you now, honey."

Melissa's breath caught in her throat at Sophie's words and she put up her hands for yet another fight. The Major didn't give her time to get much further though. Sophie bull rushed her, and the larger woman slammed Melissa back against the wall.

"Get away!" She tried to fight back. But the Major was suddenly so close she could barely move, let alone kick or punch.

"Oh, don't worry, I will get away with it," Sophie smirked. Then she slammed her fist into the side of Melissa's head, and the world went sideways.

When her eyes focused again, Melissa was sprawled on the floor, the world in front of her swimming like she was watching through an aquarium. Meanwhile, a pounding pain lanced through her head. Kneeling next to her with a cold grin, Sophie pulled out a ribbon of cloth. "Now, you'll need to come along quietly."

Melissa tried to struggle, but dimly recalled the Major already tying her wrists. There was little she could do besides moan in agony when Sophie shoved a wadded up ball of cloth in her mouth and wrapped the strip around her head so she couldn't spit it out. Right as she finished, there was a glow from Melissa's bracelet and the phone in her purse vibrated.

"Oooww… what have we here?" Sophie cheerfully flipped open the purse and pulled out the slim box with the glowing screen. "Surprise, surprise, it's from Devon," she declared. "Hmm… we probably need to do something about him too, don't we?"

Melissa tried to shake her head and scream, but all that came out past the gag was muffled nonsense.

"What's that?" Sophie mocked the helpless girl. "Don't worry, Melissa, you two will be reunited soon enough." She glanced back at the phone and read off the full name, "Devon Northrop. Shouldn't be hard to find."

***

Devon was back in his room, trying to sleep off the pounding sensation in his head. His invented excuse about the station lights giving him a headache had convinced his parents to take Evie off to dinner without him. Fortunately, his parents were pretty hands off about headaches, and his mom wasn't the sort to go and bother a doctor unless things were serious.

Melissa texting him hadn't made napping any easier. The realization that she was about to tell her dad everything had sent a chill down his spine. However, strangely enough, the panic had been slowly subsumed by an overwhelming surge of relief. It was like all the terror about what Kristina would do next, and who the Major from the video was, began to drain away. If someone had asked him to explain why, Devon probably couldn't have. But maybe it was simply that, for the first time in two days, it wasn't just him and Melissa against the world. It was about to be him, Melissa and the United States Space Force. That evened the odds a little.

He had texted her back that he liked the idea about ten minutes ago. Since he didn't expect she would get many more chances to send him updates, Devon tried his best to finally get some sleep. It should have been easy enough. He felt absolutely exhausted and he still had a knockout drug in his system. But for some reason, all he could do was toss back and forth, trying to get comfortable while his head pounded away like a bass drum.

Finally, just as he was starting to doze off, there was a click from the door. That would be his parents. "Hey mom," he murmured.

"Honey, I'm not your mom," an irate female voice snapped back at him.

Devon jerked upright and found himself staring at the woman from the video, the one who had smuggled the suitcase full of explosives onboard. "Hello, Devon," she smirked, "I take it you aren't going to come quietly either?"

Behind the major, two of her goons spilled into the room, one of them holding something that looked like the oxygen masks paramedics used. "Take him," the major flicked her hand. "We can't have him spoiling things. Not now."

Devon was still half asleep, and before he could fight back, the two men shoved him down against the bed and slapped the transparent plastic mask across his face. Devon didn't smell any gas, but when he breathed in, it was like a cloud passed between his brain and the rest of him. He tried to fight it and knock the thing away, but with each breath his struggling grew weaker. In a matter of seconds, his mind faded into a merciful, dreamless black.

Chapter 19
Adrift in the Darkness

Devon. Devon, wake up." Somewhere he heard Melissa's voice echoing through the darkness, and he became aware of his slow, steady breathing. "Devon, wake up."

Someone was shaking him and finally his eyes inched open to see Melissa leaned over him, a reddish bruise on her cheek. As his mind cleared, Devon tried to sit up. "What…where?"

"Shhh," Melissa gently pushed him back to the floor with an anxious look. "Give it a minute, they drugged you with something. Do you feel okay?"

"He'll be fine," Kristina's voice intruded from nearby. "Sophie probably just used Xenon gas. They still have a few tanks of the stuff up here from back before they installed the Mercury Ion Drives. I keep a little stash myself. Your boyfriend should be okay."

"Shut up, Kristina!" Melissa glared at her with a dark frown. "This is all your fault."

"My fault? Seriously?" Devon turned his head and saw Kristina sitting across the room with her back to the wall. She rolled her eyes in frustration. "Does Major Tannenhill get none of the blame for kidnapping you, Curls? Or is that somehow my doing too?"

"If you hadn't dragged us into this–"

"If I hadn't gotten involved, you two would have both died of asphyxiation back in water treatment, and whatever the good major is planning would still be happening. Don't get so self-righteous."

Melissa put on an air of disgust and turned back to Devon. "You think you can sit up?"

"I'm fine." The wooziness of the anesthesia had mostly cleared away, and happily, the headache from earlier had vanished as well. Devon pushed himself up to sitting to discover they were in a grey metal room devoid of furnishings and bathed in glaringly bright light. A tightly closed steel door marked the only way out. Over by the far wall, Kristina was still in the same jeans and dark blouse from earlier, although a bit more rumpled.

Melissa though – Devon had to look twice to make sure his eyes weren't tricking him. The last time he'd seen her, she had been wearing a pair of skinny jeans and a loose fitted t-shirt. The girl kneeling on the floor next to him though was robed in the most gorgeous blue and silver dress he had ever seen, with her skirt splashed out on the floor around her like a dark pool crisscrossed by shimmering silver strands.

Devon blinked when he realized he was staring and abruptly tore his eyes away. "You look…really nice," he stammered.

Despite the situation, Melissa blushed and her eyes drifted towards the floor. "Thanks."

"What happened to your cheek?"

Melissa's hand drifted to the red welt on the side of her face. "It's nothing." Her palm hovered close to hide the bruise but she didn't touch it, like the sore was still tender. "Just Sophie's way of negotiating, that's all." Despite everything she grinned as though it were funny. "It's hardly the worst thing to happen to me today."

"Are you two done making puppy dog eyes at each other?" Kristina's harsh voice sliced into the conversation. "Because if so, we have bigger problems."

That earned her a glare from Melissa, but Devon just focused on stretching out an uncomfortable kink in his shoulder. When he did, he noticed that gravity didn't feel right at all, like he had suddenly dropped a good sixty pounds. "Where are we?" he asked. "And what's up with–"

"Gravity?" Kristina didn't even let him finish. "If I was guessing, we're in one of the maintenance alcoves along the struts that connect the central hub to the outer ring. I was unconscious when they brought me here, but according to little miss prissy over there, they took her up a service elevator. It feels like about .5 or .6 g's, so we're about halfway up the strut. Pretty good hiding place, actually."

"What are we supposed to do?" Devon asked.

"I don't know, die? I suppose it depends on what Major Tannenhill does next."

"So, this Major Tannenhill…"

"Sophie Tannenhill," Melissa supplied.

"So, Sophie was the one behind all this? The explosives, killing McGregor, all of it?" Devon asked.

"Yes, probably," Kristina gave an exasperated sigh. "But you don't need to tell her *absolutely everything.*"

"Huh?"

"Why do you think she stuck us all in here?" Kristina sounded like she was having to explain that two plus two made four. "It wasn't just so that we could get reacquainted. I expect she's listening to hear what we know, so if you could, try not to mention too much."

Kristina paused for a second, and her eyes flashed around the room, like a cat planning its next move. "You can come in now, Sophie," she declared loudly.

Devon glanced towards the door, but after a moment there was no sign of anyone. "Are you *sure* she's listening?"

"Oh, Sophie's there all right. She's just waiting to make the point that she's in charge. Give her a minute to work out her ego issues."

Sure enough, a moment later there was a clank as the door unlocked, and Valerie walked in. "Hello, Kristina."

"Valerie," Kristina had a taunting grin, her tone cheery, like she was meeting an old friend. "I was wondering if they remembered to take you along. I figured they might have left you tied to that chair."

Valerie's face creased in a frown and in a few strides she moved across the room. There was a loud crack as she slapped Kristina right across the face. "That's for drugging me, you witch."

Kristina didn't seem fazed though. "If it's any consolation, you had it coming."

"Shut up," Valerie snapped back. "Now, get up, Sophie has plans for you."

Sophie's two goons walked in and pulled Melissa and Devon upright, while Valerie dragged Kristina to her feet to reveal that the Russian lady's hands were cuffed together behind her. "Move," Valerie roughly shoved Kristina into the next room.

The next room was much like the one that had doubled as their prison cell, except there were chairs waiting for the three of them and two tables situated at either side of the room. Sophie stood near one table, staring over the shoulder of a man in blue and white patterned combat fatigues. The woman watched as he poked away at a computer screen. Over on the other table, Devon spied his phone and watch piled next to Kristina and Melissa's purses.

Kristina nodded to the Master Sergeant when they brought her in. "Malcolm," she smiled sweetly, "fancy seeing you here."

"Likewise, Kristina." The man at least had the courtesy to return her smile. "It seems today is just stock full of surprises… for everyone."

"Out of curiosity," Kristina continued, nonchalant, even as Valerie shoved her down into a straight-backed metal chair, "how much did Sophie have to offer to buy you?"

Devon thought the man might be offended, but he didn't seem bothered any more than if she had asked for football scores. "Quite a lot." Malcolm turned back to his screen. "More than enough to get by for the rest of my life, and a beachside house in Macau. I'm looking forward to retirement."

"Sounds nice."

"Quiet!" Valerie slapped Kristina across the face yet again.

"Oh, do give it a rest, Valerie," Kristina grumbled. "Everyone knows you're pissed about getting your memory wiped. There's no need for hysterics."

"Why, I should–"

"Valerie, stop!" Sophie took notice and stood. "We don't need you damaging Kristina just to settle a grudge."

For a moment Devon thought Valerie was about to hit Kristina again anyway, but finally she pulled her hand back and her lips curled in a sneer. "Don't think you've won," she hissed. "What comes next is going to be a lot worse than anything I could do."

"Whatever you say, Valerie." Kristina's eyes shift to the major with a curious gleam. "So, Sophie, you're working with the Chinese now?"

"Don't be so glib, Kristina. If you think you can just laugh your way through all this, you're sorely mistaken."

"And what is *all this,* Sophie? Not a lunatic power trip I imagine?"

"How about we start with the basics." Sophie's tone grew cold. "Who do you work for?"

"Myself," she answered cheekily. "That's the whole point of owning a business."

"Okay then," Sophie gave an icy smile. "I figured it would be this way." She glanced towards Melissa and Devon with a pondering look. "Let's start with the boy first."

"Darius, Sawyer," she gestured to her two thugs, "hold them both. We don't need anyone running off."

Sophie strode over and knelt down right beside Devon, even as powerful arms pinned his wrists so tight he could barely move. "You see, Kristina," Sophie pulled out a knife and hovered it a few inches from his face, "the reason I brought these two along was so, when we inevitably reached this juncture, I would have some leverage."

Devon watched the knife hover closer and closer until he felt the cold ceramic blade resting against his face. He pressed his eyes shut and felt a flash of pain like a bee sting against his cheek. He winced and saw the tip of the knife pull away coated red with blood.

"Here's what's going to happen," Sophie explained with a merciless smile. "Until you start answering questions, your little friends here get to suffer the consequences."

"So you're down to torturing children these days?" Kristina raised her eyebrows a touch. "Did you run out of small animals to kill?"

"You think I'm joking?" Sophie twitched and Devon could barely breath as the knifepoint hovered an inch from his eye.

"How long have we known each other, Sophie? Two years? When did you become like this?" Kristina shook her head in remorse. "Is this what Timothy would have wanted? For his wife to be torturing two scared teenagers as *leverage*?"

That remark finally brought a vengeful scowl to Sophie's face. She turned, stalking over to Kristina and Devon let out a relieved sigh as the knife vanished along with her. "Don't you *dare* talk about him."

"Somebody needs to remind you. Look around, Sophie, you're selling out your country and your friends... you don't think Timothy would have objected to this insanity?"

"Maybe he would have if they hadn't killed him and..." Sophie's voice broke off at the end, and Devon could swear he saw a dampness in her eyes.

Kristina paused, her expression stunned, angry. "That's what this is about? You're upset about your husband, so you decided to take it out on a few thousand innocent people? Damn it, Sophie, he died in an accident."

"He died because the Space Force didn't care," Sophie snapped with a look of burning fury on her face. "They knew the ramjet fan blade was off balance, but the maintenance technician didn't care because it was 'within an acceptable margin of error.' The crew chief didn't care because he was late for a birthday party. And the next morning, when my husband showed up to do his preflight, the squadron commander was in too much of a hurry to listen to Timothy's warnings. No one cared, and because of that he, died."

Sophie's face turned grim with disgust. "You know what I got out of it all, Kristina? After their negligence murdered my husband? A death benefit and a sympathy promotion. As though that makes it alright. The Space Force didn't even prosecute the people responsible. It didn't matter that their stupidity killed someone. They did everything by the book, and as far as the Space Force was concerned, that made it okay."

"So, your solution is to kill more people?"

"My solution is to get what's mine. According to the United States of America, I'm worth exactly two hundred and fifty thousand dollars as a death benefit to my next of kin. According to the Chinese, I'm worth, oh… about 500 million. Let's just say I appreciate being valued."

Sophie stalked back over to Devon and brandished the blade terrifyingly close to his face. "Now, we're going to try this again. Who do you work for, Kristina?"

"Like I said, myself."

"Fine then." Sophie pulled her knife away and circled out of Devon's view.

Devon tried to move, but powerful arms kept him firmly locked in his chair. He tensed for a moment, waiting, then a white-hot fire sank into his upper arm.

Devon screamed.

The next few seconds were a blur, dominated by unquenchable pain as Sophie's knife cut him nearly to the bone. After what felt like an eternity, Sophie finally pulled the blade free. The sharp, burning agony turned to a duller but persistent throbbing that sent lances of pain down his arm, and left him struggling just to breathe between gritted teeth.

"Stop it!" he heard Melissa's desperate screams, "Please!" Half in a daze, his head drifted to one side, and out of the corner of his eye he could see the girl fighting to struggle out of her chair, but to no avail.

Sophie turned towards Melissa with a pitiless glare. "Are you volunteering to go next, honey?"

"She's Russian! Okay?" Melissa's anger mixed with the tears of helpless frustration that welled in her eyes. "She's a Russian spy. So please, just stop."

"Interesting," Sophie mused to herself as she wandered over to Melissa's chair. "Unfortunately, that's not how this game is played. The pain only stops if Kristina is the one who does the talking."

"But, I told you – you don't…" Melissa's expression turned to horror as she realized what was next.

"Sorry, honey." Sophie shrugged as she raised the knife, and Melissa closed her eyes, wincing, even as the tears trickled down her cheeks.

"Sophie, stop this nonsense," Kristina interrupted.

"I will, when you talk."

"Fine, you want to hear it from me? I do work for Russia. Happy?"

"A little," Sophie smirked. "I still have a lot of questions though, and like I said, we're short on time. If you insist on any more stubbornness, things with your friends here are going to escalate quickly. Next question, how did you know about McGregor?"

"Because I pay attention," Kristina said. "McGregor was hardly subtle about his genius plan, although killing him was a bit excessive."

Sophie shrugged. "Loose ends," she remarked, as though that justified murdering someone. "Next question, the bomb you disabled, where is it?"

"What on earth are you talking about?" Kristina smoothly lied.

Sophie frowned, "Were you not paying attention to what I said about stubbornness? Why do you think the other blast went off right when it did? I assure you, it wasn't random chance. I saw the transceiver signal a disconnection when you disarmed it and I detonated the second charge before it could be disabled."

"I've seen the investigation reports, and there wasn't any C-4B recovered from the room. So tell me what you did with it, or I'll start experimenting to see just how loud Curls here can scream."

For a flicker of a second Devon could swear he saw a pained look cross Kristina's face. The woman cast a glance at Melissa, then, with a sigh, she nodded towards the table with their things. "My purse."

"You keep high explosives in your purse?" Sophie asked, incredulous.

"Among other things, yes," Kristina shrugged. "You never know when something like that will come in handy."

Malcolm, Sophie's helper with the computer and the military uniform, hurried over and started eagerly digging through the purse. After a moment, he gasped in pain and jerked back his hand holding one of Kristina's darts. A prick of blood dribbled from one finger.

"What in the world do you have in here, Kristina?" Malcolm glanced at the woman in bewilderment.

"My things," she remarked coolly.

"And this dart, is it… okay?"

"You'll be fine, except for your pride, which apparently you didn't have much of anyway."

Malcolm dropped the dart on the table and gingerly reached back inside. A few seconds later there was a triumphant grin. His hand reemerged holding a lump of gray-white explosives, the black detonator cap and the remote trigger box. "Got it."

"Good," Sophie gave a smirk that made Devon shiver inside. "Do you have all the components you need?"

"Shouldn't be too hard. All she did was cut the wires. I can splice everything back together, and we'll be ready to go in a few minutes."

"Excellent," Sophie turned back to the Russian woman situated in the chair with her hands bound. "One last request."

Chapter 20
A Time to Kill

So, Kristina, I'm sure you're aware of the Space Force dinner tonight? I assume Captain Lawston invited you?"

"I do recall something vaguely like that. Yes."

"Good. In that case you're going to be attending."

Kristina glanced down at her rumpled blouse. "Do I at least get to change first?"

"Oh, you'll get to do more than that." Sophie narrowed her eyes. "You, my dear, are going to get the dubious honor of strapping on that C-4B charge over there and blowing yourself up."

"What?" Kristina arched her eyebrows in bewilderment. "And I would do that because…?"

"Because if you don't, the alternative is watching Valerie try her hand at skinning your two little friends alive, right before I let her have all the revenge she could ever want on you." Sophie's voice was deadpan serious as she spoke. "There are two ways out of this for you, Kristina. Either you walk down to the party, head straight for Colonel Perry and trigger that bomb, or you stay up here and watch these two suffer until they beg for death. Then we kill you anyway… just in a deliberately painful fashion."

"No matter how this plays out you die, and I am going to get what I want. The only choice you have is whether or not Devon and Melissa get to go home to mommy and daddy – although, I guess in Melissa's case it's just going to be mommy left after all this.

"You leave my Dad alone, you worthless piece of...!" Melissa jerked at her captor to try and break free, her furious glare fixed on Sophie.

"Sorry, honey," Sophie taunted. "But if it's any consolation, how about when this is all over, if you survive, I'll do you a little favor. I doubt you'll be able to afford a decent college with the pittance the military will offer you for your dad, so what I'll do is set up a little fund with some of my newfound fortune. I'll even donate it anonymously, so your mom never has to know who's paying for your education. It can be our little secret... sound fun?"

Devon saw Melissa's face twist in utter fury and helplessness. She tried to speak, but amidst the swirl of emotion no words came out.

"I'll take that as a yes," Sophie grinned. "Now, Kristina, if you'll excuse me, I'll leave you with Valerie and Malcolm here to make your choice. They can work out the details either way. In the meantime, I have other bombs to detonate and a shuttle bay to get to. Since we won't be seeing each other again... it's been a pleasure."

Without waiting for a response, Sophie wheeled and strolled out the door, leaving behind her henchmen, along with a fuming Valerie. Meanwhile, Malcolm sat over at the table nearby, busily stripping wires.

The moment Sophie was gone, Valerie's glare hardened. "So, *Miss Andrews,* have you made your decision? Or do I need to start making your friends scream?"

Kristina sighed, and despite all her mocking banter earlier, it looked to Devon like she was very much worried. "Fine. I'll do it."

"No!" Melissa screamed, still trying to struggle free, "Please don't! Don't kill my dad!"

Kristina shook her head. "I'm sorry *miliya,*" she said softly, "it's just how things are."

"No, no..." Melissa broke down into tears.

Kristina glanced towards Malcolm, "How does this work?"

"Well," Malcolm distractedly grabbed for a little device as he spoke, "once I finish reconnecting everything, we'll strap on the bomb. It's remotely triggered, so we'll put a camera on you, and when we see you get close enough to Perry, we'll detonate it. You won't have to do a thing, just walk close to him and that's all."

"How considerate," Kristina fumed.

Despite Kristina's overt hostility, it occurred to Devon that there was something very strange about the way she was watching Malcolm, more than just curiosity or anger. His first guess was that it had something to do with the dart Malcolm had pricked his finger on earlier. Except syringes didn't work if they just pricked you. Besides, he was fairly certain Kristina's drug wasn't powerful enough to dose someone with a single drop.

He stared at Malcolm for a second and suddenly it hit him… the detonator box. Was it still active? Back in sewage treatment, Kristina had just cut the wires, and if Sophie had sent the remote trigger signal to blow up the other bomb, then there wasn't any reason why it wouldn't have triggered also.

Alone, the box was useless, barely more complicated than a light switch. It would be like turning on a lamp, then unplugging it. Sure, the light would turn off, but the moment you reconnected everything, it was just as active as before. If the detonator box was still armed and Malcolm reconnected it to the blast cap… that might be bad.

Nearby, Kristina and Valerie's voices rose to a shouting match, but Devon ignored them both and kept his focus honed on Malcolm. The military technician twisted together one set of wires without anything happening. He glanced over at the two screaming women and shook his head. Then he grabbed the last two wires. Devon tensed and pressed his eyes closed as Malcolm touched the ends together.

Devon had been expecting a loud pop like a firework back home. Instead, the military grade blast cap in front of Malcolm went off like a hand grenade. A deafening concussion rocked the room, and Devon felt Sophie's henchman loosen his grip. In an instant Devon spun out of his seat and slugged the stunned man right in the mouth. Out of the corner of his eye, he was vaguely aware of a blur that looked like Kristina rushing towards Valerie.

Devon didn't pause. He barely felt the stabs of pain that lanced down his arm as he pounded the man before he could recover. Devon connected a final fist into the man's nose with a sickening crunch, and with a woozy stagger, Sophie's henchman slumped to the floor.

Then something abruptly slammed into his side, and he went sprawling on the cold steel plating with a grunt of pain. A hulking figure had tackled him to the ground, and Devon instinctively lashed out with his elbow, connecting with a bony *crack*. The hands holding him loosened and Devon scrambled to his feet. He found himself facing the other man, the one who'd been holding Melissa.

The man rose with a pained hiss and death in his gaze. Devon put up his arms for a fight, but a foot from behind sliced up between the man's legs to slam right into his groin. His mouth dropped open and his eyes rolled upwards as he collapsed onto the floor, the lower gravity making it seem almost like he was falling in slow motion.

Behind him stood Melissa, the cold rage frosting her exprssion. With both of Sophie's henchmen out of the fight, Devon turned back to see that Kristina had somehow gotten her hands in front of her, despite being handcuffed. She had then proceeded to absolutely smash Valerie into a limp figure sprawled out on the ground. Meanwhile, over at the table, Malcolm was lolled back in his chair, groaning, his face bloody from the blast.

Kneeling down next to Valerie, Kristina searched through her pockets for a second until she found a key and quickly snapped off her handcuffs. Kristina's eyes scanned the room before coming to rest on Devon and Melissa. "Good work, you two."

"What did you do to…?" Melissa's gaze fixed on the injured Malcolm.

Behind them, one of Sophie's goons moaned and tried to get up. Before he could get far, Kristina was there with a swift kick to the face to make sure he kept down. "Me? I did nothing," she remarked casually. "Malcolm over there forgot that the trigger was still armed. Idiot. It seems like everyone's underlings are a disappointment today." Strolling over to Valerie, she grabbed the limp woman's arms, forcibly tugged her back into the room where they had been held earlier, and dropped her unceremoniously on the floor. She returned to repeat the process with Sophie's two henchmen. "You ought to do something about your arm," she added with a nod to the trail of blood dribbling down to Devon's wrist.

Devon had nearly forgotten the pain amidst the surge of adrenaline. But when he glanced down at the deep gash Sophie had left there, the throbbing agony flooded right back.

"I should have something to patch you up in my purse," Kristina added with a grunt as she lifted one of the men and pulled him away.

"Come on," Melissa took his uninjured arm. "Kristina's right, you can't go walking around with a cut like that." She led him over to the second table, across the room from where Malcolm had collapsed in a bloody mess of agonized groans. Kristina's purse was piled there with the rest of their things, and Melissa only had to dig through it for a moment, before her hand re-emerged with the gauze and medical paste Kristina had used the prior night.

"Okay, hold still," she ordered in an anxious, nurse-like voice.

Devon tried not to move, but when she started dabbing at the cut his breath hissed between gritted teeth.

"Sorry," Melissa drew her hand back for a moment.

"It's okay," he shook his head, "it's not like it's your fault."

Melissa started dabbing at his arm again, more delicately this time. It still hurt, but Devon kept up the conversation as a distraction. "So, what do you think Sophie meant when she talked about getting to the shuttle bay? You think she's trying to get off Medea?"

"Maybe," Melissa didn't turn her focus away from his arm. "I don't know what purpose all this would serve if she was just going to run away though. Maybe she plans to blow the reactor or something?"

Devon shook his head. "No, if she intended on blowing the reactor, she wouldn't need Kristina as a suicide bomber."

"Fair point," Melissa nibbled her lip as she finished dabbing on the paste and began wrapping a sheath of gauze around the wound. "Either way, we need to warn someone."

Across from them, Kristina finished dragging the last of Sophie's helpers into the small room and cheerfully flung the door closed, locking them inside. "I suspect it's a bit late to warn people." She turned back to the two teenagers and paced over to see how Melissa was doing playing medic. "If Sophie is about to start setting off bombs everywhere, then people are already going to be warned that something is up. The bigger question is *what* exactly."

Kristina glanced over at the piteous form of the Master Sergeant. "Fortunately, we have someone to tell us."

Grabbing the tranquilizer dart Malcolm had pricked himself with earlier off the table, Kristina hauled the man up into a sitting pose against the wall. "Help... me..." His eyes flickered open, and Devon could see that only one of them seemed to move properly.

"Oh shut it, Malcolm," Kristina retorted. "You knew the stakes, and you would have blown me up without a second thought. Besides, it was just the detonator cap. Don't expect sympathy. Now, start talking before I decide to add to your suffering. What is Sophie up to?"

The man remained stubbornly quiet at that question. After a momentary scowl, Kristina changed her approach. "Tell me, and I'll give you this." She held up the syringe so he could see. "All that pain can just bleed away, and you don't even have to remember it. You can go to sleep and wake up in a hospital bed somewhere... or you can sit here and moan in agony until Sophie comes back and shoots you for your incompetence. Your choice."

Devon saw a flash of indecision in the man's one good eye, like he was weighing the odds of that actually happening. Finally, he nodded. "Sophie..." Malcolm murmured in a voice like even talking was painful. "She promised the Chinese they could have Medea. There's a freighter coming... would have started... transfer burn about an hour ago."

"If there was a freighter on a transfer burn somebody on the ground would have seen it and radioed up. The whole station would already know about it," Kristina said dismissively. "You'll have to do better than that."

"The messages aren't getting through," Malcolm mumbled. "Sophie controls the comms. One of her people intercepted..." His voice trailed off in a pained grimace. "No one knows."

"And the bombs she mentioned?"

"The Chinese need a diplomatic excuse to board Medea." He swallowed, wincing as he did. "If Sophie blows the whole communication grid, they can board and pretend they're trying to help."

Kristina paused for a second. "How many?"

"Too many."

"When do they get here?"

"Half an hour... maybe less."

With a deep sigh, Kristina nodded and jabbed the man in the arm with the syringe, letting the drug flood his system. "Give it a few minutes to kick in."

A grateful Malcolm nodded, and Kristina turned back to the teenagers, just as Melissa put the finishing touches on Devon's bandage. "What do we do?" Melissa asked nervously.

"I don't know." Kristina shook her head and paced for a moment. "To start, we need to warn Colonel Perry and deal with Sophie. But if she already has control of the shuttle bay, she'll probably be ready to shoot anything that comes up the elevator. It's an obvious chokepoint." She rubbed her forehead. "I suppose I'll have to send you two downstairs to warn Perry about what's going on. I'll find a way up to the shuttle bay and see if I can't eliminate Major Tannenhill."

"You can't get rid of us that easy," Melissa protested in indignation.

Kristina arched her eyes at the girl. "You *want* to come along and get shot at?"

Melissa paused for a second, but finally she nodded. "Sophie's going to kill my dad... so yeah, I'm coming."

Kristina's gaze drifted to Devon, "And you?"

For the first time that day, Devon knew with absolute certainty that going along with Kristina was a terrible idea. But he also knew that he couldn't let Melissa do this alone. "I'm coming too."

"Well, alright then. I suppose you two have proved oddly useful today." Kristina gestured towards a storage closet nearby. "There should be some suits in there, find one that fits and put it on."

Kristina pulled her phone out of her bag and held it in front of her to send a vid message. "Perry, it's me," she began the recording, "you're not going to like this, but you're about to have visitors…"

Chapter 21
The Long Climb

How am I supposed to put this on?" Melissa complained, holding the upper half of a white, form-fitting space suit, reinforced with golden bands on the arms and chest. "I'm wearing a dress."

"How about you lose the dress," Kristina remarked bluntly, even as she rummaged through the storage locker for a suit her own size.

Devon snickered and Melissa looked scandalized. "I would *never*… besides, it's your dress."

Kristina glanced back at the girl. "You've never worn a space suit, I presume?"

"No."

"Okay, step one is take off all your clothes."

"What?"

"You heard me." Her gaze flickered across to Devon. "And you, don't peek or I'll dump you out an airlock." She motioned for him to turn around. Devon grabbed a suit of his own, his face reddening. He turned away and started stripping down to fit into what was basically a leotard that went on under the shirt and pants.

"Now," Kristina's gaze slid back to the blushing girl, "Melissa, either lose the dress, or you aren't coming."

Melissa felt there was something deeply improper about pulling off her dress in front of a Russian spy, but looking at the tight-fitting space suit, she really couldn't see another way. And it *was* to save her parents. With a timid look, she turned her back to Kristina. "Could you get the zipper?" she murmured.

"Of course." There was the distinctive loosening as Kristina unzipped her. After one last sigh to sacrifice whatever sense of decency she still had, Melissa wiggled out of the dress and quickly slid into a *very* snug space-leotard, then pulled on a pair of strange pants and the compression top over it. The shirt probably would have been too tight to wiggle into normally, so instead, it had zippers along the arms and chest. She had to weave her hands through wrist holes, then zip up along the front of her arms, then zip up her chest. Same with the pants. The whole suit gripped her, kind of like wearing tights, except over her entire body. That, and the material was an unusual sort of heavy woven fabric.

Melissa stared down at her strange get-up, noting a few thin plastic tubes woven into the front of her garment. Fidgeting with the hem of the shirt, she noticed something else.

"So... umm," she'd expected there to be a pressure seal of some sort between her top and the pants. "How exactly does this keep the air in?"

"It doesn't," Kristina remarked, deadpan.

"Huh?" Melissa spun around to find Kristina calmly pulling on a gold accented suit of her own.

"Sweetie, it's a compression suit, it's not meant to be pressurized. The suit fabric squeezes you to counteract the vacuum of space. No air required. That's why it's so tight."

"But... it's safe?" Devon nervously peeked around in his own red tinted space suit.

"Well, I doubt they would have a maintenance locker full of them if they didn't work." Kristina rolled her eyes. "Besides, you all shouldn't complain. Have you ever seen an old cosmonaut suit in a museum? Trust me, these are *much* better." As if to emphasize her point, Kristina lithely stretched her arms overhead.

Melissa tried not to think too hard about it. She slid on a pair of tight gloves, laced up some heavy, but surprisingly comfortable boots, and finally looped her bag across her shoulder.

Meanwhile, Kristina grabbed a couple of – what basically looked like windbreaker jackets and pants out of the closet and handed them each a set. "You'll need these too," she cautioned. "I believe we're behind the planet right now, and it gets chilly out there at night."

Melissa was tempted to point out that there was no wind in space, and thus no *need* for windbreakers. All the same, she'd frozen her butt off enough times in Germany to learn never to say no to a jacket. She could always dump it later. Plus, the coat looked fabulous, it even matched the suit. Heavy weave beige that sported the Medea Station chest patch – a golden supernova on a field of blue.

"So, Kristina," Melissa asked, stepping into the thin pants and slipping on the coat, "What *exactly* is the plan?"

"We're going on a spacewalk," she explained. "Since I don't particularly want to try my luck taking the service elevator up and having Sophie shoot me when the door slides open, we'll get to the hangar bay the old-fashioned way." Kristina turned and grabbed a couple *N2-O2* life support backpacks out of the locker. "Now shut up with the questions and put these on. We don't have much time."

***

Meanwhile, back in the mess hall, Bryan Hale's face creased in mounting anger. "Where in the blazes could she have gotten off to? I swear Julia, if she snuck off to meet up with that boy again…"

"Yes, yes, I'm sure Melissa will come to sorely regret it," Julia remarked. "Now come on, dear, no point letting it ruin the party."

Colonel Hale grumbled but finally nodded. When he found Melissa, she was going to be grounded, at the very least until they reached Mars. Disappearing for a few minutes was one thing, but she had been gone for more than half an hour. She wasn't answering calls and hadn't told anyone where she'd be. As angry as he was, he was also starting to worry, and he could sense Julia was worried too. He couldn't miss the way she kept anxiously glancing at her phone, but he knew from experience she wouldn't say anything… not for a while at least.

Walking back to the main party, the two found their seats near the head of the table arrangement. As a Lieutenant Colonel, Bryan Hale was seated right to one side of Colonel Perry, and the Colonel glanced over with a bemused expression when he sat down.

"Missing someone?" he politely noted the empty third seat next to them.

Bryan sighed, but forced a smile. "Just my daughter. She vanished a while back, and now she isn't answering calls."

Perry chuckled and shook his head. "Children. If it's any consolation, you aren't the first to have that happen. I have two of my own, a boy just in college and a girl about to be. Both of them are nothing but trouble, and horribly expensive." The Colonel paused with a bemused smile. "Admit it though, if you could do it all over again, you would."

Bryan Hale ground his teeth at the thought but nodded. "Yes, I suppose I would. I'd do a few things differently though."

"Wouldn't we all…" Perry's voice trailed off as his phone buzzed in his pocket. "Hmmm… who would have the gall to text me right now?" he murmured.

Perry frowned when he saw the name, "Kristina Andrews?"

"You mean that sweet dress store lady?" Julia intruded in curiosity.

"Well, you might be the only one to call her *sweet*," Perry said, "but yes, that would be her. Although why she would send me a message titled, *Perry the Chinese are Coming!!!* is a bit of a mystery." His eyes searched the room. "I thought she was supposed to be here as Lawston's date." After a minute he turned back to Bryan, "She must have stood him up. Poor Lawston is looking about as glum as you are over your missing girl."

The colonel set the phone on the table in front of him. "Well, knowing Kristina, this promises to be interesting."

He tapped the play button while Bryan and Julia both crowded around. "Perry, it's me," Kristina began. "You're not going to like this, but you're about to have visitors. Chinese visitors, and not the sort looking to invest in real estate either. It's a long story, but Sophie Tannenhill is a traitor, and she's about to let Chinese soldiers storm the station. I'm not sure of all the details, but they should be here in half an hour. Tannenhill is currently camped out up in the shuttle bay waiting for them to arrive. I'm headed up there to try and knock off Sophie, in the meantime–"

"Wait, *what* are these?" a girlish voice intruded from off camera.

"Just shut up and put them on," Kristina snapped. "In the meantime," she turned back to the camera, "I suggest you get everyone you can find, break out every bit of light weaponry you have on this station and get up there before the Chinese start pouring in. And this isn't a joke by the way. I'm sure by now you've found McGregor's body in his room. I know who killed him and why. That should be enough to drag you out of that fancy dinner of yours." She paused for a second and her expression softened a little, "*Udachi,*" she murmured. "Good luck, Perry, you're going to need it." The screen flashed to black as the message cut off, and Perry glanced to Bryan and Julia, only to find Julia's face deathly pale and Bryan's mouth hanging open.

"You two see something I missed?"

"The other voice in the video," Bryan explained, even though the words kept getting stuck in his throat, "that was our daughter, Melissa."

"You're sure?"

Julia nodded, "It was her."

"That can't be right what she said about Major Tannenhill though," Bryan added. "We were just talking with her earlier."

"And since then?"

"Well, I guess we haven't seen her since about…"

"Since about when Melissa vanished," Julia said in a shaky voice. "You don't think…?"

Perry shook his head, "Best not to speculate. We'll get to the bottom of this." He raised a hand to get everyone's attention. "Quiet!" he shouted over the dull roar of a hundred voices.

It took a minute, but slowly silence fell over the room. "Does anyone know where Major Tannenhill is?"

"She was here a little while ago," someone spoke off to the left.

"And is she here now?"

There was a long moment as everyone glanced around trying to locate the Major, but the only answer was a mounting chorus of no's from all across the room. Perry's face grew grim. Then, just as he was about to speak, a series of groans ripped through the station, like an angry god had grabbed a hammer and unleashed a flurry of blows on Medea.

****

Two hundred meters overhead, Sophie pressed the detonator button and muttered a curse to herself as she wandered the deserted hangar bay. Next time she was going to have to find competent help. She didn't understand how it was possible. She had left four adults to watch over Kristina and those two children of hers and yet, somehow, neither Valerie nor Malcolm were answering her calls.

That could only mean that those three worthless annoyances had somehow managed to get away. That also meant that Kristina would no doubt be running off to spill whatever she thought she knew to Colonel Perry. In which case, no point delaying the next stage of her plan and letting Perry's people find the bombs she had hidden in the com relays.

It took less than a second for the echoes of the blasts to ripple through the station, and Sophie tensed at the sound. That was it. The die was cast, and the Chinese had their excuse to board Medea.

Hopefully, even if Perry did find out what was going on, he would assume that the station's point defense cannons would stop any attackers from coming too close. That finally brought a smirk to the brooding major's face. Dealing with those had actually been the easiest part of her plan. Since the distances and speeds in space were much too large for humans to target accurately, the whole system was completely computerized. All Sophie had needed to do was pull up the targeting program and remove a single zero, so that instead of 60 arc seconds in one arc minute, the computer now thought there were 6. A simple, elegant change that turned them from some of the most precise weapons ever created to something that, quite literally, couldn't even hit the broad side of a barn. With fifty thousand lines of code to check, it would take days of debugging to find her sabotage, and Sophie was quite confident that Perry had nowhere near that long.

Now it was just a waiting game. She had disabled the comms, cameras and all but one of the elevators. She had her two remaining people stationed there with guns and orders to shoot anyone who came up. They didn't need to hold the bottleneck for long, maybe fifteen or twenty minutes. Then the Chinese would arrive, and it would be lights out for Medea. Hopefully Perry would still be trying to sort out what was going on.

Casting a quick glance at the two dead servicemen who had been standing sentry duty up in the hangar bay, Sophie couldn't help but feel a twinge of regret and anger. Kristina shouldn't have tried to fight. If she had done her job and taken out Perry, this all could have gone much more smoothly. Instead, now there were going to be a lot more like those two by the end of the day. People who she regarded as friends – dead. With a sigh, Sophie tore her gaze away from the bodies. Oh well, there was nothing she could do about it now. After all, the die was cast.

***

Devon nervously touched his helmet's glass faceplate as the airlock door slid shut behind them. The indicator light above the door flipped from green to red, and there was an audible hiss as the air was slowly vacuumed out of the room. Even worse, despite the fact that it was supposed to 'protect' him, Devon could definitely feel the pressure drop through his compression suit. An uncomfortable tightness tingled his skin, accompanied by a chill that crab-walked over his body like he'd just climbed out of a pool into a stiff breeze. Fortunately, the tightness seemed to level out after a moment as his suit squeezed back. The air pressure dropped, until even the hissing of the atmosphere being sucked away faded to a silence broken only by his own breathing.

As the last of the air was pulled out of the room, Devon felt a gloved hand clutch his, and turned to see Melissa looking just as scared as he was. Overhead, the indicator light flashed green, and the door to outer space slid open in an eerie silence. Devon knew Melissa couldn't hear him through the emptiness, but he gave her hand a comforting squeeze and was rewarded with a nervous smile on the girl's face.

"Alright, let's go." Devon nearly jumped in shock when he heard Kristina's voice in his helmet.

"Wait, we can talk?"

"Obviously," Devon couldn't see Kristina's face, but he could definitely hear her sarcasm. "Now remember," she added, "we are in space, riding on a gigantic spinning wheel. If either of you let go, you're going to fly off into the void, and I can't save you. Understand?"

"We get it," Melissa nodded.

"Good." Kristina reached down to her belt and tugged up a retractable clip attached to a thin steel cable. "Last thing, this is your lifeline. There should be a bar that you can hook it onto by the ladder. Make sure you attach it, so if you do fall, it'll stop you."

"Is this going to be kind of like rock climbing?" Devon asked. He and some friends had done that a few times at the mall back home.

"No idea, but probably." Kristina led them out of the airlock. They stepped onto a narrow platform, illuminated only by a few bright floodlights, with the sun veiled away behind planet Earth. "That said," she continued, "if you fall, instead of splatting on the ground, you just keep tumbling forever into the darkness until you run out of air and asphyxiate, or if you're unlucky with your trajectory, you might burn up in the upper atmosphere in an hour or so. Not sure which is worse."

Devon followed her outside. When the miniature flashlights on the sides of his helmet clicked on, he took a few steps forward and found himself standing on the precipice of a void, with only a black infinity beneath him. Off to his left, the nighttime mirage of Earth swelled up to consume nearly his whole field of view, a vast sheet of blackness pockmarked by ribbons of twinkling lights. Amid the dark, it took him a half second to realize that they were flying over the US East Coast. The whole planet currently appeared to be upside down and slowly rotating. It took him a moment to register that it was actually Medea Station that was spinning, and regardless, the effect of seeing Earth moving in such an unnatural way was enough to give him pause.

He didn't have long to look. Close to the airlock stood a simple ladder that ran up the side of the station, and far overhead sat the hulking shuttle bay, the mammoth hub in the gigantic wheel that was Medea. They were about halfway up one of the spokes that ran between the outer ring and the inner hub. Through a rectangular slit cut in the platform, Devon could see that the ladder ran all the way down to the main ring *very* far below.

"So… we have to climb that?" Melissa asked. The radio in Devon's helmet made it sound like her voice was coming from right next to him, even though she was a good ten feet away, staring nervously at the ladder.

"That would be the idea." Kristina clipped onto the safety bar. She grabbed hold of the ladder, swinging out above the hole in the platform, to begin her ascent. "On the plus side, spin gravity should go down the higher you climb, and a hundred meters isn't that far. Just remember, be careful. Space isn't always intuitive." With that, Kristina started climbing, slowly but steadily gripping each rung.

For a few seconds Devon and Melissa both watched, but finally Devon glanced over at her with a shrug. "I guess, ladies first."

Melissa didn't look very happy to go first, but after a moment's hesitance, she clipped on her safety line and grabbed a tight hold on the rungs. As she started climbing, Devon could hear a faint murmur over the radio, "Dad's going to kill me."

Well, he mused, at least she wasn't the only one with parents who were going to be ticked when they found out about all this. He waited for Melissa to move a little way up, before tugging out the carabiner attached to the metal cable in his belt and latching it on. Gripping the cold metal rung as tight as he could, Devon's eyes drifted down to the stomach churning drop below, then upwards, past Melissa to the hub of the wheel far overhead. He swallowed down the lump of fear in his chest, then swung himself out onto the ladder, his arms working less than usual in the lighter gravity. As a darkened planet Earth zipped by below, he began pulling himself up into the cold night.

Chapter 22
The Shuttle Bay

Even in the low gravity, Devon still found the climb nauseating and exhausting. The freshly bandaged gash in his arm wasn't helping either. The station had some lights along the way, but mostly he was forced to rely on the twin lamps mounted on his helmet. With everything else veiled in the dark gloom of space, he found himself wishing they would get around to the sunny side of the planet already.

He was also extremely glad he'd taken the jacket and pants. Even with his heart pounding, he still fought back a shiver at the chill that washed over his whole body, like he'd stepped outside in the dead of winter. Despite the insulation of his compression gloves, the bitter cold from the metal rungs leached through to his hands. And, just to cap it off, every step higher the ever-pulsing Coriolis force grew stronger until he wanted to puke.

The Coriolis force was the worst. Whenever he hauled himself up to the next rung, it kicked in like someone gently shoving him towards the wall. Then he would stop, and it would vanish, only to reappear when he hauled himself up to the next rung. Once or twice was fine, but after a hundred feet the nausea was almost enough to make him lose his grip.

It must have been getting to Melissa too. "Can we stop for a second?" She sounded like she was about to be sick.

"Yes, please," Devon panted in agreement.

Kristina's voice sounded strained. "We can pause for a minute, but we don't have long."

Along the ladder, every twenty feet or so, there were small segments where someone had installed a steel framed cage that wrapped around the rungs. Climbing up a few last rungs to the cage immediately above him, Devon leaned back against the steel strips. He positioned himself so he could let go of the cold ladder rungs for a moment. He tucked his hands inside his jacket to let the warmth flow back into his frigid fingers.

Overhead, Melissa had stopped at the next alcove above him, and Devon saw her cringe and pull her arms close like she was shivering. "I don't get it, how am I freezing to death and burning up at the same time?"

Devon tried to catch his breath as he spoke. "I think... it has... something to do with convection."

"Huh?"

"On Earth... your body loses heat to the air, but... up here there's no air to exchange heat with. Your body isn't designed for this sort of environment."

"That still doesn't explain why I'm freezing cold."

"It's because you're sweating."

"I am *not* sweating," Melissa snapped back. "My skin's so dry I could use some moisturizer about now."

"No... I mean," Devon tried to explain it. "It has something to do with low vapor pressure."

There was a pause, "You don't know what you're talking about, do you?"

"I do too," he protested. "You forget, my dad's an engineer, and he's been talking about space for weeks now. I think, because space has no pressure and these suits aren't pressurized either, all the moisture on your skin is instantly evaporating. Evaporating water cools you down, which is why your skin is freezing. Since your body can't lose heat through convection with the air, it doesn't know what else to do, so it keeps on sweating because your core is still hot. But because it evaporates so fast, your skin stays cold."

There was a petulant silence from the girl, "Well, I could still use some moisturizer."

"Melissa, Devon do you two *have* to do this *right* now?" Devon could almost hear the eye roll accompanying Kristina's scathing tone.

"Sorry," Melissa muttered, her teeth chattering. Devon felt a pang of sympathy for the girl. She was from Texas after all, it barely even snowed down there. No wonder she was freezing.

"Let's just get moving." Far overhead Kristina started climbing again, and with a reluctant sigh, Devon put his hands back on the rungs and began hauling himself higher, the nausea surging back as he went.

For another few dozen rungs, all three labored upward in silence. Finally, Melissa spoke up, "Kristina, why are you using my name all of a sudden?"

"You prefer Curls?"

"No," she said quickly, "I just… I was curious."

"If you must know, you've started acting more like a big girl recently, so I figured you deserved a big girl name. Although, frankly, you aren't doing yourself any favors. Now hurry up, it's not much further."

By the time they reached the top, Devon couldn't help but feel that Kristina had lied to them. It had been quite a way. Somehow though, Kristina didn't seem remotely bothered by the freezing cold of the station or the way their skin had turned nearly to ice. He suspected it was because she was Russian. They were probably immune to the cold in Siberia.

Regardless, he breathed a deep sigh of relief when he scrambled up onto another platform and unclipped his safety line. There he found Kristina opening an airlock, while Melissa hugged her arms to her chest, trying to keep warm.

Devon had almost gotten used to the oppressive silence of space, but seeing the airlock door slide open without a sound was still enough to unnerve him. Once they were inside though, the red light blinked on, and it was a relief to hear the hiss of air and feel his skin loosen a little as the pressure equalized back to a standard atmosphere. There was a beep when the light finally flashed green, and Kristina flipped up the glass visor on her helmet so she was in the open air. "Well, that was fun, now wasn't it." She strode into the hangar bay.

Devon raised his own visor and glanced over at Melissa, so they weren't talking over the radio. "You okay?"

"Yeah," she nodded, "just a little cold, that's all."

"Kristina, do we still need these oxygen tanks and everything?" Devon thumbed to the life support pack strapped to his back.

"Depends on whether or not you think the shuttle bay is going to decompress once the shooting starts. There's a good chance it doesn't, but I would rather be prepared than not."

That was enough to make him abruptly reconsider dropping his life support pack. He hastily tightened up the backpack straps. It wasn't that heavy in the low gravity anyway.

"So, what now?" Melissa finally stopped shivering long enough to ask.

"Well, I suppose you two can run off and do whatever you want, but personally–" Kristina still had her bag looped across her body, and now she calmly pulled out her dart gun, "first stop is to go find a real weapon."

They had come out in what Devon could only guess was the cargo segment of the hangar bay. When they had docked at Medea, he had only briefly seen the cavernous docking port and the gleaming entryway, but it seemed the rest of the hub was one gigantic storage shed. There were tools, replacement panels and structural beams stacked together in towering piles. He saw crates scattered everywhere, banded with various colors of tape, and rows of shelves crammed with more electrical and mechanical widgets than he could count. Kristina ignored all that and made a beeline straight to a small arms cabinet. There they found the doors already flung wide open and several empty slots where assault rifles would have fit.

Melissa's mouth fell open when she saw it. "That's not supposed to be…"

"Open?" Kristina's eyes twinkled in amusement. "You forget who you're playing against, sweetie. Sophie knows all these little secrets too, probably better than I do." Reaching inside, she grabbed the one remaining M20 Rifle and a few pistols that had been left behind. "I was counting on something like this. A dart gun may be nice, but it isn't a match for automatic rifles, and arms locker keys aren't exactly easy to come by. This is good though. It means Sophie doesn't suspect we're up here."

Kristina deftly popped a fresh magazine marked with a band of blue tape into the pistol and tugged back the action to chamber a round. "Do you two know how to shoot?"

Next to him Melissa nodded as Kristina handed her a pistol and magazine of her own, but Devon tried to hide a surge of embarrassment. "Ummm… well it basically like Ringworld, right?"

Kristina narrowed her eyes at him, "Have you ever *actually* fired a gun?"

"Not… in person."

Kristina sighed, "Melissa, you've been to a range before, yes?"

"A few times." As if to make a point, Melissa repeated the same process Kristina had just gone through of inserting a magazine, flicking off the safety and racking the slide to chamber a round.

"Good," Kristina nodded in approval as she tossed Devon an empty weapon. "Keep tabs on your boyfriend then, and make sure he doesn't shoot anyone by mistake." Kristina dug an armful of ammunition out of the locker. She snapped one magazine into her M-20, then stuffed the majority of the remainder into her bag before parceling out the rest between the two of them. "Okay, yellow magazines are normal 9mm NATO ammo, good for smashing stuff. The blue are tungsten penetrator flechette rounds, they're like a miniature anti-tank shell, very handy if the Chinese roll up in battle armor. Try not to be wasteful," she warned, as Devon slid the ammo into several pouches on his belt.

She glanced through the locker and grabbed a few little plastic cases, tossing them one each. "Don't forget some ear plugs too. These are the fancy kind, 80 dB cutoff. You'll hear fine when you're talking, but once the shooting starts, especially in close quarters like this, you won't be able to hear a thing without them."

"You'll also need these." Kristina grabbed three sleek boxes that looked kind of like little wallets with belt clips. She tapped a button on the top of each so a green indicator light started blinking, then clipped one on her belt and handed the other two to Devon and Melissa. "Keep these on you at all times. They're drone scramblers – a combination of high-power active jamming and script-hack countermeasures." Kristina patted hers with a sentimental grin. "Probably the most beautiful little thing to come out of the US in a while."

"Last thing," she grabbed several tubes, that looked like miniature grenade launcher attachments and passed them out. Each was about three inches wide by six inches long, with a flat mounting bracket on top and with a sort of trigger in the back. Kristina slid hers onto the rail beneath the barrel of her rifle, then locked it in place.

"These are short range microwave pulse emitters." She explained, taking each of their weapons in turn and sliding the tube onto the attachment rail beneath the pistol barrels. "If they start using wire-guided quadcopters, you point this baby in their general direction, and fire. You won't see anything, but it should fry the electronics. It shoots a pretty wide beam, so you don't have to be too careful when you aim. But you only get one shot before the capacitors have to recharge. You'll see a red indicator light on the back, when that turns off it's good to fire another pulse. Usually it's about a minute to recharge and five shots until the battery dies."

She finished up, handing Devon his weapon back with a dauntless grin. "Now come on, kiddos, it's time to go hunting."

Kristina strode off, making for a service stairway down the hall, but Melissa shot Devon a curious look. "How have you never fired a gun?"

Devon shrugged, "I live near Chicago, nobody has guns up there."

Melissa seemed to find something humorous about his statement, but she nodded anyway. "Well, the main rule is don't ever point it at anything you don't want to shoot, particularly me."

"You two coming?" Kristina called back. "Or am I interrupting something?"

Melissa scowled, "One second." She took Devon's weapon, and quickly loaded it. "Okay," she handed it back, "the safety is off, so just point and pull the trigger. And *please* try not to shoot me."

***

"So, we can't contact anyone?" Colonel Perry stalked back and forth in the CIC, working a boiling rage.

"I'm sorry, sir," the hapless serviceman stammered. "Every external comm relay on the station was destroyed by the blasts. We can probably patch something together, but it will take time. Until then we can't send anything."

"How much time?"

"A few hours, possibly longer if the Chinese ship out there doesn't intend on being friendly."

"Well, that's a given." Bryan saw the Colonel turn away and grit his teeth in frustration.

"We have a second contact diverging from the main ship!" someone shouted. "It looks like they've launched a shuttle. It's burning straight towards us, LADAR reads 15 kilometers and closing. Current ETA is six minutes."

"Can we signal them off somehow?"

The first serviceman shook his head.

"The Chinese are sending a message asking if we require assistance," a third controller called out. "They're saying if we don't respond they will board us and assist with any repairs."

"Like hell they will," Perry snapped. "Are the point defense cannons still online?"

"Yes, sir." The captain in charge of overseeing the station's defense systems looked up from across the CIC. "We have a firing solution on your command."

"Good. Put a few signal rounds across their bow. Preferably close enough to make their pilot over there wet his pants. That should send a clear message."

The captain grinned gleefully, "With pleasure, Colonel."

A few seconds later, a single point defense rail gun rotated onto a computer calculated firing vector and pumped out three tungsten tracer rounds at the relatively slow velocity of one thousand meters per second. The tracers weren't normally used, but they were kept on hand as the space version of signal flares that burned a mixture of white phosphorus and oxidizer to give off a blinding glow. The idea was to give the Chinese pilot something of a light show to scare him off but–

"What the…?" The captain's confused voice demanded, "That can't be right. Recalculate the vector heading and fire again, one round."

"Sir," the young officer turned back to Perry with a stunned expression, "there ummm… there seems to be an issue with the fire control systems. They don't appear to be calibrated properly."

"What?" Perry snapped, and Lieutenant Colonel Hale stepped close to see for himself and check the computer's firing solution. It wasn't a difficult one, and it took maybe ten seconds to see that it was correct. The problem was that the actual shots had gone off in a totally different direction. "Zero the gun, then retarget," Bryan suggested.

The operator tapped a button and waited a few nervous seconds with the station commander hovering over him. Finally, the weapon was recalibrated by setting it to a fixed zero position. The young serviceman let the computer recalculate the firing vector and retarget the gun, then pressed the button to fire off a single low velocity tracer.

There was a chorus of muttered curses as they saw that, once again, the shot had been completely wrong.

"Sophie," Colonel Hale murmured, "She must have sabotaged the point defense guns." He glanced at Perry, "Sir, if she did something, we may need to reload the whole system's software. I'd wager she also corrupted whatever backup copy you might have had on Medea. Until we can reestablish communications to upload a fresh version, there may not be much else we can do."

"We have two more shuttle contacts," a serviceman loudly announced, "also from the Chinese transport."

Perry scowled, "Captain, get everyone you can to skim through the fire control code and sort out what Sophie might have broken. If you *can* get the cannons working, you don't need my permission to make that freighter or the shuttles out there disappear." He turned to Bryan, "Colonel Hale, do you have any experience with ground operations?"

"Minimal, sir."

"Too bad. We need every available person we can muster to get up to the shuttle bay. Grab some guns, get together anyone you can find who isn't working on Sophie's sabotage, and head over to find Lieutenant Colonel Mayweather at the elevator. If Sophie is bunkered down up there, I intend to root her out, preferably alive so she can fix our systems."

Chapter 23
The Scary Spetsnaz Lady

Melissa cringed and pressed herself against a nearby wall when she heard the echoed cracks of gunfire in the hall. It wasn't aimed at her – the sound was too muffled to be nearby. That meant it was Sophie and her people, probably fighting it out with the rest of the Space Force. She murmured a quick prayer that her dad wasn't included.

"Sounds like Perry finally took my advice," Kristina remarked, her eyes drifting across the corridor as the three crept forward. "He sure took his sweet time getting around to it though. We beat him up here, and we took the stairs."

"We have to help them," Melissa insisted.

"Relax, we will." She led them down the hall until Melissa could see the corridor ahead widen out into the cavernous docking bay. Kristina suddenly put her arm up, and pressed them back against the wall, "Quiet." She held up a finger before they could ask any more questions.

Melissa craned her head to one side and her breath caught when she saw a troop of soldiers in combat armor disembarking from a docked ship.

"*Suka,*" Kristina hissed to herself.

Devon bit his lip as the soldiers vanished down the hall towards the elevator, "I take it that's not good?"

"Chinese soldiers in Tianlong Battle Armor are *never* good." Kristina shook her head. "*Der'mo*. Look, if the Chinese are already here, we're going to have to change plans. If they keep pouring in like this, your Space Force friends aren't going to last long trying to reclaim the hangar. We need to slow them down and give Perry a chance to mount a defense, maybe downstairs at the elevator."

"You have a plan in mind?" he asked.

Kristina shook her head. "Maybe it's best if you two find somewhere to hide. I'd hate to see you both get killed."

"We didn't come all this way to hide," Melissa protested, indignant. "We want to help."

"Well," Kristina considered for a moment, "if you and Devon want to make yourselves useful, get a ship, head out there and see if you can't do something to blast whatever sort of cruiser all these Chinese shuttles are coming from. Knowing the Chinese, they brought along a full battalion, and we need to cut them off before they're all on Medea."

"And what about you?"

Kristina sighed and unslung her rifle. "Only one way to solve this sort of problem, sweetie. It'll be just like the Battle of Baikal – fight until the Chinese learn to run away."

"You fought in the war?" Melissa regarded the Russian lady in surprise.

"14th Spetsnaz Brigade," a grin tugged at Kristina's lips. "I was a sniper in Irkutsk. This will be the same thing, except back then I had a better gun and actual air support. Now go, I'll make them bleed, you two just need to stab them in the heart. And if we don't see each other again, it's been nice working with you both – despite our differences."

Melissa stared at Kristina for a moment. "Why are you doing this?" she asked. "This is an American station, but you're willing to die to save it? To save us?"

Kristina smiled, "Perhaps I have a bit of a soft spot for Americans and their optimism. Or maybe it's just not in anyone's interest for the Chinese to control Medea." She shrugged, "Maybe I've already seen too many dead children in the world to want to add two more. I'm not entirely sure myself, but at this point I don't suppose it matters. You two do your country proud. Okay?"

"We will," Melissa nodded. "And, Kristina… thank you."

"Always a pleasure, Curls," Kristina remarked cheekily. "Now, get moving. I believe you Americans would say it's about to light up like the Fourth of July around here."

***

Kristina waited until Melissa and Devon had both vanished back down the hallway. Nice kids, even if they were a little nosy… stubborn… downright foolish sometimes. She allowed herself a whimsical grin, hopefully they'd find a ship and use it to get the heck out of here.

Oh well, Kristina took a deep breath and peeked out at the docking bay. The first group of soldiers was gone, but it seemed another shuttle had just docked and a second contingent was pouring forward. They would work.

Kristina gripped her M20 and tried to remember everything she knew about target shooting. She had practiced enough with her dart gun to know that the spinning on Medea would screw up precision shots. Probably not a huge issue operating in close quarters with supersonic rounds, but it might be helpful if there were grenades tumbling around.

The rules was that shooting spinward caused the shot to drop, while shooting anti-spinward caused it to curve upwards. Lawston had tried to explain relative motion in rotating reference frames to her once. But, by the time he'd finished all his hypotheticals, she had just felt more confused than before.

But even if she didn't understand why they worked, Kristina had the rules memorized by heart. The only question was which way was spinward. Holding her weapon straight out in front of her, she let it drop. In the .2 standard gravity of the station hub, it fell so slowly it almost looked like it was drifting through water. Eventually though, she saw the gun curve away from her as it fell, the Coriolis force at work. That meant she was facing spinward so she should aim a hair high. Definitely not as much as if she were down on the main ring. Lawston had been very

217

particular about that point, something to do with lower tangential velocities.

She snatched the falling carbine rifle out of the air, took a half second to steel herself, then swept around the corner and fired.

The Chinese were bunched up, and versus flechette rounds in the close quarters of the station, their light battle armor wouldn't really help them. Kristina leveled her rifle and pulled the trigger, feeling the three round burst kick like an elephant to the shoulder. She didn't wait to see if she hit as her aim drifted on to the next, and the next after that. There were thirty rounds in her magazine, and in less than eight seconds she had emptied them all at ten different targets.

She heard the distinctive click of the depleted magazine and slid well back into cover. Dropping her old magazine to the floor, she jammed a second one in and deftly chambered a round. In about three seconds her rifle was reloaded and ready to fire.

Of course, she couldn't do that again. The Chinese had seemed surprised to see her, but now they were spraying her position with a hail of automatic fire. Thankfully, this part of the station was built like an orbital bunker. Given how fast the main ring spun, the shuttle bay was really the only way on or off Medea. Her understanding was that the Space Force had reinforced the walls to allow them to set up strongpoints on the defense. Medea's heavy steel walls kept her safe, but Kristina didn't fancy stepping out into all that lead. Instead, she retreated back down the hall to the next intersection, pressed herself against the wall and waited.

The assault rifle fire slackened, and she heard the distinctive whir of a drone copter zooming closer down the hall. The noise grew louder then hesitated as her active jammer kicked in, before fading as signal loss triggered the return to home function. Knowing exactly what came next, Kristina started a quick mental countdown in her head. When she hit zero, she took a deep breath, swung out of cover, and squeezed the trigger.

Three soldiers had come down to investigate, two stared at her ejected magazine on the floor while the third aimed down the hallway. She shot the alert one first, three rounds straight in the chest, then switched her fire, dropping the other two before they could even get their weapons up. Her chamber wasn't empty, but even so, she dashed forwards, ejecting the half-spent magazine and reloading as she ran.

Retaking her old position, Kristina popped out and got off two more bursts at the rest of the squad before they started up again with the smash of counter fire, QBZ-95B by the deeper sound. That was one of those noises she could never quite forget. The same way the crack of an AK-12 could still make her eyes mist over, the Chinese rifle brought back a different part of her. The terrified eighteen-year-old girl, watching as the 65th Group Army storm the outskirts of Irkutsk.

A particularly heavy burst of gunfire sent shudders through the wall, snapping Kristina back to the present. Scavenging hand grenades off the bodies like it was her birthday, she waited until the fire slackened a little. When it finally did, she leaned back out, rapidly burned through the last of her M-20 ammo and tossed it aside. Reaching down, she plucked the bullpup rifle from one of the limp figures at her feet along with a few more magazines. Kristina managed a fierce grin. She had always thought the QBZ was a trashy weapon. Oh well, time to make new memories. There was a fresh magazine still loaded, and retreating back, she took a new position and waited for the inevitable counterattack to start picking off those PRC *suki*.

∗∗∗

Melissa cast an anxious glance backwards as the echoes of automatic weaponry reverberated from the direction they had left Kristina. "You think she's okay?"

"I thought you, and I quote, 'hate that woman'?" Devon remarked in an amused voice.

"Well, that was before she saved our lives."

"Actually, I believe you said it right *after* she saved our lives."

"Oh shut up," the girl fumed. "I can change my mind. And you're forgetting which of us actually knows how to shoot."

"Is that a threat?" Devon grinned like he actually enjoyed getting a rise out of her.

219

"It's a warning," Melissa glowered. "Now come on, we need to find a ship."

"And do what? Honestly, Kristina has no idea what she's talking about. Neither of us know how to fly those things, and unless I missed the secret missile pods, they don't even have weapons."

"Well, we have to do something," Melissa said, frustrated. "That's my dad fighting downstairs, and unless we stop this, I'm never going to see him again. Do you have a better plan?"

"Look, you aren't the only one with a family on Medea," Devon snapped. "But if we just hop in a space-ship and go out for an adventure, we won't help anyone."

He paused, "Kristina must have had something in mind. She knows these ships aren't armed… what would her crazy Russian solution to this problem be?"

"Get drunk and wreck the ship," Melissa muttered.

"Oh…" Devon's eyes suddenly lit up.

"What?"

Devon didn't answer; instead he pursed his lips and frowned like he was working out an idea. "That could work, I think."

"What could work?"

"Your crazy Russian plan."

"You want to get drunk… now? Are you insane?"

"No," Devon shook his head, "not that part. I mean wrecking the ship. Look, let's get to a shuttle, I've played with a few space flight simulators before, so maybe I can work out the basic controls. I'm pretty sure the computer does most of the flying, so it can't be *that* complicated."

"And then what? You just said they didn't have any weapons."

"We won't need weapons." Devon acted as though it all made perfect sense. "Come on, we don't have much time."

As though the universe wanted to hammer in the urgency, Melissa saw a soldier suddenly round the corner behind Devon, an assault rifle aimed right at them. "Stop!" he shouted in a thick Chinese accent.

Melissa had zero intention of doing that. "Devon, drop!"

Devon pushed to one side and hit the ground while Melissa threw herself towards the hallway wall, bringing up her pistol as she went and pulling the trigger. By all rights they should have both been dead, but the soldier hesitated for a critical instant. Maybe it was the fact that they were kids, or he just didn't expect to see a girl with a gun. Regardless, it saved their lives. He only got off one burst with the semi-automatic and it went straight down the center of the hallway, completely missing Melissa as she hugged the wall.

Melissa didn't miss though. She couldn't remember actually pulling the trigger fifteen times, but she must have, because the next thing she knew her weapon clicked empty and the Chinese soldier slowly sank to the ground in the low gravity, dead. For a half second she stared at the body in shock. She'd never cared much for the People's Liberation Army. Not since she had understood what her dad did for a living but... Oh God, she had just killed someone.

Melissa's gun clattered to the floor and suddenly she couldn't breathe. "No."

"Melissa," somewhere far away Devon shook her, "you okay?"

"I killed him," she whispered breathlessly.

"I know, good shooting. Now come on, we need to go before his friends show up."

"Don't you understand?" Melissa covered her mouth in horror. "I killed him."

"Yeah," Devon forced her to look him straight in the eye, "it was him or us okay... you chose us." He pressed his gun into her hand. "Now come on. Like you said, you're the only one who actually knows how to use this thing, and we have to get to a ship."

He pulled her down the hall, and Melissa finally tore her gaze away from the dead man on the floor. She couldn't get the picture out of her mind though, and she shuddered at what she had just done. She tried to tell herself it was like fighting Valerie earlier – self-defense – but it didn't feel that way. It felt like murder. The man had hesitated, and she hadn't... so he was dead.

With a sudden urgency, Melissa jerked free from Devon's grip and ran back down the hall, kneeling next to the lifeless body sprawled out in the intersection.

"Melissa what – we have to go!"

She wasn't listening to Devon. Instead she found the dog tags around the man's neck and jerked free one of the two rectangular metal ID's. It was inscribed in Chinese, but she could translate that later. He at least deserved to have someone know his name.

"*Tìng! Tìng!*" Melissa looked up to see another soldier twenty or thirty feet away, coming from the same direction as the one lying next to her, his rifle raised. Whatever *Tìng* translated too, he didn't sound friendly, especially not with his compatriot dead at her feet.

The body was sprawled out into the intersection, but Melissa was already half hidden by the wall. A quick glance at the pitiless fury in the man's eyes told her that now wasn't the time to throw up her hands and surrender. She scrambled back out of his view as a hail of automatic fire tore through the spot where she had knelt a half second before. There was another deafening burst of suppressive fire, until suddenly… "*Cao!*" She heard the distinctive rattle of him pulling out a magazine. That meant either that he was reloading or the gun jammed. Her chance. Clutching Devon's pistol, she jerked back around the corner and pumped three rounds into the man, sending him drifting to the floor in the low gravity.

Her eyes lingered on the second body for an instant, but then they flickered back to the first man beside her and her mind clicked into survival mode. More soldiers would have heard that. She grabbed the man's assault rifle, slid a spare magazine into her belt and dropped two hand grenades along with Devon's pistol into her bag. At least now they had a fighting chance.

"Melissa, we have to go!" Devon shouted from down the hall.

"I'm coming." The girl calmly stood and flicked her new rifle into single fire mode. She jogged back down the hall with a cold expression. "Let's find a shuttle."

Chapter 24
A Jump Into the Void

Melissa and Devon rounded a corner, as behind them the echoing clatter of automatic fire beat at their earplugs. Further down the hall they could see a stairway. Melissa recalled from their arrival that the layout would lead up to an airlock and a shuttle. Pressing herself against the wall, Melissa gripped her assault rifle and winced as more weapon fire raked the hall. "Devon, keep moving and get to the ship!"

"What about you?"

"I'll hold them off for a few minutes," Melissa tried to sound optimistic. "Just get to the ship and let me know when you're ready to go."

She could see from the pained look on his face that Devon disagreed with her hanging back, but fortunately he was smart enough to know there wasn't time to argue. With a nod, he ran for the stairs, vanishing up towards where Melissa really hoped there was a ship they could use. The air split with more blasts of suppressive fire from the Chinese soldiers who had been chasing them, and Melissa stuck her gun out to return a few blind shots down the hall.

The response was a sustained volley from the Chinese that left her wondering how they all weren't running out of ammo. Huddled behind her wall, she tried to figure out what to do next. Just firing the rifle had left her shoulder stinging like *she'd* been shot, and it was only a matter of time until she ran out of bullets. There were at least six of them that she had seen, probably more behind, and they actually had training. Her only combat experience was when her dad had taken her to the shooting range or dragged her off for a weekend paintball. Somewhere deep down a little voice echoed what she already knew – she was dead. Even so, she whispered a desperate prayer for a miracle… for anything, some path that didn't end with her and Devon dead in a cold corridor four thousand miles above Earth.

There were more shouts from the soldiers that Melissa couldn't understand, orders by the sound of them. Maybe they were going to send another drone at her. At least the microwave emitter had worked like a charm. She leaned back out with her single shot assault rifle and fired off several more desultory rounds until 'click'… her heart turned to ice. She was out of bullets.

With a loud curse, Melissa grabbed at the second magazine in her belt, then caught herself. The Chinese had suddenly gone very quiet. They would have heard the click of an empty rifle too, and they were waiting to hear if she reloaded. Maybe it was best to give them what they wanted.

Looping the assault rifle strap around one shoulder, she quietly slid a grenade out of her purse, took a tight hold of the pin and waited. In a few seconds there were more shouts from the soldiers, "*Zǒu, zǒu, shā biǎo zi!*"

That didn't sound good. Melissa heard footsteps moving closer and jerked out the grenade pin. She wasn't sure what the fuse time on Chinese grenades was, probably about four seconds, same as American ones. She let the striker lever flick up and tossed it down the hall like a hot potato. There was a distinct ping as it struck the floor. Suddenly the corridor echoed with panicked shouts.

She pulled the pistol out of her bag right as the whole world was drowned by the deafening blast. The tight halls helped focus the shock to the point where, even hidden behind a corner, the detonation wave made her skin tingle. Behind the blast front the world was suddenly transformed into a confused haze of acrid smoke and pained screams that echoed from every direction.

Leaning out, Melissa couldn't see more than five feet in front of her, but that didn't really matter. She emptied her pistol blindly down the hall and was rewarded with more shouts.

When her weapon finally stopped kicking at each pull of the trigger, Melissa dropped back behind cover just long enough to eject one magazine and ram another in. Dodging back out, she squeezed off a few more shots to sweep the corridor. Now that the smoke had cleared some, she could see the wreckage she had left behind. Scattered across the hallway lay three dead soldiers amid a ring of charred and dented metal, marking where the grenade had detonated.

Had she been thinking clearly Melissa probably would have been sick at the sight, but with the adrenaline coursing through her, all she could think of was the next fight. With a deep breath she pressed herself back against the wall and wasted a few seconds fumbling to reload her assault rifle. There were sharp cracks from enemy rifles at the far end of the hall but nothing like the hail of bullets from earlier. If she had to guess they would take a few minutes to regroup then...

She caught a metallic clang as something bounced off the floor, and Melissa glanced down to see a grenade five feet away—

Then the world washed with a fiery concussion.

She should have died.

Had the grenade fuse been a second and a half shorter, she would have. As it was, Melissa turned and dived, hitting the ground maybe fifteen feet away right as the fragmentation grenade went off with a reverberating roar. Even with earplugs, the only thing that saved her from permanent hearing damage was that she was face down and wearing a helmet. The only thing that saved the rest of her from ricocheting grenade fragments was, oddly enough, her suit.

It wasn't technically body armor, but the heavy mesh space suit was designed to offer the wearer at least some protection from micrometeoroid impacts. The bouncing grenade fragment that ricocheted into her back was little different from a shard of space debris. It left an awful pain, like someone punched her right in the kidneys, but the suit mesh held and dissipated the worst of the blow.

Instead of bleeding out on the floor with a shrapnel hole in her, Melissa, stunned but alive, fumbled in her purse for the one grenade she had left. She knew exactly what was coming next. In about five seconds the Chinese would be around that corner and after just killing three of their people, she didn't expect an ounce of mercy.

Melissa jerked free the pin and tossed it back down the hall. Otherwise though, she didn't move. Amid the smoky haze the Chinese wouldn't be able to see any more than she could, and standing up would just make her an easier target. Lying face down on the floor, she gripped her assault rifle and squeezed off a couple blind shots back down the hall. Over the crack of her own weapon, she heard the telltale shouts of the Chinese moving closer, and more gunshots snapped by overhead.

Then her grenade went off, and another pressure wave body slammed her against the steel plated floor. In the aftermath, all Melissa could manage was a pained groan. Everything hurt. Her ears were ringing, and frankly, she was tired of things blowing up. She managed to struggle to her feet though, her shoulder screaming from the rifle kick as she pumped off a few more shots into the haze of smoke and staggered back towards the stairs.

As bad of shape as she was in, Melissa could see that the Chinese had by far gotten the worse end of the deal. Amid the confusion of the fight, they hadn't noticed her grenade until it was too late, and Melissa could make out at least two motionless forms who had taken the blast at point blank range. She really hoped that, with half a squad dead, the Chinese would have had enough. But even as she withdrew, another grenade tumbled forward in a second attempt to clear the intersection.

Melissa turned and made a run for the stairs a few seconds before the blast went off. Behind her came a concussion and a sharp sting at her side. She barely noticed as she stumbled up the steps, pausing just once to fire back a quick suppressive burst. Sprinting up through the airlock, she found it docked to a midsized shuttle with Devon up front messing with the controls.

"How's it looking, Devon!"

"Huh," he glanced back at her and his mouth nearly fell open. "Melissa, what happened–"

"Can we launch or not?" the girl demanded as she stumbled up behind him and more or less collapsed into the copilot chair. "Because I'm running low on ammo, and if we're stuck, I don't think they're in the mood to take prisoners."

"I ummm… probably." Devon tapped a button and the door slid shut behind them. "Yeah, we can go. The controls are pretty simple, mostly automated. Although I don't think we're going to be able to close the airlock behind us."

"And…?"

"Well, I guess it doesn't really matter." He pressed another button and there was a *thunk* sound from beneath the shuttle, like something had just switched off. "I can detach the docking clamps, but we'll vent the hallway to space when we go. Sucks for the Chinese I suppose… literally." There were a few flashing warnings that popped up on the screen, but Devon just ignored them and switched on the docking/undocking autopilot. Beneath them, Melissa felt slight pulses of acceleration as automated maneuvering thrusters boosted them off the floor, nudging the shuttle this way and that, until it hung suspended, motionless in the center of the hangar bay, with the whole of Medea station spinning around it. Finally, the autopilot fired a sustained, low g thruster burst and their ship coasted out of the hangar bay and into the orbital space around planet Earth.

With the shuttle underway, Devon turned and gave her a concerned look. "Melissa, what happened?"

"I ummm…" Melissa tried to form words but suddenly she felt absolutely exhausted. She glanced down at the persistent stinging in her side and was surprised to see a gash in her space suit. She pulled back the jacket to reveal a growing patch of blood staining the milky white fabric. More in shock than anything else, she touched the wound and winced at the pain as her finger came away slick with blood. "Oh…" she murmured in a faint voice.

"Don't move," Devon cautioned, floating up from his chair and scouring around for a medical kit.

With the ship coasting in null gravity, and her whole body too weak to do much of anything but sit, Melissa wasn't going anywhere. Instead, she stared at her side, watching as the blood began to pool into floating droplets in zero gravity. As the adrenaline from the fight drained away, the pain worsened. Melissa couldn't stop a tear from trickling down her cheek as the reality of what she had just done sunk in. She had just killed… how many people? At least seven, maybe more. The first one had bothered her but… none of the others. How was that possible?

The tears began to pool in her eyes as Melissa's mind drifted through everything. What was wrong with her? How could she have just… she didn't even feel sorry.

"Hey, it's going to be fine," Devon floated around next to her with a first aid kit. "Just hold still and I'll get you fixed up."

Reaching down he started to roll up her shirt to get at the shrapnel gash in her side, but when Devon got to the wound, Melissa's side flared in an agonizing pain and she screamed.

For a moment Melissa's whole world was consumed by the fire in her side. When her vision finally did clear, she was gasping for breath and Devon was peering at her bloody cut with a worried expression.

"Are you okay, Melissa?" his eyes flicked up to meet hers.

"I'm sorry," she murmured, "It just…"

"I know," he took her hand with a sympathetic nod. "Just hold on, okay? We'll figure something out."

With a shuddering breath, Melissa glanced down at her wound, "It's still in there, isn't it? The shrapnel?"

Devon gave a grim nod. "I think the space suit was heavy enough to slow it down but not to stop it completely. It's all tangled up down there now, I can… well it's going to hurt."

"Okay." Melissa gave his hand a desperate squeeze, "Do it, just, please…"

She couldn't find the right words but somehow Devon met her gaze and his face softened in understanding. Melissa took a deep breath and braced herself, but suddenly Devon's eyes shifted out the cockpit window with a bemused look. "That's weird."

"What's weird?" She turned to see, and suddenly there was a jerk at her side. Her wound lit up in searing pain, she screamed, and her eyes defocused until the whole world was little more than an agonizing haze.

The world finally came back into focus as the pain began to fade. Melissa wasn't sure how long it had been, but it seemed the worst was over. Her side still burned, but nowhere near as bad as before. She had been dimly aware of Devon sticking a patch over the hole in her inner suit, and now he was firmly wrapping strips of gauze around her midriff. "That was a dirty trick, Devon," she muttered with a hurt frown.

"You prefer the alternative?"

Melissa didn't, but that didn't stop her from glowering at him as he finished with her bandages.

"Well, that's the best I can do." Devon finally rolled her heavy compression shirt back down over the gash. "I guess we'll have to hope it holds until we get back to Medea."

"Speaking of which, what exactly is your plan?" Melissa finally took an interest in the world beyond their cramped space-ship. They had been coasting out of Medea for several minutes now, and the station was likely some distance behind. Through the heavy, composite-glass cockpit, she could see more shuttles ferrying troops onto Medea from the small dot in the distance that marked the Chinese freighter. Although, how were they supposed to take on a cruiser like that with nothing more than an unarmed jump-ship? Melissa had no idea.

"Well, you're not going to like it," Devon began. "Basically, we do what you said, get drunk and crash the ship, except we don't have any alcohol, so we'll just ram the Chinese instead."

Her mouth dropped open in astonishment. "That ... is the stupidest plan I've ever heard."

Devon massaged his forehead as he explained. "Yes and no. The fact is, we need a weapon, right? Most weapons in space are just kinetic projectiles, essentially things moving really fast. If you think about it, this shuttle is just a very large missile. Plus it's loaded up with rocket fuel and oxidizer, so let's use it. If we boost it up fast enough, it should tear through that freighter like a cannonball."

"Did you forget that we're *on* the shuttle?"

"That's the cool part," Devon supplied cheerfully, "we can just jump out the back."

"Have you gone insane?"

"Possibly," as he spoke Devon absentmindedly used the null g to spin himself upside down, tilting his head to one side as though he suddenly had a different view of her from that perspective. "Look, Melissa, I know this isn't a very appealing plan, but it is the best option we have at the moment. You want to stop the Chinese? This is how we do it."

With a huff of displeasure, the girl crossed her arms. This was verifiably idiotic. How could any thinking person want to jump out of a moving space-ship, and yet there was Devon, hanging upside down in midair with his overconfident grin… or was it a frown? Melissa wrinkled her nose in distaste. How was she supposed to talk to someone acting like a zero g monkey?

Pushing herself out of her seat, the girl nudged herself into the same upside-down orientation as Devon, taking special care not to jerk around and make the slash in her side worse. At least now she could look him in the face. "Devon, how are we supposed to get back to Medea then? We are literally out in the middle of nowhere."

"Not exactly." Devon flipped himself back upright and glided over to his seat where he brought up a map on the shuttle HUD. "We're currently two hundred and thirty-seven meters from Medea and drifting away from the station at .70 meters per second. If we don't wait too long, I can set the autopilot on a collision course with the Chinese. It'll probably get angry at me, but it should work. Then, we jump out the rear door and coast back to Medea."

Devon pushed out of his chair and launched himself towards the rear of the craft, where he dug around in a supply locker for a minute. "We'll be needing these." He reappeared holding four fresh life support packs, two of which he gently tossed at her. "Swap out your old one, might as well start with a fresh pack, then strap the second one around front."

"Okay," Melissa sighed, "it's great that you're trying, but we can't switch out life support packs in space. I'm pretty sure we would die."

"Melissa, you don't get it. These aren't to switch out. We're going to use the second backpack as a thruster pack. One keeps us alive and the second provides reaction mass. Don't worry, it'll work."

"Devon, you realize if you're wrong–"

"If I'm wrong then we die together, and you can have the satisfaction of saying *I told you so*" he remarked calmly. "But I'm not. I know this sounds scary but I'm telling you, we can do this. Besides, it isn't like we have any other choices. We can't just fly the ship back to the dock, and we have to stop the Chinese somehow."

"Devon, if this doesn't work, I'm going to… to…"

"Kill me?" he smirked. "Good luck with that. Now come on, every second we're getting further away from Medea, so get ready to jump and I'll get the autopilot set up."

Devon was right about the ship getting angry with him. Almost every time he pressed a button, the HUD popped up yet another safety warning. There was an impressive variety, 'Warning: Calculated burn exceeding safety margin!' 'Warning: You are on a collision course!' 'Warning: Retrograde burn required for intercept!' Apparently, the ship thought his plan was dumb too.

Melissa tried not to linger on it. She busied herself unplugging her old life support pack from the panel on her stomach and latching on the new one. She tweaked open the air valve, waiting to feel the cool breeze near her face to confirm she'd hooked it up right. By the time she finished, Devon seemed to have everything set up and after letting the ship's computer do a quick simulation run, he turned to her. "I think we're good."

Melissa looked him right in the eye. "You're sure this is going to work?"

Devon opened his mouth to speak, but for a moment nothing came out, and she glimpsed the fear lurking in his own eyes. "I…

it should work. If it's any consolation, I'm stepping off the ship with you."

That wasn't much consolation at all, but even so, Melissa flipped shut her helmet visor and the little control patch on her wrist flashed a 'Overpressure Test' option. For a few seconds there was a building pressure around her face, as the suit did a quick check for leaks, before finally the pressure normalized, and the control patch flashed green. Next to her, Devon was just plugging in his own pack, and after a few quick tests, he looped the second backpack around his front and gave her a tentative thumbs up. "We're good to go. Ready?"

Melissa gave a small, terrified nod, watching as he tapped a few last buttons and the rear hatch slid open. For maybe a quarter second, she could hear the rush of venting air then... nothing.

"Okay," Devon explained over the radio, as he kicked off and floated himself towards the rear of the shuttle, "we have sixty seconds until the engines fire, so we need to get to the back of the ship and jump." He caught himself on one of the rails towards the rear and Melissa repeated the maneuver to catch up with him a few seconds later.

"Stand here and be sure to jump straight up." Devon crouched down on the boarding ramp with one hand still on the rail.

Melissa found it was actually a difficult spot to get into. The null gravity made it feel a lot like trying to move around underwater where her arms had to do most of the work. Finally wiggling into position, she looked back towards the slowly spinning Medea Station, now seeming very small in the distance. "Ummm, Devon..." she suddenly had a worrying thought, "shouldn't we jump *back*, not *up*?"

"Yes, but the engines fire backwards, and I have no intention of getting cooked to a cinder when they go off in thirty seconds," he explained. "Now, go in 3... 2... 1... jump!"

Melissa took a terrified breath and kicked off. She launched out into the empty nothingness of space. Medea loomed far in front as their shuttle slowly fell away beneath. And off to her right the Earth was shrouded in a fading gloom as the first hints of light peeked around the edge of the planet.

Chapter 25
The Light of Dawn

Bryan Hale leaned out of cover and fired a few quick bursts down the concourse towards the advancing Chinese soldiers. One of them went down with a wound to the hip, but there were just too many to stop.

Crouching behind the wall he had been using as cover, the Lieutenant Colonel shook his head. Ever since the first elevator had slid open and a wave of Chinese marines had poured out, things had rapidly gone from bad, to worse, to absolutely awful. To start, there were simply too many civilians on Medea. Many of the servicemen who should have been holding back the red tide were instead off herding panicked civies back to their quarters, trying to keep them calm as the station came apart around them. On top of that, there flat-out wasn't enough ammo on the station, and most of the servicemen on Medea hadn't done target practice in at least a month. That been a perennial grip across the Space Force. Ammunition was heavy and there wasn't the budget to ferry large amounts up into space. Besides it wasn't as though there was room for a shooting range anyway.

Just to cap it all off, the rotating station was throwing off everyone's aim, not much, but enough to scramble all his instincts and make him overcorrect.

Overhead a quadcopter buzzed and he snapped up his aim, pulling the trigger for his pulse emitter and sending the drone tumbling onto the concourse. Meanwhile, off to the left, two more Chinese soldiers pushed forward. Colonel Hale aimed for the chest and fired. This time he landed a square hit on the front-runner and the rest of his squad managed to finish off the other with sheer volume of fire. He should have been please, but he couldn't escape a looming dread, knowing there would just be more soldiers to follow. It was like fighting a hydra, kill one and two more popped up to take his place.

Given the size of the Chinese freighter lurking out there, they could have crammed a thousand soldiers – a whole battalion – onboard. Sure, the freighter's life support systems would give out… eventually. But they didn't have *eventually*. At this rate they had hours, at most, until Medea fell.

They were helpless to stop it too. Normally they could have blown the reactor core when the station was truly lost, a final act of defiance, but with so many civilians onboard that was no longer an option. It probably explained why the Chinese had attacked when they had. Frankly, if it came to that, which it very quickly was, Bryan wasn't entirely sure what he would do. Personally, he'd made his peace with dying. It came with the job. But with Julia and Melissa onboard, he couldn't just stand by if Perry tried to turn the station into nuclear slag. The thought set his mind to worrying for a moment. What on earth was going on with Melissa? He kept telling himself that there was no way she was involved in all this but… that had been her voice on the warning video, he was sure. So what was going on?

A long burst of gunfire shattered his thoughts, and leaning back out of cover, he saw more soldiers pouring forward. A grenade arced overhead, and one of his men went down to the suppressive fire. Bryan Hale did the only thing he could, he fired back until his magazine ran dry, then slammed in another and kept shooting.

***

Devon couldn't help but feel a little nervous as they kicked off into the void. He tried not to let it show though. Melissa already seemed terrified enough for the both of them. And he… he believed his plan would work.

While Melissa had been busy getting herself blown up, he had been puzzling over exactly how much compressed air they needed to get home. Devon didn't know the exact math, but their air tanks were pretty highly pressurized. They only needed 2-3 meters per second of velocity change to get back to Medea and there were at least 4 or 5 pounds of gas in each that would come out at the speed of sound, so about 350 meters per second. That felt doable… hopefully.

Glancing to the side, he saw Melissa drifting a touch further away but still close. He'd been afraid the jump might separate them, but after accounting for everything, it appeared their strength to weight ratios were pretty similar. Meanwhile, maybe forty or fifty feet below, he saw the shuttle engines suddenly flare up like a miniature star against the black void. For a quarter second it seemed like the shuttle wasn't moving at all, a blazing feather suspended in the breeze. But then it rapidly began to lurch forwards. In a few seconds the craft pulled away beneath them, rocketing off into the blackness as its computer made a beeline for the Chinese freighter.

"So, what now?" Melissa's frightened voice interrupted Devon's satisfaction at seeing his plan kick into motion.

"The extra air tanks," he explained, fumbling around in his belt until he pulled out what looked like a laser pointer. "Basically, point the nozzle opposite to the direction you want to go, open up the choke a little bit and it acts like a simple thruster. Just don't get too eager, we only have one shot at this, so we need to be careful. I also grabbed this," he waved the laser pointer. "It's a rangefinder and…" Shining it back towards Medea, he waited a few seconds until it flashed a distance reading of 425 meters. "We can use it to make sure we're going in the right direction."

"And what if we get separated?"

"Just don't panic and overreact," Devon cautioned. "If we start to drift apart, say so. We'll both close our tanks and take a minute to work out how to get back together. Sound good?"

"Not really." Devon couldn't see the frown that he suspected was written on Melissa's face, but he could see the way she shook her head. "It's not like we have a choice now."

Even in space it was possible to turn around, although it took Devon a few seconds to sort out how. He had to swivel his waist, kind of like he was using a hula hoop, and in doing so his whole body would start spinning. The nice part was, as soon as he stopped moving, his rotation would stop too. In short order he was facing away from Medea, with the nozzle to his spare air tank pointed in what he hoped was the correct direction.

"So, for our first thrust, hold the nozzle near your center of mass, around your waist. Point it straight ahead and up, then open the regulator valve a half turn. I'll count to five, and then close it again. Then I'll see if we're heading in the right direction."

He gave Melissa a few seconds to turn herself around, hoping that the motion wasn't too painful for her. "Ready?"

"I guess," Melissa sounded nervous, even over the radio. "Let's do this."

"Valves open in 3… 2… 1… open."

Keeping a tight hold on the air hose, Devon tweaked the regulator open and was rewarded with a stream of white gas puffing away into the void. He could definitely feel it pushing on him too, not very hard, but enough to know his plan was working. He counted aloud to five over the comm, then they both shut off the tanks. Thankfully, the air pressure hadn't changed too much, so they should have plenty more boosts like that available. Wiggling around, Devon took a new range reading, '469 meters.' Hmmm that wasn't great, but the number did seem to be going up much slower this time.

They were about to repeat the process when a flash of light in front of them momentarily bloomed so bright Devon had to cover his eyes. Only for a second though, then it faded like a dying star. When Devon lowered his hand there were just a few far away twinkles of light, secondary explosions that marked what had once been the Chinese freighter. Well, at least that part of his plan had worked. Now they just needed to get home.

***

Kristina knew she was doing something right. The Chinese were starting to panic, just like they had at Irkutsk. After Russia had stopped accepting the worthless Yuan as payment for raw materials at the end of the last war, the Chinese had swept north to take what they needed by force. Kristina still recalled just how confident their recon units had been, strolling into town like they expected her people to just roll over and give them whatever they wanted. That had lasted for… about five minutes.

She could still remember it vividly. One moment it was quiet, except for the far-off rumble of APCs. The next there was the roar as their artillery began a rolling bombardment on the edge of town, then from overhead came the buzz of drone swarms, the black dots tumbling out of the sky, one by one, swatted by the invisible beams of the laser air defense batteries.

At the time she'd been paired up with a bubbly girl named Anya, and between them, they had managed to rack up something like nine kills in the first few days. Afterwards, the Chinese had gotten a bit more circumspect and lost a lot of their 'middle kingdom' bravado. They were doing that now too. At first, they had just wastefully charged at her… which was fine. If they had a death wish, she was happy to oblige them.

Now though, she was dealing with more measured attacks. That was also fine, it meant she could be as aggressive as she wanted. Pulling the pin on yet another grenade, she took a deep breath and lobbed it down the hall, tensing as the detonation roared back a few seconds later. Hopefully that would keep them back for a little while. Jogging off down the hall, Kristina found the next corner, raised her rifle and waited for the inevitable counter grenade, from the Chinese. She had been having fun like this for a while, stinging them whenever they tried to push forward, then gently giving ground. It didn't really matter, the whole station was a circle after all. They could chase her forever for all she cared.

Sure enough, after about ten seconds a counter grenade tumbled forward where she'd been standing and detonated to no effect. She was expecting them to follow right behind, but the

Chinese stayed put and a few seconds later another grenade blast shook the hall. So, they were trying to be clever, were they? Well bring it on. She leaned out and as the first soldier snapped around the corner, Kristina fired and dropped him like a rag doll. Obviously, the rest of the squad was right behind so she pulled the pin on… wait, was that her last grenade? Regardless, she sent it spinning down the hall. When she checked her bag, she found it mostly devoid of weaponry except for a single assault rifle magazine and a few dozen pistol rounds. Hmmm, maybe that meant it was time for a tactical withdrawal, at least until she could rearm.

Down the hall her grenade went off with a thunderous boom, but Kristina was already shifting away from the fight. She ducked into a side hall and was trying to decide what to do next when Devon and Melissa's voices cut into her helmet radio.

"Okay, point it down a little," Devon was explaining, "just like that, then give it a quarter turn for about two seconds. That should get us back together for the final approach."

"You sure?" Melissa asked, her tone hesitant. "I think we may be going a little fast."

"Not really, we should be fine, so long as we're lined up pretty well."

"Okay," Melissa gave an audible sigh, "here goes."

Sliding into a defensible spot for a moment's pause, Kristina flicked on the microphone in her own helmet. "Sounds like you two are having fun."

If Melissa could have jumped in outer space, she would have when Kristina's voice sounded in her ear. As it was, she nearly lost her hold on the air hose she was using to boost herself a little closer to Devon. For a second there was an awkward pause. Finally, Devon managed, "Morning, Kristina."

That part was actually true. It might be nine-thirty in the evening on Medea station, and they both might have been utterly exhausted, but looking down, Devon and Melissa were currently zipping over the Indian Ocean nearly to Australia, and down there it was morning. The sun had just peeked out from behind the planet a few minutes ago, and despite how reassuring it had been at first to feel the soft tendrils of light warming her, that was getting old really quick.

Honestly, Melissa had concluded that just about everything to do with space was uncomfortable. The rooms were cramped, the air was stale, the water was just recycled– well she tried not to even think about that. Outside was just as bad. It was all the worst parts of the Arctic and the Sahara Desert rolled into one. Her skin was bone dry, and froze whenever she sweated, which was apparently all the time, because somehow she was burning up inside. On top of which, she was desperately thirsty, probably because she was sweating so much. Then, of course, the sun didn't help things either. It was blindingly bright, and beat down with the heat of… well, the heat of the sun. Apparently that was worse in space too, even if her jacket seemed to take the brunt of it. So now, she was dealing with the most unpleasant sensation of half her body being furiously heated by a nuclear-powered fireball, while the other half froze to death as she sweated even more.

At least it was almost over. After twenty minutes of floating in the void, the Medea shuttle bay loomed large in front of the two. She wouldn't admit it aloud, but Devon's plan had actually worked pretty well. If anything, it was easier than she had expected. All she would do was jet her air tank for a few seconds, then wait a minute while Devon took distance readings and talked about how fascinating space was. Then they would drift apart, one of them would make a correction thrust… and wait some more. It was a lot like being in the Space Force she suspected, complete with a bunch of people telling her exactly what to do.

"Might I ask where you two have been hiding out?" For some reason, Kristina sounded amused of all things.

"We're outside."

"Oh, well that's… creative. Do I want to know what you've been up to?"

"We rammed the Chinese," Devon declared proudly. "Sent their ship up like a fusion powered bonfire."

There was a pause on the other end. "Hmm, gutsy... stupid, but gutsy, I like it. Does that mean I need to find a shuttle of my own and go pick you two up?"

"Actually, we're almost back. We'll be in the shuttle bay in a minute or so."

In truth it was a lot sooner than that. While Devon had been talking, they had coasted on into the hangar bay, and all of a sudden, the back wall got *very* close *very* fast. One meter per second didn't sound fast when you were a half kilometer away, but now that there was a wall in front of them, it was fast enough to make Melissa twist open her air canister to get one last bit of thrust and slow down.

It *mostly* worked. Instead of crashing into the back wall, she just bumped up against it and grabbed at a handhold before she could float away. They were pretty much in the center of the shuttle bay, and along the back wall, ladder rungs traced downwards from the center to the hangar floor a hundred feet below. It was still a bit of a climb, but just holding onto something firm after floating back for what felt like an eternity was enough to make Melissa breathe a sigh of relief.

Next to her, Devon yelped in pain as he hit the wall a bit faster than he should have. "Told you to slow down," she smirked.

"Everything okay out there?"

"We're fine," Melissa answered, feeling the slight pull of spin gravity returning as she pulled herself down the ladder towards the hangar below. "Except for Devon, his pride is a bit bruised I think."

"Well, you two hang tight out there," Kristina cautioned, "there's a lot of fireworks still going on in here. It might be safer to stay outside until the Chinese decide to evacuate."

"Any luck knocking off Sophie?"

"Unfortunately, no. I nearly had a shot, but someone stepped in front of her. A real bummer. Try not to get in too much trouble out there. I'll be around in a little while."

Melissa was tempted to ask what that meant. Kristina made it sound like she would be dropping in for a friendly visit. But whatever, if Kristina wanted them to bunker down and stay safe, they could definitely do that for a change.

Flicking off the microphone in her helmet, Kristina paused for a second as she tried to work out what to do next. She probably needed to make sure that Curls and her boyfriend didn't get into trouble, or at least any more than they already had. She couldn't suppress an amused grin – ramming the Chinese, whose idea had that been?

Regardless, with the hallway clear of soldiers, Kristina made a beeline for the nearest airlock. When she finally got there, she peeked out to see Devon and Melissa crawling down the back wall. For a second she couldn't quite believe her eyes. She had assumed that they had taken two ships, but from the look of things, those two geniuses had actually floated back to Medea. That was… idiotic didn't even begin to describe it. It was a genuine wonder they were still alive. Flicking down her helmet face piece, Kristina checked her pressure seal and air gauge before cycling the airlock that led out into the hangar bay.

Devon and Melissa were just getting to the bottom of the ladder when she strolled up behind them with a loud, "Hello, Curls."

Kristina wasn't normally the sort for practical jokes, but the way a startled Melissa lost her hold on the rungs and slow motion tumbled the last meter to the floor was enough to make her burst into laughter. She had the good sense to mute her mic though, and in the soundless void of space, Melissa was none the wiser when she scrambled to her feet.

"Kristina, you're uhhh… here."

"How observant, Curls."

"I thought we weren't using that name anymore," Melissa scowled.

"Well, after discovering you two just floated your way home, I'm reconsidering." Kristina shook her head, "I suppose it worked out alright. So long as I don't have to break any bad news to your parents, we can stick with Melissa… for now."

Devon drifted down the last few feet and landed next to them. "So, what's the status inside? Have we won?"

"Effectively, yes, but I'm not sure the Chinese realize that yet. Until then they're still dangerous."

Even as she spoke, one of the Chinese shuttles detached from the section of the bay far overhead, firing off white thruster bursts to slide into the center of the hangar before boosting away into the blackness of space.

"I wonder where they think they're going?" Kristina mused.

"They might be hoping to land back on Earth," Devon chimed in. "I believe the Pacific is coming up in a few minutes."

"Not in that thing they aren't." Kristina shook her head, "That's an orbital transfer shuttle, no heat shield. If they try and re-enter the atmosphere, they'll end up incinerated."

Kristina glanced around for a minute before pointing to a shuttle closer by with a more airplane-like design. "That one, on the other hand…"

As she spoke, several people appeared in the transparent plastic tube that connected the shuttle to Medea station, among them, Sophie Tannenhill.

Kristina's rifle popped up to her shoulder and there were a few noiseless puffs of smoke as she fired. "*Suka,*" she cursed at seeing Sophie vanish into the shuttle. "Of course that witch would choose the right sort of ship."

"Melissa, Devon, do either of you have any grenades?"

"I'm out," Melissa shook her head. "But we can't just let Sophie get away."

Kristina grimaced, and in a fury fired a few desultory rounds at the shuttle. "Well, unless you have a plan–"

"Wait, do you still have that C-4B?" Devon asked out of the blue.

"Yes, but without a detonator cap it won't do any good."

"Is there some other way to set it off?"

"Yes, but you'd basically need an explosion to trigger it. Not sure where you'd find one of those around here."

Devon grinned, "You think the combustion chamber of a rocket engine would work?"

Kristina cocked her head to one side with a calculating look, then reached into her bag and tossed him the lump of C-4B she had been holding onto. "Have at it, kid. I'll cover you."

Fortunately, she didn't need to worry about anyone shooting at Devon. Her first shots had punctured the plastic tube and with the air quickly venting into space, she saw the shuttle door slide closed. It was probably Sophie and a bunch of PRC officers trying to escape, and of course they wouldn't be waiting for anyone as lowly as their own foot soldiers. It took Devon less than a minute to sprint across to the shuttle, jam the hunk of C-4B into the rocket nozzle on the starboard engine, then jog back. He was returning just as the control thrusters on the shuttle fired and boosted it up into the center of the launch bay.

Sophie was in such a hurry that she didn't even wait for the ship to stabilize before firing the long monopropellant thruster burst to slide her vessel out into space. For a minute she coasted to a safe distance, all three watching, waiting to see what happened next. With her secondary thrusters accelerating her away from Medea, Sophie finally tried to fire up the main rocket engines. The left one worked fine, but the right one puttered for a quarter second. Suddenly it bloomed into a raging fireball that consumed half the ship as a mass of hydrazine and oxidizer went up in a single brilliant inferno.

Kristina shielded her eyes from the flare. When she looked back, what was left of Sophie's ship was spinning an eternal cartwheel as it tumbled away from Medea with a gaping hole in its side. "Well, I think that did it," she declared cheerfully. "Come on you two, let's get back inside."

Chapter 26
Until We Meet Again

Melissa had never been claustrophobic. Even so, she couldn't wait to pull off her helmet the instant the airlock cycled open. Letting her messy brown locks spill out above her shoulders, Melissa took a deep breath. The air was tinged with the acrid scent of spent explosives and gunpowder, but not having to breathe through a hose on her back more than compensated.

Flipping up her helmet visor, Kristina's gaze fell to the red patch of dried blood soaked into the uniform at her side. "Are you hurt?"

"I'll manage," Melissa shrugged. "Nothing a doctor can't fix… I hope."

"Well then," Kristina smiled, "the Chinese are on the run, you two are relatively unharmed. I'd say my work here is done. Now, it's off to my dacha in Crimea I think."

"Wait, what?" Devon frowned. "You're leaving… after all this?"

"*Mili*, we might have just saved Medea Station, but I still work for a different government than yours. Perry might be happy to not have the Chinese in charge, but I assure you, he will definitely *not* be happy to find out who exactly I am either. Best I vanish before things get any more exciting around here. In the meantime, you two should probably bunker down until the Space Force roots out the last of the *Kitaiski soldati* up here."

"And what are we supposed to say when they find us?" Melissa bit her lip and nervously glanced at the unmistakable gash in her side. "Like... how do we explain this?"

Kristina's expression softened a little at her consternation. "Well, to be honest, you two are both about to be grounded forever." She dug an old fashioned notepad and pencil out of her bag as she continued, "As far as getting arrested and thrown in jail though, I might be able to help with that." She scribbled a quick note before ripping it off, folding it in half and handing it to Melissa.

"Last I heard there was a fellow up on Medea named Evan Banks." Just the name brought a scowl to Melissa's face. "Ahhh, I see you've met him," Kristina grinned affectionately. "He's a wonderfully tactless fellow, but unlike myself, he actually *does* work for the CIA. We've had a few... encounters in the past, and if anyone can help you two out of this mess, he can. Tell him Kristina Androkova sent you."

Devon shuffled his feet uncomfortably. "We... might have already burned that bridge."

"Oh please," Kristina waved dismissively. "Have you learned nothing? In this game things change, always and forever. Banks will come around if handled properly. Just explain the situation and you should be fine."

"And what about everyone else?" Melissa asked.

"I suppose you can tell them whatever you want. Personally, I suggest the truth. They'll probably separate you two for interrogation, and frankly, the both of you are horrible liars. The best way to keep things straight is to be honest."

"Speaking of honesty," Kristina dug around in her purse for a second, pulling out two things, an old-fashioned paper coupon and a small electronic box with a simple screen and keyboard. She quickly typed in something on the box and pressed a big red button, eliciting a beep from the device.

"If anyone asks why my office is now a charred wreck that smells of rocket fuel, you can say I was redecorating. And," she grandly presented the coupon to Melissa, "this is for your dress."

"Huh?" Melissa stared at the slip of paper. "What do you mean?"

"I mean that every girl should have at least one nice thing, and since your last dress was ruined, this is for you. It's a coupon for a free outfit, anything in my store you want, no questions asked. I always keep a few on me if I need to bribe someone, but in your case, I think you well and truly earned it."

Kristina stepped back and smiled at the two. "Now, if you'll both excuse me, I'm going to have to get creative to find a reentry window for somewhere in Siberia on the next orbital pass."

"Wait," Melissa asked at the last second, "are we ever going to see you again?"

"Well, if you're ever in Moscow you can look me up on Codex. I'll give you a tour if I'm in town. Otherwise," Kristina shrugged, "we'll see. Mars is a long way out there, but who knows? Either way, it was a pleasure working with you two." She smiled, "*Do-svidaniya malyshi.*"

Melissa watched as Kristina turned and strode off toward the small shuttle where they'd come back inside. The airlock door slid shut behind the woman, and in a few moments, Kristina had undocked and was boosting her way off Medea Station. Melissa watched until Kristina's shuttle broke right and vanished from sight. All that remained in view was the exhaust plume of a retreating Chinese shuttle.

"So... what do we do now?" Devon finally asked. "Find an out-of-the-way spot and wait for the Space Force to come to the rescue?"

They were currently at the top of a stairway leading down into the rest of the hangar bay, with only a steel and plexiglass airlock to separate them from the outside. It made for an incredible view of a slowly rotating planet Earth cruising by beneath. Wandering over to the wall, Melissa slid down and took a seat with her back to it. She cast a quick glance back towards stairs but didn't see or hear any other soldiers coming. With the shuttle on this pad gone, there wasn't really any reason. "I suppose if we're waiting for my dad to show up and kill us, this is as good a spot as any."

"You mean kill *me.*"

"No, I mean *us*. Trust me, he will not be pleased." She stared at the ground for a moment. "What about your parents? How do you think they'll take all this?"

"They probably haven't noticed I'm gone," Devon remarked deadpan, sliding down next to her. "They'll manage."

Melissa crinkled her nose in disapproval. "You don't have to be like that, you know."

"Like what?"

"Pretending that no one cares. I know your sister does for one, and your parents wouldn't have gone through the hoops to take you two to Mars if they didn't either."

For a long moment Devon didn't respond. "Maybe," he finally shrugged. His eyes drifted to the note Kristina had handed her. "What does that say?"

"No idea." She flipped it back and forth between her fingers in obvious curiosity. "I suppose we ought to read it, just to make sure she isn't going to antagonize Banks even more than we already have."

Melissa flipped open the note, and Devon leaned in to get a look:

Dear Teddy Bear,

I hope you still think of me now and again. I'm sending these two little ones your way, so don't be too hard on them. They were just in the wrong place at the wrong time, and they've done their best to save Medea, so do play nice. I'll drop by next time I'm around. Maybe sooner than you think.

Miss you always,
Your Little Tsarina

For a minute, Melissa stared at the letter in wide-eyed surprise.

"That's... kind of weird," Devon finally spoke for the both of them.

She folded up the note and slid it into her pocket with a skeptical frown. "Well, it's… something."

She looked up as more roars of automatic weapons echoed in the hanger. Except this time, she heard a distinctively different cadence to the gunfire. Those weren't Chinese rifles. Instead of the slower, more spaced-out whip-cracks from earlier, these shots came sharper and faster so the reports almost blurred together.

"Sounds like the Space Force is finally coming," Melissa observed, taking a worried breath. "What do you want to tell them?"   Devon shrugged, "The truth, I guess. Just… let's not mention Evie or that French friend of yours. No point getting them involved."

Melissa gave a tiny nod and took Devon's hand in hers. For a moment they both sat there, hand in hand as the gunfire marched ever closer. Finally, Melissa's anxious eyes flickered across to him. "Devon, if we ummm… if we don't get to see each other again, I just wanted to say thank you, for everything."

That finally brought a smile to his face. "You too, Melissa." He gave her hand a reassuring squeeze.

Nothing had changed, but somehow Melissa felt her heart lighten a little. Out in the hall, a jumble of voices speaking in English for a change. She caught footsteps then someone barking out a sharp command to push forwards.

"Well, here goes." She took a deep breath, "Help! We're up here!"

There were more shouts from nearby, and a moment later three servicemen armed with carbines stormed up the stairs. Had the situation not been so serious, Melissa might have laughed at the way their mouths fell open upon finding two teenagers, both in space suits, one with an obvious wound in her side, calmly lounging around in a war zone.

"Who…?"

"I'm Melissa Hale and this is Devon Northrop," she explained. "My dad is Lieutenant Colonel Bryan Hale. Do you know if he's okay?"

None of the servicemen answered her directly. Instead, one of them shouted back down the stairs, "Captain we uhhh... you need to see this."

A minute later Melissa was explaining everything again, except this time to a captain, instead of a staff sergeant. "How did you two get up here?" he demanded.

"We took the ladder outside," Melissa shrugged. "Look, can you please just check to make sure my dad is okay?"

The captain glared at her but finally he pulled out a radio. "Can I get a copy from Lieutenant Colonel Bryan Hale?"

For a moment there was heart wrenching silence until, "This is Colonel Hale, what is it?"

Suddenly Melissa could breathe again. Her dad was okay. No matter what else happened, she still had that.

"Sir, I don't know how to say this, but we found a girl named Melissa. She says she's your daughter."

"Where are you?" her father snapped back.

Melissa winced. Dad didn't sound happy at all. She spent the next two minutes waiting for him to show up and dealing with a rapid-fire burst of questions from the captain. Every time she or Devon would try and answer, he would just hit them with a different one, so by the time her dad appeared, the captain still had absolutely no idea what was going on.

Finally, Melissa's dad strode up the stairs, and for an instant looked her straight in the eye. "Hi, daddy," Melissa bit her lip. She was expecting him to scream at her or shoot Devon or... something, but instead he just wrapped his arms around her so tight she almost couldn't breathe.

"Melissa, what happened?"

He finally let her go and Melissa could only stare shamefaced at the ground. "I... I need to tell you some things," she murmured, "but could we please talk somewhere that's not here."

To her dad's credit, he didn't try to probe for any more information. He didn't even ask about the obvious gash at her midriff. He just helped her to her feet, gestured for Devon to get up and turned to the captain. "I'll take these two downstairs to the infirmary. Finish securing the hangar."

With so many others badly injured from the fighting, Melissa and Devon were dead last on the list of people to get medical attention. When her dad brought them in, the doctor glanced at their bandages, then immediately passed them off to a harried nurse. She found two white-sheeted beds for them in the low priority wing of the infirmary, then hung around just long enough to enter their information in the hospital database. She handed them both green triage bracelets with a barcode, told them to stay put, then left.

With the nurse finally gone, her dad's severe gaze drifted between her and Devon. "I think the two of you have some explaining to do."

The way he looked at her nearly made Melissa burst into tears, not because dad seemed angry, but because she finally realized that she should have just admitted everything the prior evening. "I'm so sorry, Dad," she said in an ashamed voice. "Devon and I… we got into really deep trouble with a Russian spy, and things just kept getting more complicated." As she spoke the words began to tumble out of their own accord. "I was going to tell you tonight, but Sophie kidnapped us, and tortured Devon, and she was going to kill everyone. Then the Chinese attacked and, and…" Her voice broke down in sobs of relief, and shame, and exhaustion, and terror. All of it bottled up inside and swirled into an overwhelming emotion that she couldn't describe and couldn't stop as it welled in her breast. "I'm so sorry."

She had been expecting a lecture from her father, but instead Dad wrapped his arm around her shoulder to pull her close in a reassuring embrace. "It's okay, it's over now."

For some reason that just made Melissa cry even more.

Chapter 27
The Endless Answers

When Melissa's eyes flickered open on Wednesday morning, she was lying beneath a light cotton sheet. She was still wearing her blood drenched space suit, and still hadn't had a doctor look at the impromptu bandage around her waist. She felt a lot better though. Sure, every muscle in her body was punishingly stiff, and there was a persistent ache where the shrapnel had hit her. But for once no one was trying to kill her, and there weren't any secrets to keep.

Rolling her head a little to one side, she saw her parents fast asleep in two chairs next to her bed. Farther past them, two people she vaguely recognized from the shuttle ride up as Devon's parents were sleeping beside his.

The whole of last night was a bit of a blur. By the time her dad had gotten them to the infirmary, it had been at least ten, and when she had broken down into tears trying to explain everything, he had finally just told her and Devon to get some sleep. She could recall collapsing on the bed, thinking just how wonderfully soft her pillow was and how much she could use a shower. She must have dozed off, because after that her memory was blank.

Glancing across the room towards the clock, she saw it was a little past six in the morning. Unlike the chaos of the prior night, the infirmary was largely quiet. She was about to lay back and catch another hour of sleep except for… footsteps, coming closer. Probably what had roused her. She watched a second, then her eyes widened as Evan Banks strolled into view past the white partition curtain and paused at the end of her bed with a calculating half smile.

"Good morning, Melissa," he said quietly enough not to rouse anyone. "I was wondering when you were going to wake up."

"Banks," she managed a nod, "what brings you here?"

"Word gets around fast," the CIA man remarked. "It sounds like you and Devon here had an exciting evening. I expect Perry will be by sometime, but I confess my curiosity got the better of me. I wanted to come down and see if I was correct in my assumptions when we talked yesterday."

"If you're looking for a straight answer, you of all people should know you won't get one." Melissa dug into her pocket and pulled out Kristina's note. "This is the best I can do. A little Tsarina left it with me." She leaned up enough to hand him the slip of paper. "She said it might convince you to give us a hand. I expect we'll be needing all the help we can get when Perry shows up."

Banks glanced over the note, his smile almost imperceptibly widening as he read. Finally, he refolded the note and slid it into his pocket. "What was her last name? The little Tsarina who gave this to you?"

"Andrews."

"Her *real* last name?"

"Androkova," Melissa answered, "Kristina Androkova. I don't suppose you would mind telling me where you two met?"

"Harbin," Banks remarked half to himself. "I saved her life, and now from the sound of things, she might just have evened the score." As he spoke, his smile grew visibly softer and more sympathetic, like there really was emotion behind that arrogant veneer. It just required a special kind of woman to bring it out. "Anyway," Banks offered her a half nod, "it appears you have a recommendation from a woman who gives those out very rarely. I need to go make a few calls about this, but I'll see what I can do for you and your friend."

He took a few steps like he was leaving but paused for a second. "I do have one question though," he dug into his pocket and pulled out a silver necklace with an emerald pendant and butterfly charms on it. Melissa had only seen it for a moment down in the sewage plant, and it was gleaming clean now, but even so, it wasn't hard to recognize Evie's lost necklace. "They found it after the explosion down in water reclamation," he explained. "I was mostly curious who it belonged to, you or Devon's little sister. My bet was his sister."

"You would be correct." Melissa didn't bother trying to lie. "I'm sure she'll be ecstatic to get it back."

Banks regarded the little silver necklace for a moment, his finger brushing the jewel pendant. "Such a small stone," he murmured, right before tossing it into her lap, "and yet such big waves."

With a nod, Banks turned to leave. Once he was gone, Melissa scooped up the sterling silver necklace and dangled it in front of her eyes for a moment, before eventually laying it on the counter between her and Devon and nestling back down into her pillow. A small stone indeed.

It was good that Melissa had gotten a couple extra hours of sleep. When she woke up again it was almost eight, and with everyone else already awake, there was little hope of getting any sort of rest. A doctor had finally come around to check on them, and he was busy re-bandaging the deep gash on Devon's arm. Meanwhile, both their parents were crowded around, peppering him with waves of questions, while he had the defensive look of a deer surrounded by a pack of wolves.

It was enough to make Melissa almost pretend to go back to sleep, but before she could, her mom spotted her. "Melissa, you're awake."

"Morning, Mom." She managed a tepid smile.

"Sweetheart, we were so worried." Her mom's eyes drifted to the blood red splotch in the side of her space suit. "Your father said he found you up in the shuttle bay, hiding from the Chinese? What happened? How did you...?"

"I uhh..." she tried to think of a good way to explain what had happened but ended up just blurting out, "I took a frag grenade in the side."

"You did *what*?" Her father overheard and now he crowded around her too.

"When I was fighting the Chinese," she explained. "They got a lucky hit on me. The suit stopped another one. It could have been a lot worse."

Her mom looked like she was about to be faint at the thought, but her dad simply nodded in approval and let the matter drop. "And what exactly are you two doing wearing space suits?"

"We were in space."

"You mean actually *outside* Medea Station?" her mom's eyes went wide.

Melissa nodded, "Yeah, it kind of sucks actually. I think I prefer planet Earth."

"Melissa," her mom took a seat on the bed beside her, "how did all this start? Why are you suddenly fighting the Chinese and wandering around outside the station?"

"Devon and I... the night before last, when the bomb went off in sewage treatment, we ran into a Russian spy lady." She caught the surprise on her dad's face when she mentioned the explosion. "I'm sorry, I was going to say something, but I was afraid, and things just spiraled out of control from there."

"What's this about a Russian spy on my station?" someone interrupted. Her dad turned and Melissa saw Colonel Perry standing at the foot of her bed with a scowl. Behind him Banks was watching with an entertained spark in his eyes.

"When I told you to check into things, Colonel Hale, this wasn't exactly what I had in mind," Perry added. "Now, would someone here like to explain why the Chinese tried to invade my station last night? Or why everything seems to be exploding lately?"

Melissa gulped nervously, but behind the angry colonel, Banks gave her a quick wink. It wasn't much but it was enough to calm her nerves. "I can tell you some of it, sir," she said quietly. "It's a long story though."

It was, in fact, a very long story. Even tag-teaming their explanations, with all the pauses and questions, it took Melissa and Devon almost until lunch to explain everything. Colonel Perry didn't make things any easier, thanks to his habit of pacing and talking to himself. There was also a break when Perry realized that Valerie and Sophie's henchmen were still locked in a room in a maintenance alcove. He spent a few minutes dispatching people to scoop them up, then went back to pacing back and forth while they explained. By the time they were done, the doctor had patched them both up and told them they could leave so long as they came by for a checkup the next morning. Evie had even wandered in at one point and interrupted both of them with a flurry of hugs when she saw her necklace waiting for her… Right before realizing that she wasn't supposed to have lost it in the first place and abruptly pretending that nothing had happened.

Despite all that, they managed to cover most of the high points. Of course, there were some things they left out – Evie following them down to the sewage plant, Gabrielle, and a host of little private moments that neither wanted to share in front of their parents.

When they finished, Perry just nodded. He offered them both a small thank you for their efforts, told her dad to come talk with him later, then he just left. Melissa wasn't sure what to make of that, but from the look of pride on her father's face when they were done, it couldn't have been that bad.

Once Perry and Banks were finally gone, Melissa couldn't help but slump back down in her bed. Even after a good night's rest, all the questions had left her exhausted. She was still in her dusty, damaged space suit from the prior evening. But thankfully her mom picked that moment to grab her backpack form the corner and oven it to reveal a spare set of clothes.

"Would you like to change, sweetheart?" It was like Mom could read her mind. "There's a restroom right over there."

Melissa couldn't hide a sigh of relief at the chance to finally get back into normal clothes. Slipping out of bed, she winced, her whole body hurting when she moved. Yet compared to everything else, it felt almost trivial. Taking her backpack and wandering into the bathroom, Melissa found a modest, light blue t-shirt and a pair of leggings inside.

She spent a moment washing her face in the sink, then emptied out her pockets and paused as she pulled out the dog tag from the soldier she had murdered the prior night. She had tried not to think about it, she had even glossed over that part recounting her story earlier, but to have the metal tag in her hand brought all the emotions surging back.

She kept telling herself that Devon had been right, that it had been her life or his. It didn't help things though; it didn't make her feel like any less of a monster. In truth, when she looked in the mirror, she didn't really recognize the girl who looked back, the cold dangerous girl with a patch of blood on her side and an ocean of it on her hands. That wasn't supposed to be her. She went out with friends, had lunch, played games, did homework... but that wasn't the girl in the mirror, and if it wasn't then... who was she? Really?

Staring at the metal tag with its unreadable Chinese scrawl, Melissa finally opened her purse to drop it inside. She was stunned to find the pistol and ammunition still there.

Apparently, no one had bothered to check her bag. Melissa shook her head. Maybe her parents hadn't thought that a girl like her would...

Whatever the reason, there was no point giving it back now. If last night had taught her anything it was that weapons were life, as horrible as that sounded. Just another token of the new girl in the mirror, she thought with a grim sarcasm. She spent a moment rearranging the ammo magazines so they wouldn't rattle together too suspiciously, before dropping in the dog tag, zipping everything up and giving it an experimental shake.

With her pockets empty, Melissa finally got down to the main reason for going to the restroom, fresh clothes. In a moment she had stripped off her space suit, and despite her dour mood, she couldn't avoid a surge of exuberance when she slipped into a comfortable pair of dark leggings. It was a strange sensation. She had nearly forgotten how much the compression space suit was squeezing her, and to suddenly be in normal clothes was a tremendous relief. Her hair might be little more than a ragged mop, and there was still the persistent ache from the hole in her side, but she felt…better. Until she could find a shower, that was enough.

Wandering back outside with her bag looped across one shoulder, Melissa found Devon had also been busy swapping into new clothes. Their parents were standing around like they were eager to get out of the infirmary and put all of this behind them.

"Melissa," her mom caught her eye, "the Northrop's invited us to go get pizza with them. Does that sound okay? Or did you just want to go back to our room for a little while?"

"Pizza's fine," she nodded, and her eyes drifted despondently back towards the floor.

A moment later she felt her mom's arm around her shoulder. "Is everything alright?"

Honestly, it wasn't. She felt like a murderer, but apparently she had killed the right people, so no one cared. She was walking around with a gun in her purse, because how could she ever *not* be afraid again? The clothes were the same ones she had worn a hundred times before, but it felt like a different girl was wearing them. For a moment she tried to bottle it all up, but then the dam burst, and Melissa broke down into wordless sobs.

She felt her mom pull her close in a hug, "Shhh…it'll be okay."

Melissa glanced up through tear-stained eyes, "How?"

"Oh, Melissa," for some reason the question brought a soft, sympathetic smile to her mom's face, "I love you sweetheart. Your father may have a strange way of showing it, but he does too. God will always love you, and I think Devon over there may be set to join the club. I know it's been tough moving to Mars and having all this happen, but it will get better. I promise."

For a long moment Melissa stood there sobbing into her mom's shoulder. Finally though, it was like she ran out of tears. Maybe her mom was right, things would get better. Maybe, in a way, they already had. Melissa's eyes drifted up and she found her mom smiling back at her. "Are you hungry, sweetheart?"

Now that Melissa thought about it, the last time she had eaten was her lunch with Devon at Seoul Express the prior day. That had been almost twenty-four hours earlier, and the moment the possibility of food crossed her mind, her stomach grumbled in agreement. The thought of eating brought a hint of a smile to the girl's face. "That does sound pretty good."

***

It was a little past four in the afternoon when Melissa found herself standing in the hall outside KA Dresses and Accessories, idly flipping Kristina's coupon for a free dress between her fingers. The store didn't look like it was in great shape. The coffee shop was still open, with a few patrons sipping their drinks. But the dress shop was empty, the display windows shattered from the fighting the prior night and a few soldiers with weapons were now posted at the entrance. A cashier and a few other women hung around near the register, chatting aimlessly but there didn't seem to be many customers. Clearly the battle combined with Kristina's abrupt departure had thrown things into chaos. The fact that Perry had probably tried to raid her self-destructed office earlier likely hadn't helped.

After realizing what she had been up to the last few days, her parents hadn't wanted to let her out of the room alone. Melissa had been forced to make a whole host of promises not to get in trouble before they would even open the door. In a way it was kind of like being grounded, except she knew her parents weren't angry, just worried.

That wasn't what had Melissa fidgeting nervously with Kristina's slip of paper though. She had a very different question on her mind. Should she even accept the free dress at all?

She knew it sounded silly. There were no strings attached to this dress, just Kristina's way of saying thank you. But every time she tried to take a step towards the store, she couldn't help but think back to the prior evening. She was stuck in that moment, when she'd realized just how much Kristina's first dress had really cost and promised herself that she would never accept another one.

She tried to make herself take that first step, but some part of her absolutely wouldn't. In a way, it made sense. She didn't want to open her closet every morning to a reminder of nearly being killed a half dozen times and almost having her memory wiped. Still, the other part of her knew that Kristina really had intended it as a gift. Despite their disagreements, Melissa felt bad about just tossing away something like that.

She ran through the arguments in her head, and yet all she found was indecision. And she needed to decide soon. The attack by the Chinese had delayed their departure to the Persephone, but every day they waited complicated the transfer orbit to Mars. Despite the attack, her family would be departing for the colony ship midday tomorrow. Then her chance to use Kristina's gift would be well and truly gone, forever.

As Melissa's gaze drifted across the storefront like she was hoping to see an answer there, a thought suddenly popped into her head. Why not let somebody else enjoy it? Just because she didn't feel comfortable in another one of Kristina's dresses didn't mean that there weren't a dozen other girls on the station who wouldn't jump at the opportunity. A slow smile spread across her face at the thought. She knew exactly who to give it too.

Five minutes later, Melissa was standing outside a grey steel door. After a moment's indecision, she knocked on the cool metal.

"*Une seconde,*" a boy's voice echoed from inside. A moment later the door swung open to reveal a handsome young boy about her own age. "Hi there," he smiled and nodded to her with a charming French accent. "Can I help you, *mademoiselle*?"

"Is Gabrielle here?"

"Melissa?" She heard Gabrielle's voice, and a moment later the French girl appeared in the doorway with a big smile. Gabrielle did her weird, pretend kissing on the cheek routine, and finally she pulled back. "You are okay? *Non*?"

"I'm good," Melissa reassured her. "What about you? The attack didn't cause any problems?"

She shook her head. "There was fighting downstairs I think, but nothing up here. What about your father? You said he was in the military? He is okay?"

"He's fine," Melissa glanced at the boy. "Is this...?"

"This is Martin, *mon frère*," Gabrielle introduced them.

"A pleasure," the boy flashed her a roguish smile.

"So," Gabrielle went back to mostly ignoring her brother, "what brings you here?"

"Well," Melissa shuffled her feet, "I was wondering if you wanted to go dress shopping with me?"

Gabrielle's eyes lit up at the offer, but she cocked her head to one side. "You mean to actually shop for dresses, or do you have more *compliqués plans*?"

"Just dresses this time," Melissa assured her. "There's sort of a sale going on at the moment."

Gabrielle regarded her closely, "And your Russian friend? She is…"

"She's not really around," Melissa explained. "Besides which, we kissed and made up…metaphorically. Like I said, just old-fashioned dress shopping."

"Hmmm," Gabrielle still had a suspicious but excited gleam in her eyes, "so long as there are no more spies involved. Let me get my things." She vanished for a second and reappeared with a small handbag looped around her arm.

"So," Gabrielle closed the door behind her, leaving the two alone in the hallway, "how is it that you and *madame* Kristina are suddenly friends?"

"Honestly, it's a very long, very weird story."

"Well then," Gabrielle grinned as the two girls set off down the hall, "it is a good thing we are going dress shopping, *non*? You will have plenty of time to share."

THE END

260

Afterword

If you enjoyed the book and want to help others discover it, I'd also encourage you to leave a review on whatever platform you use. Those reviews are very important to the continuing success of the book. For those reading on online that can be as easy as flipping to the end and offering a rating.

If you're interested in my other works, I've also penned several Biblical historical fiction novels. I'd encourage you to start with *The Days of Elijah*. You can learn more about me as an author at *www.jnoblewrites.com* as well as reach out to me at *Johntheauthor1@gmail.com*.

With that out of the way, I just want to say that this was one of my favorite books to write, and hopefully you've enjoyed it also. I've always been fascinated with outer space. As a kid I watched every sci-fi show I could find, and that love was a big part of why I became an engineer.

Since I am an engineer, and I *dearly* love details, wherever possible I've tried to do the actual math regarding what's happening in the book and incorporate real, or at least plausible, technologies. I should also add that, while this book covers a lot of geopolitical speculation about the future, it's just that speculation to help tell a cool story. So don't take it too seriously.

As usual, this book wouldn't be anything like the one you've read without the contributions of my mom, Carol Noble, who sat through endlessly long hours of editing. If you see commas in the right places and sentences that don't drag on to infinity, that's mostly because of her very hard work. That includes an insistence on going through the book twice, to make sure we got *almost* everything. Things may have gotten a little tense at points, but she dedicated a lot of work to making this book the best it could be. I also wanted to thank my younger sisters Kayla, Sarah and Rachel for all being positive when they read the story. That includes Rachel, who more-or-less refused to read it until she had literally *nothing* else to do, then wouldn't put it down for a straight five hours and kept pestering me about how it ended.

I also want to thank my dad. What I haven't mentioned is that, partway through writing this book (the original manuscript was penned some years ago), I found myself laid off from my existing job, a quite depressing situation. During that time, my dad graciously allowed me to move back in while I combination wrote/job-hunted. Without that I don't know where I'd be today, and I certainly doubt you would be reading this story. So, thank you.

I really hope you enjoyed reading Starbound as much as I loved writing it. And maybe we'll meet again on a new adventure, somewhere not too far in the future and a million miles from home.

THE END

FOR NOW